A FACET FOR THE GEM

A Facet for the Gem

The Tale of Eaglefriend

Book One

C. L. Murray

For Grams

THE

EAGLE MTHS

VELDERE

oAVRETH

REALM OF THE

EAGLEMASTERS

The SILVER RIVER

Speaking River

o DRALVIND

oVIRENSOR

VELESEOR
o

FEROTAUR
WILDLANDS

0   50   100

SCALE   IN   MILES

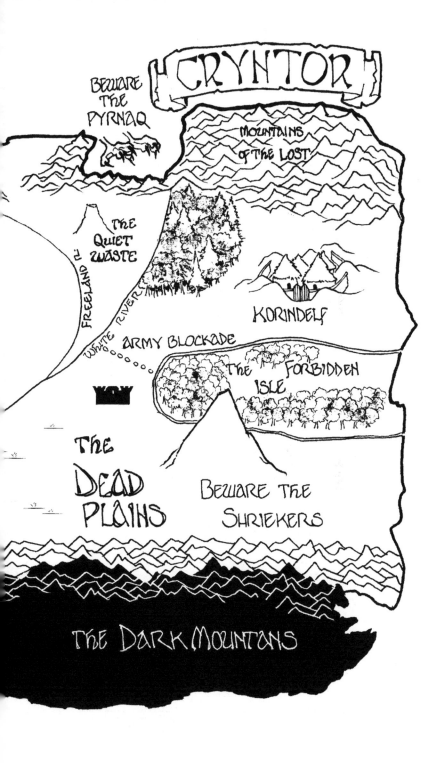

CHAPTER ONE

MOLE

ORLEN TASTED NOTHING but smoke as he forged through the woods, straining for a look at the destruction beyond. He emerged to see a toxic shroud approaching from the border that guarded Korindelf's lands against enemy invasion, and could not be certain whose side burned. Still, he felt no worries over friends and family as most would on this day. His lack of both was a luxury now.

He traveled on the edge of a horse-drawn cart laden with skins and venison slabs that would sell handsomely in a city fearing siege. An agitated whinny protested the exposure to floating flakes of soot, but regardless, the northerly-moving curtain could bring much-needed concealment when the other boys came after him.

Surveying as far as present conditions permitted, he tried to glimpse the blockade of fortresses that edged the Dead Plains, but the spreading plumes must have enveloped it hours before. Korindelf's horns would likely sound tomorrow, blaring either to celebrate the army as it marched back in triumph, or to warn of the horde it had failed to repel.

Often he dreamed of fighting the beasts that plagued the world of men. He hoped valor could wash clean the shameful reputation that had followed him for all of his sixteen years growing up in the city. But most in Korindelf would lock themselves behind its walls if the border was breached, and their admiration would be short-lived if he made a stand outside. He would slip in, trade his goods, and slip out again, wishing them the best of luck.

Urging the horse onward, he peered at his cargo. Every cut of meat was secured in rabbit pelts and twine, which would ward off flies for hours. Whether he could hold larger pests at bay remained to be seen, and he ran one hand up the soft yet leathery length of his deerskin quiver, thumbing the feathered ends of the arrows it held.

His white ash bow was marked by an indelible smudge where a hand larger than his own had gripped it many times, and it looked modest compared to others. But not once had he envied his fellow hunters their weapons, instead reading the foreign fingerprints smeared onto his only rightful possession as a tale left deliberately for him, and no other. Passed down from a father he'd never known, it offered volumes about adventure and toil, pursuit and loss, and all that had led up to his own life of dodging scornful eyes.

A violent disturbance of crows at the forest edge soon made him uneasy, and he ducked while glancing back toward the commotion.

"Mole!" came the familiar call, his adoptive name in circles where the loudest voice was most persuasive. "What ditch have you run off to now?"

"Careful calling him that," joked another. "He may transform and crawl up your trousers."

Morlen could make out at least five or six carriages maybe thirty yards behind, and kept head and shoulders low while imploring the tall grass to guard his course. But a wake of drooping stalks could soon betray him.

"He left in such a hurry, I'd almost think he caught something he didn't want to share," taunted the first boy.

Morlen envisioned the fresh start that his haul could purchase: his meager knife cast aside for a modest dagger; perhaps a rugged old horse, not borrowed like this one, nor quite as gaunt; a winter cloak, moth-eaten but warm. Such a trade could send him far on his own way, now that he finally had more cause to take his chances out on the frontier than reside in Korindelf. A full day's journey stretched between his goods and any suitable offer, though another bargain would come much sooner now, one he was most unwilling to make. Swiveling forward, he whipped the reins against the horse's ribcage, though worried that the wagon's creaking axles divulged his path through the haze. But if they wanted what was his today, catching him would simply be the beginning.

"That's him!" shouted one of the boys. "I'd know that squeaking anywhere."

"Come back, Mole!" their leader continued to mock. "You know better than to sneak off like that, before we've taken our fill."

"How big a kill do you think he has there, Jathidd?" asked another.

"Well," Jathidd laughed, "you've all heard what Mole does in the wild—crawls up so close behind the deer he's got their stink dripping brown and wet off his head before they hear him coming, and then it's too late. I'd wager he knocked off a full-antlered stag just to get cozy with a doe."

"I heard from another camp that he walked right through a herd," one more joined in. "And none of them ran away, like he wasn't even there. And the hunters watching didn't shoot... like they were afraid of what he'd do."

"Afraid of Mole?" Jathidd scoffed. "He's nothing to be concerned about. Though, I remember one night about three years ago he kicked me right between my legs, and the next morning I sprouted hair down there."

Morlen risked shattering his flimsy cart to pieces if he maintained the current pace, and they rode in sturdy vehicles led by animals that his own couldn't hope to match. But there were other options.

"Anyone spot him?" a boy rasped in the enclosing smoke. "Sounds like he's slowing now."

"I can hardly make out your lumpy gut spilling onto your lap," said Jathidd. "Did you see that walking carcass he drove out from Korindelf? It'll collapse by midday, no question. Then Mole will be the first to greet whoever survived that battle down there," he nodded toward the engulfed South. "Maybe he'll give us some warning if they couldn't hold the shriekers back this time."

"His squeals could be louder than theirs," one chuckled. "Korindelf's watchmen won't need to sound the horns."

"Don't joke about them," scolded another. "What if they actually broke through the blockade? All of them! They'd claw their way into the city before anyone could push them back. Imagine having to see them up close—taller than men, gray and slimy, with hands that could take your head off and jaws to fit around it."

"The Eaglemasters would come rain fire down on them before that happened. Korindelf would be under siege for a day at most, and we'd have seats to watch it all happen."

"The Eaglemasters were probably in the heart of the South fighting, like Korindelf's men! Maybe there aren't any of them left to help. And even if there are, how are they supposed to see anything from up high through all of this?"

"An Eaglemaster is deadlier on the ground than in the sky," replied Jathidd. "I expect they'd recruit the city's best to join them on foot, and throw out the lot of you as decoys. They might even find a use for Mo—"

Two rough slices against leather and a ringing snap suddenly interrupted, followed by a yell on their flank. "I've been cut loose!" alerted the rightmost of the group, struggling to hold the reins that soon slipped away as his horse left him behind. Quick footsteps running around their perimeter sent all heads darting in vain to glimpse the culprit, and one strike after another scattered the team away from Jathidd, whose transport was the last left intact.

Charging past his hindered companions, Jathidd homed in on the whine of old spinning axles and came to Morlen's cargo and horse, which were unattended. Unable to detect anyone nearby, he climbed down to sift through every fat parcel, when an arrow zipped with a resonating thud into the wooden frame inches below his hand. Slowly turning his head while keeping the rest of his body rigid, Jathidd traced the projectile's visible path through the murk and saw Morlen stepping closer, smoke sealing behind him while he drew his bowstring for another well-aimed shot.

"I'm leaving; do you understand?" Morlen's voice deepened threateningly. "I'm taking what's mine to Korindelf, all of it, and getting something in return. Then I'm leaving, and none of you will follow me. You won't see me again. Not ever. Understood?"

Jathidd's shoulders relaxed somewhat, his arm retracting while he straightened up, unshaken. "Mole, you think we haven't learned by now that you would've bloodied us all long ago if you had the stomach for it?"

"We may all get bloody tomorrow anyway," replied Morlen. "And I'm only just starting to learn what I can stomach."

Stiffening slightly at this, Jathidd furtively glanced for any sign of the others, all of whom could be heard scrambling to round up their unharnessed horses. "Just give me half," he said. "That miserable creature can't haul everything. I'll take half and let you go on, and we won't do anything to you."

Morlen's bow creaked as he drew back farther. "It's always half. And a bit more for them afterward. Then a little more for you. I'm finished crawling back to the city with what's left. Turn around and salvage everything you can, and I'll be gone. Or—"

"Or…" said Jathidd, "one more warning shot, and then we'll see just how far you can crawl."

Morlen held the weapon steady, and neither he nor his target flinched as the stinging fumes gathered between them. The string choked the blood from his fingertips while he desperately hoped to break Jathidd's certainty that he wouldn't follow through. But, grinding his teeth against the strain of the draw that demanded immediately to be sprung or let down, he finally eased up on the taut cord, withdrawing its arrow.

Jathidd sneered as though knowing the standoff's outcome all along. "Now that you mentioned it, Mole," he mocked, "a bit more than half will do nicely."

Suddenly a mounted boy dashed behind Morlen and wrenched the bow from his left hand, trotting away to join the others, who were all closing in on horseback. Each horse had been saddled earlier on the hunt to be ridden through denser parts of the wood, where a cart couldn't pass. Now, with nothing else to carry, they could more easily pursue their prey.

They circled the scene like buzzards while Jathidd left his cart and climbed atop one of their horses. "Mole is cunning in the shadows," he yelled, following Morlen as he turned to run. "But now he has no place to dig." He drove Morlen farther out past his cargo, the rest herding him with kicks to his shoulders.

Morlen pushed hard against the hide on his right and barreled out through a small gap. But the others crowded in again, this time whipping him more vengefully until Jathidd directed them to fan out.

"Let him breathe a moment," he laughed, and Morlen stopped in the center of their perimeter. "The chase is only starting, Mole," Jathidd warned, sensing he meant to be moved no more. "You should get ready."

But Morlen stayed firm, even as they formed up twenty yards

away. Then they came at him again in a rapid gallop, charging head-on while still he refused to budge.

"You'd best get running!" Jathidd urged. "You'd leave too big a mess over all of us."

Morlen saw them pounding closer, so close that to bolt in any direction would leave him bruised and scarred, but he stood his ground. They would ram, kick, and trample, and he would bleed. The earth shuddered beneath him, and he saw the thrill in every eye that watched, waited.

"STOP!" he screamed with arms thrashing out, and all five horses abruptly dug hooves into grass and dirt, neighing shrilly while skidding to halt before him. Jathidd careened so violently forward that his face slammed into the back of his animal's head before it bucked him off, sending him flailing to land with a snap on his side. The others clung tightly when their carriers reared up and thundered down again, looking on through the frenzy at their fallen captain, who rolled to a stop several feet past Morlen.

Jathidd's mouth was full of blood, his two front teeth glistening in the reeds beside his head, which lay studded with brown thistles, and his right arm bent backward at the elbow. "Uaggh…" His groans traveled far as he propped up to let a red puddle spill from his lips onto his chest. Three boys jumped down and ran to his aid, careful not to exchange any glance with Morlen, who remained fixed in place while only beginning to understand the damage done.

"I told you it wasn't just stories," one hissed, gingerly tucking himself under Jathidd's crooked limb amid louder whines. "We need to do something. In case he tries anything else."

"Next he might come looking for us," another whispered. They lifted Jathidd's torso and realized his legs were too weak to lend any support, finally picking him up at either end.

Morlen kept silent, transfixed by the hateful glare that now had fright at its core, so reminiscent of looks he got frequently at Korindelf. Then, a clenched hand bashed a jagged rock against his head, dropping him to his knees.

Dizzily steadying himself with both hands on the ground, he tried to stand as a boy rode up and kicked him squarely in the jaw, knocking him sideways. He had no chance to counter as the two pounced together on foot and pummeled his back and ribs. The second assailant was the one who'd taken his bow, which he glimpsed only momentarily as it was repeatedly brandished and rapped against him, until it cracked in half with one last blow that numbed his arm entirely.

His vision darkened as a low hum slowly built in his head, and he saw them turn away satisfied after a long while. They helped lay Jathidd inside the lead wagon, and then moved on to claim the cart with which he'd hoped to escape, releasing the frail beast that stumbled aimlessly forward while they gave a stronger specimen its bridle. With their own recovered spoils packed against Jathidd, they abandoned the other carts to proceed in a caravan around both loaded vehicles, and none cast even a brief look back.

On the edge of consciousness, Morlen reached out for his bow and found it splintered into two lesser arcs. The string lay useless nearby, so he tied it to the broken pieces and hung them around his neck. Now, any hope of escape was a distant dream. Elevating his head to reduce its throbbing, he gradually regained enough sight to spot his pitiful horse plodding through a column of dust, and forced himself upright.

He limped on behind those who would profit once again from his diligent harvest, and had to lean his whole body against the animal before daring to lift one foot to a stirrup. Eventually able to climb up to a seated position, he tapped both heels into its rear flanks. His long hair was matted with enough dirt to match the brown tatters he wore. In fact, if hostile eyes approached from the

Dead Plains, he could dive from his mount and blend perfectly with the undergrowth. But such a life of constant concealment was one he saw worth losing.

Korindelf sat on the obscured horizon, and only tomorrow would tell its fate. He wished his own needed not be caught in the balance, but as resources were few, the city was his only haven. And if truly no warriors remained to defend it, he felt his loss today would soon appear minuscule.

As he rode farther, an unprecedented gust from high above drew his gaze, and thousands of immense, brown-feathered wings tore through the clouds. With his head tilted back, he discerned the silver gleam of armored legs astride each bird and broad red capes that billowed over every tail. The Eaglemasters were flying from their city nestled in the mountains, plunging toward the densely veiled South. And the sight of them in full force was more overwhelming than he ever could have anticipated.

He drank in one gulp after another of clean air that poured down from their soaring formation, having to shield his eyes against the burst of sunlight that flooded the rift they opened. Just as his vision adjusted, the last in their ranks passed by, leaving him in silence again to watch the radiant window stretch in their wake, and reseal.

Shrouded once more by unending gray, Morlen savored the picture, etching it into memory that none could rob. Then, with another prod to the horse, he continued on his way.

CHAPTER TWO

THE EAGLEMASTERS

K NIGHTLY WARRIORS IN beaked helms, feathery silver armor, and regal capes of deep red, mounted above wide-spanning wings, the men of Veldere assembled to fly into battle. Each had a lengthy spear and full quiver strapped over his shoulder, with a longbow gripped in one hand, and a sword sheathed at his side.

Their dauntless birds puffed out broad chests under plumage interspersed with brown and white, and their golden beaks, below piercing bronze eyes, threatened worse than any blade. A line of trumpeters cracked the air with notes that were answered by ringing calls only the heartiest of beasts could muster, and lethal talons sprang off in flight. Soaring toward Korindelf's lands, the Eaglemasters were three thousand strong, wreathed by the rising sun—a sight to fill even the most brutal foe's heart with dread.

One man among them held a shining spear, its upper half and sharp head crafted of crystal, with a silver shaft and bone horn filed to a razor edge at its base. He was scarred and weary, yet had a sureness of direction that commanded great trust from all following behind. Peering into the distance, he grimaced as though to inspect a patch of sores that would never heal, since he could not look out upon his own kingdom without seeing the atrocities prowling at its edges.

Three who flew closest along his path watched him diligently, keeping a slight distance. "Father flies heavy today," said one, loud enough to be heard over the wind at such altitude, though careful not to project past the two on either side of him.

"No heavier than you, big brother," replied the one to his right. "Six years' peace with nothing but a few dozen ferotaur skulls beneath your sword has made you fat."

The first who'd spoken laughed at this. "Peace has never met the stomach of any Velderian, mine least of all, brother. A true Eaglemaster would vomit at the thought."

"You think yourselves true Eaglemasters?" said the third and youngest. "Our little sister holds more sway over the birds than do the likes of you." He spurred his carrier on to fly a deft loop around his two brothers. "Neither of you could beat me in flight even if I had four goblets in me."

"No," said Verald, the eldest, "we'd stay back and watch you fly boldly into the Wildlands, with a leg of lamb where your spear ought to be."

"Besides," added Ivrild, second eldest, "I was there when you took your very first flight, remember? Snatching Father's eagle so brazenly, only to tread air like an infant before being flung down through the aviary."

Young Ondrel lowered his head, pride slightly deflating as he raised his voice over their chuckling. "I still remember lying there at the bottom in a heap of feathers and cow bones, and—" he sighed, wiping some ill-remembered feeling from his hair. "Father came down to find me, and then he gave me a lashing I still can't forget. The flat of his blade left its outline on my back for months."

Suddenly the one they watched out in front slowed his eagle,

11

gradually flying abreast with them. His presence was welcome, though all three instinctively straightened their posture when he approached.

He furrowed his brow at his youngest son, showing wrinkles made by laughter he dared not let anyone hear, and said, "I've never struck you before in your life."

Confusion reddened the prince's jovial expression as it turned between his father and brothers. "But," he replied, "I remember, you said—"

"Oh right," Ivrild blurted, "something to the effect of, 'Son, this hurts me more than it hurts you.' And what'd Verald say when it was his turn to have a go?" he snickered.

"You did all the talking as I recall," Verald answered with a light smirk. "He was so delirious from the fall, he would've taken a naked drunk for Father."

Ondrel held them both with a look of stubborn disbelief, which eventually broke under the strain of his own widening smile. And the three were glad to share a moment of levity with their father before he broke away again, flying in solitude out ahead.

As King Valdis led his army through the clouds, he uneasily took in what little he could past a net of smoke creeping northward from the Dead Plains—the very territory they flew to strike. They had not calculated the attack alone, though; it had been coordinated with Korindelf for months to be sprung on this night, and no sooner. Fire and thick plumes made them of little use to the plan now, and such a glaring deviation compelled him to ready his blade for their ally as much as for their foe.

"What disturbs you so much?" asked the eagle he rode, Clodion. "I suspect it's neither arrow nor dripping fang you fear."

Valdis ruffled every familiar contour beneath his longtime companion's neck feathers with a seasoned hand, proud and grateful that, had any other man been within earshot, he would have merely heard the subtlest screech, and nothing else. An eagle's words, like its wings, were won.

Trust, yielded openly and returned, forged the pairing that his people's ancestors had sought out of sheer necessity with the colossal mountain birds, when pitted against hostile mouths on all sides. Now, that trust maintained the time-honored union that had elevated what once was a crumbling pocket of humanity into a thriving domain, though still its borders were under constant assault.

Theirs was a fighter's kingdom, and any who grew too relaxed would be lost to the hungry wretches they had long struggled to keep at bay. True, his people lived contentedly enough, spread across five cities, but every keep in the realm had been born in blood. To this day, the four settlements beyond their well-nestled capital were bergs in perilous waters, held fast by beloved sons no older than his own. And many sons had been lost.

"Will you not say what worries you?" Clodion repeated, flying far out in front.

As if it weren't taxing enough defending their own land from relentless masses, their spears were pledged to guard Korindelf always. This pact had led both kingdoms toward prosperity from the early days of tribulation, opening channels of trade and calling on Korindelf's army to aid the West in times of dire threat. Friendship and fierce loyalty were etched into such a lasting alliance. But as of late, those ties had been strained indeed, and he would sooner stroll unarmed through the teeming Wildlands beyond his realm than allow one soldier of Korindelf safe entrance.

Glancing back at the thousands holding to his course, most of them younger than thirty, he wondered how many were still bound for death here, even above what looked to be the fresh ruins of a centuries-old enemy. "I cannot count the times we've flown to these parts, thwarting one advance after another," he answered, turning forward again. "Or the gaps that always linger in our ranks on the journey home, like open wounds in our shadow as it passes along the ground. I fooled myself, hoping today we'd finish it, finally end all campaigns here and be free to focus solely on our own borders that crack every day, before it's too late."

Clodion was glad to hear him break his silence, which often could persist for hours on end. "I see no inch of space around the flames where any creature survives, even those whose screams are shriller than ours. And the men of Korindelf sit at ease atop their horses on the plains, as though no danger approaches, only awaiting us, it seems."

"Are you past the days when you would regard us as danger to those below us?" Valdis asked.

"Of course not." Clodion raised a stubborn beak. "But to the soldiers down there? Never have we had cause for that."

"I suspect we have for a long while," replied Valdis. "And only today will we begin to learn just how much. Something of this magnitude tells me he razed the tower itself, which both armies united never came close to capturing."

"He?" asked Clodion, with a curious turn of his head.

Valdis sat up more rigidly, indignant at having to utter the name. "Felkoth," he said. "The only man I've ever seen step among the shriekers and come out unscathed."

Their faraway country shrank from view when the Eaglemasters finally passed over Korindelf's outer territories, which appeared to be free of any intrusion, and they descended to the frontier bordering the Dead Plains. The king and three princes sat at the front ranks, and the banners of their realm flew high on either side, showing a silver eagle with a spear of crystal clasped to its chest, flying against a red sky.

The ground shook as Korindelf's cavalry rode toward them, numbering over five thousand, clad in bronze, yet Korindelf's flags were nowhere to be seen among their battalions. They halted opposite the Eaglemasters with mouths tightened in displeasure and noses wrinkled as though wading through manure.

Prince Felkoth, their commander, wore dark robes over sleek iron armor, forsaking the colors of his kingdom, and was quite pale, with long black hair that rested on broad shoulders. His eyes delivered a chill to Valdis that even the smothering heat of battle couldn't stifle. No matter how quickly he met them, they always seemed to have been trained on him long before, and he felt them now like constricting coils.

"Where are your flags?" Valdis spoke calmly, trying to suppress his contempt at Felkoth's lack of greeting. "Do you not wish to celebrate your kingdom in the ashes of its worst foe, so far ahead of schedule?"

Felkoth sneered at him. "The celebration has only just begun, Valdis. We've a great feast ahead of us, and though it is customary that uninvited guests pay tribute to warrant their presence, I'm afraid poultry was not on our list."

Valdis jumped down from his eagle to stride with dwindling patience toward Felkoth, who remained on horseback, indifferent to his approach. "I assure you," the king said, projecting his words for all to hear, "had I allegiance to you as I do your father, we would have come last night for fear that you might suffer drastic loss of life in such a rash advance. Instead we arrive now, flying to fulfill our pact with Korindelf like those before our time, against the enemy we share. But, if we intrude here, mark your line where I've overstepped, and see if I withdraw."

Felkoth laughed, unthreatened. "You and my father," he mocked, "both drawing your plans so long for this with trusted advisors, forgetting that we alone hold the ground you see each day on parchment. But, as I am sure your ever-watchful spies ascertained last night, victory has already been had, and your late attempt to claim a portion of it only makes us uneasy about what else you might try to take. And, when we grow uneasy, we may act even more rashly."

Valdis's pulse was steady, and he paced casually to observe Felkoth's men. "Victory indeed," he praised falsely. "Why, I can count no scratch on any of them, no limbs lost though I've seen many stronger and more tested torn clean, armor and all. Outnumbered at least three to one, you must have employed some ingenious strategy that none in nine centuries before you ever dreamed.

"Yet," he continued, "my scouts report the army was encamped here when the smoke broke out, which I am more inclined to believe, as it surely would not be the first time you engaged the shriekers singlehandedly and came to no harm."

Felkoth appeared pleased by the implication. "This preoccupation with my activities sounds quite consuming," he replied. "It's no wonder your realm lies stagnant within shrinking borders while mine is expanding. I'd almost think you expect my ailing father's reign is near its end, and naturally you lie awake wondering what's to become of the bond between our two kingdoms, now that you need us much more than we need you."

Valdis's fingers turned white around his spear, angling it for an upward thrust that he fought to restrain. "What I need," he said through gritted teeth, "is for the cost paid dearly on this very grass over the years, in the mingled blood of our countrymen, to gain us more than nothing."

Felkoth savored his choice of words. "I suspect it will gain you much. Certainly I am not one to withhold from others what they have long deserved, especially when they bring it to my attention day in and day out."

"And I cannot begin to know what *you* deserve," answered Valdis. "Pity, as we would gladly pay you in full. But I spoke only of need, as these times hardly afford us anything more than necessities. And today, after six years of wondering why our foes have been so lenient toward you, I am beginning to understand what you've needed all along."

"Then tell me," said Felkoth, "before I fall from my horse."

Valdis grinned subtly this time, opening his stance a bit to show himself at ease. Though each man behind him kept silent, he knew they now looked sharply for any signal to strike, and all on Felkoth's side made no attempt to disguise their eagerness for such an opportunity.

"I have heard tales of a sword," began Valdis. "Forged in the black mists that shroud those mountains beyond the Dead Plains. None in recent generations has claimed to have ever seen it, but, those who did long ago called it the Dark Blade.

"They said it has a poison, a curse, woven through its metal, and any who is even slightly cut by it succumbs to agonizing death. It is what killed my ancestor, the first king of the Eaglemasters, at the Battle of Korindelf. And the one who wielded it controlled all the shriekers."

"Such a weapon would be formidable indeed," said Felkoth.

"I would assume as much. Its earliest keepers built their empire in the South, waging war on Korindelf. But, I have long believed that their bloodline spread past those boundaries. And if indeed an heir existed here who found himself embattled with the ghouls that often struck these lands, perhaps they'd scatter from him, smelling the blood of their rulers in his veins. It would stand to reason they might not deter him from traveling into the heart of their domain, where he could claim the instrument that would put them under his power."

Felkoth's spine remained rigid, legs tightening on either side of his horse, and he gave no response, only keeping the silence that veiled nothing.

Valdis held him with a look that needed no answer. "I am

not saying I know what you've done, or what you plan to do. I've watched you strengthen your hold on this army, tainting its ranks with thieves and vicious outlaws who swore loyalty to keep their heads off the block. Your father has heard my worries many times over, and I could offer him nothing new. But, be certain that if I ever see that sword in your hand, that is the day you are my enemy."

Felkoth lifted his chin while taking in a long breath. "And, on the day we are enemies," he mused, "will we settle our differences, just the two of us? Will these fine specimens who follow you see fit to follow me, after it's finished?"

With the speed of a trained battle archer, Prince Ivrild set an arrow to his bow and pointed it at Felkoth's chest. "Enough banter," he seethed. "I'll do what we all know needs to be done, right now."

Hundreds of swords hissed from their scabbards as Felkoth's closest men rallied around him, ready to charge if so ordered. But Felkoth held up a hand to stay them, fixing his watch on the young challenger. Mouth curling upward, voice smooth, he said, "Quite shrewd of you. But, careful you don't make more enemies than you know what to do with."

Valdis turned to Ivrild. "Not yet!" he steamed. Then, as he sternly faced Felkoth again, his tone left no room for objection on either side. "Not today." With reluctant obedience, Ivrild lowered his bow.

"Charitable, Valdis," said Felkoth. "A prince assaulting a king. Much too barbaric, even for my taste."

"You are not king," Valdis resounded. "Not of Korindelf, or any other part."

"You and my father may be the only ones who share that view," Felkoth replied, pausing to let Valdis take in his vast forces.

"Until tomorrow, at least, when he can finally rest easy in his infirmity, and step down. Then, you may find yourself all alone."

Valdis sought any recognizable humanity in Felkoth's stare, turning away after finding none. "I bid you safe journey to Korindelf," he said, "and we will gladly return to our own country without loss of man or beast." He remounted his eagle gracefully, letting the dizzying pain in his old joints remain a well-kept secret. Then he leaned forward to address Felkoth one last time. "We'll be watching, and you'd do well to keep in mind that no matter what you tell your father, he knows the Eaglemasters will still fight for Korindelf any day.

"And," he said as he prepared to leave, "should you ever find yourself on the battlefield with us, remember: we're deadlier on the ground than in the sky." With that, their trumpets sounded again, and they lifted off in one elegantly woven flock, flying far toward the West, the way they had come.

Felkoth soaked in the wafting notes of their departure, seated at the head of thousands who would rather choke on the enclosing ash than complain. Nefandyr, his lieutenant, rode slowly forward to wait at his right, careful to halt inches before aligning side by side.

"He suspects a great deal, my lord," said Nefandyr, his white hair caked in soot. "Should we fear their eyes see farther than we anticipated?"

Felkoth's colorless lips stretched in a thin smile. "Fear." He savored the word. "Fear is ten thousand mouths that would devour you were it not for the single solitary whip that splits any tongue out of turn. Fear is a ruler long past his prime who shields himself with one arm, asks for aid with the other, and finds both severed. Fear, Nefandyr, is very much on our side."

Pulling his horse around to address the awaiting soldiers,

Felkoth announced, "We return to our forts! Save your strength. We must prepare for tomorrow's celebration at Korindelf."

Quick to obey, every battalion left the long-dreaded South scorched far behind, its distant tower a flaming ruin in lands littered with rubble and dust—but not one corpse, no trace of the creatures that called it home.

The three princes flew closely around King Valdis now, their battle-hardened faces distinctive reflections of his own, each troubled by questions that none dared voice. After leading the army back over the mountainous northeastern corner of his realm, Valdis broke off toward a nearby peak with his sons in tow, and they landed together as every battalion returned to its respective outpost.

Unwilling to wait any longer, and assuming it his duty as next in line, Verald braved the silence caused by their father's harsh expression, which threatened to unleash fire at the very mention of Felkoth. "Six years, Father." He spoke tentatively, gauging the king's reaction. "Six years since we last fought the South with them. All that time surveilling, strategizing, waiting for the enemy to make one move. He violates our pact, and we indulge his deception? We return home, just like that?"

"All we know for certain is that his army hadn't yet advanced when the fire began," young Ondrel replied. "We don't know who or what sparked it. They may very well have moved in afterward, and the shriekers would have been smoked out like gophers, right into their trap."

"We won't know until the smoke clears, will we?" chided Ivrild. "Clearly it wasn't his design that such a screen be lifted before our eyes, leaving us no choice but to watch from afar or really get our noses deep into whatever was unfolding, and maybe not come out to tell about it. I should've finished him when I had the chance, and we'd be extracting the truth from his men. Believe me when I say the three goblets I reserved for us at the Broken Beak are all mine tonight."

The king somewhat relaxed as he exhaled loudly, silencing his sons. "Six years," he repeated. "Six years since the shriekers poured out from the South in full force, since I flew to reinforce Korindelf's blockade with all Eaglemasters. Your first battle away from home," he added, tilting his head toward Verald, who gave a light nod in acknowledgment.

"Felkoth's first battle as well," he went on. "A mere princeling determined to prove himself. We arrived as the horde was a mere hundred yards out, and dropped volleys to suppress their advance. You two should consider yourselves lucky you were too young to go," he said to Ivrild and Ondrel. "You'd be surprised the shots they can take... the kind of shots that would put a ferotaur down. The things you can do to their flesh, and still they keep coming for more. And the sound they make when your arrow pierces them, as though out of the thousands of men swarming above, they know it was you.

"They were becoming so intermingled with the blockade that soon we'd have to descend into the fray, and that is when a lucky death is by the sword. But then, like the ripples of water from a dropped stone, they all abruptly moved back, centered around one man.

"It was when I saw that this was none other than Felkoth, who stood whole before the legions that had once swallowed my own father, scattering them back to their master's wasteland, that I suspected he would have a larger role to play in the war ahead. And now, six years since he was named commander, after corrupting the army beside which I once proudly fought, he's shown that he had but to eliminate the threat at their borders—or assimilate it."

The brothers exchanged earnest looks, each hoping another

knew the answer that seemed to dangle at the end of their father's words, though it remained elusive. "So which has he done?" Verald broke their collective silence with an impatient tone.

The king's sight reached the broad Speaking River, which under cleaner skies sparkled like a road paved with sapphires, stretching beside the dense forest that extended for miles northward to the snowcapped Eagle Mountains, at the base of which glistened their capital. Looking out on his kingdom lovingly, he pitied his people, who hoped to soon meet the beginning of a new age.

"Tomorrow will tell," King Valdis answered before taking off again, and they followed. "I shall have to send word to Korindelf detailing our account of what transpired today. But, regardless, I think it is more than sound to assume that our alliance will soon be at an end."

Felkoth led the army an hour north, and the smoke was thinner now than what had surrounded them the previous night. It had blinded even the keenest eyes then to those who crossed the border unchallenged for the first time, those whose concealment was imperative. Coming at sundown to the fortress line that had protected Korindelf for centuries, Felkoth halted and faced his men once more, finding them instantly quiet.

"Korindelf's people urgently await their saviors," he announced. "They see destruction carried on the wind from their most threatened territory, and realize what emerges shall mean life or death. Undoubtedly now they place far greater value on the luxury they have so long taken for granted, passing all responsibility for their own security, for their very livelihood, to us alone.

"The Eaglemasters feel Korindelf owes them a great debt, for services rendered long before any of us ripped our way into this world. And make no mistake, what we do not offer, they will try to take, and the thousands we've guarded with our lives will merely yield to the stronger pull. And so, we must protect the people from themselves. We must teach them we are all that has ever stood between them and the grave, even if it means burying those who resist. We must let none wander so far that he might be taken by those who wish to topple us, and the Eaglemasters will wish it, of that I'm certain.

"That is why I acquired our new allies last night, those who are loyal to my bloodline alone. Before, though they would not harm me, neither would they obey my command. Now they have no master left but me. And henceforth, I assure you, they will obey.

"Tomorrow, those who have reaped the fruits of our vigilance shall finally pay us dearly, and even before I am named king, they will recognize beyond doubt who has ruled them all along. But, with our homecoming imminent, I wish first to know that every link in our ranks is strong and unshaken. So let any man who objects to my design step forward now, and be heard."

All battalions remained rooted to the ground, every soldier subduing even the slightest breath that might set him apart. Soon it became clear that any man with the gall to voice dissent would likely be run through by those nearest him, and be concealed long before Felkoth cast one scornful eye in their direction.

Taking their unified silence as a clear answer, Felkoth's expression lightened. "Then water your horses and go to quarters," he ordered. "Eat, and gather all the provisions you can carry. We won't need them here any longer."

With that, the army broke off, making ready for its overnight march to Korindelf while Felkoth withdrew to the central fort, descending into its deep tunnel that had been secretly dug in the years since he assumed command. Dank, with a palpable stench of flesh on the cusp of decay, it ran for dozens of miles, and its tall, hairless, emaciated occupants sniffed anxiously at his arrival with broad snouts over twisted, elongated fangs.

Proudly facing the shriekers as they drooled down gray, scaly stretched necks, he unsheathed from within his cloak the ancient Dark Blade, taken from those who had once commanded these dreaded masses. It collected an aura of arrested torchlight like dust to a corpse the higher he brandished it, and the humanoid brutes gazed with obedient wonder, jaws open, panting excitedly.

"Heed me well, and you will never know hunger," he promised, inciting a chorus of yelps. "Remain here, out of sight, and listen for my call, as it will come when I have the greatest use for you. And, with the greatest use, follows the greatest reward."

Then Felkoth left his new servants in hiding, relishing the images of their impending emergence. The densely packed channel reverberated with their tantalized frenzy, opening under wide fields just a mile outside the gate of Korindelf, which would soon open to welcome the conquering heroes, for as long as they wished to stay.

CHAPTER THREE

THE TREE AND
THE GOLDSHARD

MORLEN REACHED KORINDELF late the next morning, having allowed his faltering horse a pace slow enough not to be a death sentence. The city was shaped like an engrailed crown with its high walls curving to bridge six encircling hills, each of which was capped with an ornate watchtower. Its two southern walls slanted sharply inward, forming a narrow corridor that led to the gate.

He slowly advanced into the tapering channel while several bowmen lining the battlements above trained their weapons on him, a reception that was no precaution for what approached from the South. There would be no questions as to his business here or his place of origin—he was a citizen they recognized well. And the report they must have gotten from the other returning hunters clearly left no room for rebuttal.

As he neared the sealed stone entrance, a rectangular hatch creaked open at eye level, through which a guard's inhospitable glare accompanied a protruding arrow. "Any closer and you'll be a stain on that sagging hide!" the voice reverberated coarsely.

"I was attacked on the road," he said. "I've come back for shelter."

"You'll find none here," the watchman scathed. "We've just seen what you did to the boy, heard what you made the horses do. You think we'll permit your corruption inside these walls again? We should've shut you out long ago."

"I have no intention to stay," Morlen insisted. "But I need provisions. All that I had was taken. And this horse—I borrowed it, with a promise to bring it back."

The guard scoffed. "Then whatever you traded for it was too much. I suggest you turn around, ride that beast as far as it'll go, and then eat it. The people are stirred up enough as it is— word has only just begun to travel that the shriekers have been defeated. Now that those foul wretches are gone, your face is the last any will want to see."

"Defeated?" Morlen whispered, looking back at the surrounding lands, still bathed in a residue of battle. "And the army?" he asked, wondering what kind of force could have possibly exterminated such an enduring threat.

"Soon to arrive," the man replied with greater hostility. "And you'd better be gone before they approach! If Prince Felkoth finds the gate closed to his procession of triumph because of you, starvation will be the least of your worries. Now off with you! I'll give no more warning!"

A drawn bowstring put more power behind the arrow aimed at Morlen's throat, and he pulled his horse around. From his waterskin he took a weary swig that did little for an empty stomach. Wiping his mouth, he surveyed the open expanse and doubted he would get far. But, while he made his way out all disgruntled mumblings around him fell quiet, as though every guard now cast their attention on someone else, inside.

"You will admit him at once!" a familiar voice echoed out from behind the closed barrier.

Daring to halt and pivot back, Morlen waited for any sign of change, listening for a defiant retort that never came. Silence kept him firmly in position, and he suspected that any sudden movement might trigger a nervous shot from one of the archers, until finally a great winch began to crank on the other side. Korindelf's gate slowly swiveled open into the city, revealing a host of guards who spitefully lowered their weapons. They parted along either side of the central road in which a single man stood, hooded in silver-blue robes, old and of tall stature, with a thick pale beard projecting far past his chin.

"Nottleforf." Morlen breathed a sigh of relief, trotting closer to the threshold though stopping short at the disdain from each sentry before him.

"You may enter now, young Morlen," said Nottleforf, his tone prohibiting any action to the contrary.

No longer hesitating, Morlen quickly rode past them, cantering a safe enough distance to ensure no further interference, and was smothered by the bitter attention of many onlookers. Soon he dismounted and strode between Nottleforf and the horse in a way that shielded him against the dozens who would not let him pass so easily.

"You don't belong here!" scolded several beside the road, pushing closer through the crowd.

"Now he turns our animals against our children!" screamed another. "He brings danger wherever he goes!"

Morlen kept his head low while maintaining a brisk pace, dodging debris and brown clumps of lettuce flung in his direction, though Nottleforf seemed unfazed, refusing to bend.

"Well, Morlen, only sixteen years old and you're the talk of the city. In case you've not yet ascertained as much, the people of Korindelf are not exactly comfortable having you here among them anymore. Since your most recent altercation, there is a growing call to exile you permanently."

"I'll save them the trouble," Morlen replied. "I came back for supplies, food, that's all. I was going to trade everything I gathered on the hunt—you should've seen it. I was going to have all I'd need to make it for years out there, but…" He trailed off, expecting little consolation. "I'm still leaving, today if possible, with whatever I can get. I might go north of the Quiet Waste. Maybe you could help me."

"Ah yes, the wide frontier," said the old man. "So beckoning to the young and adventurous of heart, and so littered with their bones."

"I'm not staying here! I never asked these people for anything, never disagreed when they said something about me wasn't right. But they never gave me a chance to change."

"A man may consider himself changed," replied Nottleforf, "merely after finding what was always hidden in him."

Morlen sent over a suspicious look, uncertain toward what course he was being nudged. He did not understand why Nottleforf had tried to aid him through most of his early life, when many would have left an infant of low birth to follow its mother to the grave. Whether would-be guardians came and went, or humble households offered scraps and a cold night's sleep, Nottleforf had always brought him from one to the next. And now that he was grown, they were quite distant. Yet there was an ever-present impression that, while Nottleforf purposely remained detached, he was secretly watchful.

"When I was younger, one of the families that took me in had two other boys close to my age. Do you remember?" he asked.

"I do," said Nottleforf.

Morlen was certain the wizard had heard the stories that had circulated about him over the years, though he'd never been asked for his own accounts. "The father was a blacksmith, strict," he continued. "But the mother was kind, and told her sons to treat me like their brother. After a month had gone by, I thought I might finally be home. Then one day, the boys were sparring too close to the hearth, and the one with his back to it didn't see that his tunic had caught fire. I pushed him out of the way, even though his brother saw what had happened and did nothing, and he hit his head. His parents came and found him unconscious with me batting out the smoke at his side, and his brother told them I'd done it all on purpose.

"The father cornered me against the fire and tried to beat me, and I was so panicked that I grabbed the iron poker from the flames and hit his hand with it. His fingers broke and were badly blistered. He screamed that he'd never be able to work in the smithy again, and I ran out and never looked back. After that, I've always sensed something in the way people look at me, and it's as though I can only be what they think I am.

"You used to take such an interest in my welfare." Morlen laughed, shaking his head. "Looking in on me, like someone who wants to be seen but not needed. All I need is to not be this, anymore," he said, rigidly crouched beside the horse, wiping more refuse from his hair.

Seeing Morlen's snapped bow dangling toward the dirt from around his neck, Nottleforf withdrew the broken arc, untied the string and delicately balanced both halves in wrinkled yet nimble hands. Interlocking the jaggedly split pieces with slight pressure between his thumb and index finger, he plucked a long hair from his ample beard and wrapped the grayish strand twice around the fracture. Then he applied more force that sent a popping heat from his fingertips, melting a now luminous thread to flood every gap in the break, until, with no scar to be found, the bow was whole.

"You were lucky with this," said Nottleforf, offering it back to him. "There is much I cannot mend so deftly."

Morlen accepted the weapon slowly with raised brows, surprised by the greatest amount of care Nottleforf had displayed in many years, and restrung it securely. Then, he drew back on the bowstring to find it sprang with strength and flexibility renewed.

"If you are to leave Korindelf," Nottleforf went on, "why not head due south?"

"South?" Morlen muttered. "There's nothing but miles of fields, a little too close to here for comfort. And then"—he stopped, realizing what Nottleforf meant—"the Forbidden Isle?"

Nottleforf's ageless eyes sharpened. "Not forbidden to all."

Suddenly a chorus of horns at the gate announced the sighting of Prince Felkoth's army, which would soon funnel into the city in a victory march. Conversation now proved difficult under eruptions of cheers, but Morlen was glad to no longer be the focus of everyone's attentions.

Knowing that Nottleforf would have matters to attend to in the castle, as he often served as King Fendon's advisor in military and diplomatic affairs, he was content to take his leave with a gracious nod. Then he went as inconspicuously as possible toward the stables, to return what might be the best transport out of Korindelf he could ever get.

Felkoth grew restless as Korindelf lay only a short stretch ahead, his rightful seat that victory had now secured while lineage alone may have left some doubters whispering. None would doubt him after this day, though, not even Valdis and his bird-keeping squires, whose intrusive presence adjacent to his own realm would have to be swept clean. But, he now had only sufficient strength to repel them here, if they dared interfere with his rule. To overwhelm them in their own territory, choking them with a tireless grip, there was one more thing that he needed. And he would have it, very soon.

Studying the thick blue mists that surrounded the Forbidden Isle south of the city, he recalled the story of its most renowned inhabitant, who had struck the first blow in the Battle of Korindelf nearly a thousand years earlier. Many accounts described a warrior emerging from the vapors leading a great horde of lions, driving the shriekers away from Korindelf for good.

The following generations who lived behind those same enchanted borders were always reputed to fight when needed, but their power and influence seemed to have dwindled; they had not been seen in years. If any still survived, surely they were too weak or few to show themselves, or they would have done so long before now.

The mysterious domain eventually shrank far behind, and thoughts of potential threats it posed vanished from his mind when he entered the gateway of Korindelf, where many throngs cheered overhead. He led his army on horseback, filing through the narrow opening in a celebrated parade flanked by people of the nearby territories. Droves had flocked to the city as the smoke rose, not knowing whether friend or foe would soon be coming.

The glorified cavalrymen rode tall along Korindelf's central road, a path scattered with flowers by those applauding their passage. Lined by rows of wooden and stone huts that composed numerous bustling villages, it ran for about eight miles, linking the gate at the southern edge to the castle of Korindelf far on the other end.

"Do you hear that, Nefandyr?" Felkoth asked his lieutenant. "Those are the cries of thousands who crave authority as though without it they would be lost. We will give it to them. We will ensure that their efforts serve a greater purpose than they ever have before, just as we served them for so many years."

"I doubt many will resist, my lord," Nefandyr replied. "It is as if they already know their true king has come home."

Felkoth grinned. "The throne's current occupant does seem to have faded in their minds. I became king the moment that gate opened. Any other notion is a lie."

"You've called him your father all this time. One lie in exchange for another, then let him see the power you'll use to rebuild the kingdom that grew soft under his feet."

Eyeing the citadel that rose high in the distance, Felkoth knew he would soon gaze out from its towers and watch his borders spread each day, until finally no other borders remained. "There was a time when I tried to be the prince he wanted me to be," he admitted. "I played the diligent pupil to his tedious advisors, who spoke of loyalties and traditions that I would be duty-bound to uphold. But they painted a future that would see me a slave, not a ruler, shackled to distant allies who could strike no blow better than I, and obligated to expend my resources for their betterment.

"And after years of their lessons in diplomacy, I realized allegiance is for the fearful, who hold it up like a quivering shield to an indifferent storm. But if you are that storm, you owe nothing to the world of men but a thrashing of its feeble structures, which, when broken, reveal it as the absurd collision of flesh and dirt it always has been. And when it lies peeled and exposed, unable to deny its powerlessness, you can mold it again as you see fit."

Gradually picking up speed now, he broke out ahead of his men, letting them fill the city while he made for the castle. The dying monarch awaited him, unable to turn a blind eye to his arrival. And their reunion was long overdue.

After returning his borrowed horse to the stables, humiliated to have no spoils to show from his excursion, Morlen pushed through dense crowds that clamored on tiptoes to salute the army's triumph. Getting out of Korindelf now would be nearly impossible, especially with all the supplies he'd hoped to acquire.

He moved on through the city, where hives of decrepit shacks in which he'd spent most of his childhood gave way to modest cottages, with merchants on every corner selling questionable meat on spits, and pelts big enough to be used only for shoes and caps. Farther in, loftier houses were spread up the road, with spacious gardens tended by those who profited off their surplus crops, while often trading what was near-spoiled or worm-eaten to the poorer quarter. More stately places of limestone rose on either side as the road stretched farther toward the citadel, marking sections of the city where people of low class seldom gathered.

He felt innumerable insect-bites of contempt from those he passed as he traveled to the sunlit courtyard of Korindelf's castle. Then, a balm of elation followed when a familiar flash of gold caught his vision, reflected from within a tightly twisted branch of the large tree he visited when dispirited.

Legend held that it had been planted as a mere seed by the ancient being, Korine, shortly before his death. Founding the city as a haven for many against abounding enemies, he was said to have installed a high order of one hundred warriors, known as the Blessed Ones, to protect the people in his stead. But soon after, the One Hundred fell to an ambush from the shriekers, leaving the city vulnerable to invasion. It was when liberation had been won at the Battle of Korindelf that the tree sprang from the ground, offering a gift to the generations that would follow.

Stepping nearer, Morlen ached for the comfort it provided without fail, and began to speak to it, as he so frequently did. "Talking Tree, tell me about the Goldshard."

At his request, the tree's rough, gray bark crackled with a long opening across its face that parted into wooden lips, forming a broad mouth that recited the song he knew well:

"King of Korindelf may here retrieve

This offered Shard of Gold

And with it, gladly take his leave

For great power does it hold

It can change its keeper in any way

That he so desires

Granting youth enduring every day

Or all strength that he requires

But if you take it now, I warn

Though your kingdom it may aid

The kings to come may need it more

And will wish you had delayed

So then let him who needs it most

Withdraw it from my guard

And count himself above every host

While clutching this Goldshard."

Its message resonated throughout the courtyard, and as it subsided Morlen stared upward, wishing to take the enticing Goldshard and transform into someone admirable, someone none could ever harm again. But, he could not do that. It was only for Korindelf's king.

Nearing the citadel, Felkoth was emboldened at the sight of the mystic tree growing in a lushly decorated courtyard, and his eyes latched onto the golden object clasped tightly in one of its branches. He paid little attention to the unkempt boy who turned a captivated stare away from it to watch his arrival.

As he dismounted he was met by the king's guards who stepped aside to permit him farther. He returned no greeting, however, as their pledge of loyalty was not to him. The great hall swam with sunlight that poured through windows cut into the thick stone, casting rays on the banners of Korindelf that displayed a wreath of white stars on a blue field. Across from the entrance sat the king's granite throne and table, with a hearth carved several feet behind. Traditionally, after a battle, the king of Veldere and a contingent of Eaglemasters would join the men of Korindelf here for a shared feast of merriment and friendship. But not today, nor, he sensed, any day to come.

In the peak of the citadel rested the royal chamber in which, he surmised with loathing, the king now sat: the fool who had housed and wed his mother when she escaped from the Dead Plains. He strode through the great hall and into its rear stairwell, swiftly scaling its stone steps past corridors that led into the adjoining towers, and finally emerged in a hallway that stretched toward the king's quarters.

Asking no invitation, he wrenched the door open and burst in, where the king faced him on an armchair yellowed with sweat, looking even more gray and frail than he remembered. Nottleforf, the wizard, stood at his side. "Father," he announced, "at long last I've conquered our oldest enemy, even without the support of our allies."

But, to Felkoth's displeasure, he was not welcomed with praise. In fact, the king's sallow eyes held him with resentment. "Yes," he rasped, "I have just heard what took place between you and the Eaglemasters, though your story differs from the one they offered me."

Felkoth's attention fell on the wizard, who bent down to the king and said quietly, "I shall leave you now and carry out the task to which you appointed me."

Then Nottleforf swept away toward the door, but Felkoth stopped him. "What part are you playing here?" he demanded, breaking free of all amiable pretense.

Nottleforf's thick beard and silvery hair cut the air sharply as he turned to answer, and Felkoth was startled by the flare in his eyes. "I never play only one part," he answered. "And neither do I have a tolerance for your lying tongue."

"The Eaglemasters refused to comply with our plan of attack, yet I burned the stronghold of the South and laid waste to its surrounding lands without them—"

"And who holds the Dark Blade now?" Nottleforf interrupted. "Who commands the creatures it summons?"

Felkoth had no immediate words, trying to remain calm. "They are slain," he said hoarsely. "All of them."

Nottleforf looked at Felkoth sourly. "We shall see, young prince. We shall see." Then his long cloak swished out of the room as he left, narrowly missing being caught in the door as it closed.

With the wizard gone, Felkoth glanced back at the king who, despite being ill, began to speak with a passion he had not displayed in a very long time. "Do you mean to say to me that Valdis, a man I have regarded as my own brother since boyhood, who has spent many lives and risked his own defending my kingdom, simply deserted us?" he snapped.

"Perhaps he was too vain to go to battle with bird stains between his legs," Felkoth replied coolly.

In a surge of fury, the king leapt up and knocked him back a foot with a strike to the face. Felkoth merely stood quietly as the taste of blood filled his mouth.

"Nottleforf advised me to leave your army at the gate," King Fendon fumed. "He said it would be a mistake to allow you inside, that there was something… not to be trusted in your victory. But the people have been terrified for so long under this specter of annihilation that whatever feeble incentive they had to farm, to build, to keep this kingdom from collapsing, vanished when that smoke rose near the blockade. This celebration of theirs is the only thing that gives them the heart to resume work tomorrow. And they know as well as I that you command the army on the field, but each man in its ranks serves me! So I will ask you again"—he panted, shivering slightly from Felkoth's cemented focus—"what happened between you and the Eaglemasters?"

Felkoth spoke slowly, his eyes never leaving the king's. "I have already told you. The men of Veldere betrayed us."

"Liar!" the king shouted with a breaking voice. "Valdis sent word before you arrived here, which I and Nottleforf accepted. He said you disgraced them and spoke treason against me!"

"That is absurd," Felkoth insisted, losing patience. "Do you not see what is happening? The wizard knows your life is near its end and that the time for my reign has come, so he works now to turn you against me because he wants the kingdom for himself."

"Do you deny that you rebuked Valdis for honoring our alliance, which has lasted over nine hundred years? That you turned him away when we needed his army most?"

"Father, I… we do not need Valdis or his men. We are stronger than they are. We proved that by winning this war without them."

"You fool." Fendon sighed gravely. "This was about unifying both kingdoms in triumph after centuries of hardship. And you spat on our allies so that you could keep all the glory for yourself! But tell me, and let this be the last grief you set on me: Did you truly, in front of Valdis and all the Eaglemasters, name yourself Kordindelf's king?"

"Father..." Felkoth persisted. "I confronted the challenge posed to us and left it in ashes behind me. What greater victory could have been achieved to secure the future of our kingdom?"

"You need worry no longer about the future of *my* kingdom. I tell you now it shall never be yours." His expression slowly changed from one of anger to regret, regarding Felkoth as though he were the embodiment of all his life's failures.

"When I decided to wed your mother," the king went on wearily, "all of my counselors strongly advised against it. They said no one could have escaped the clutches of the South in such good health as she had. But, in my youthful ignorance, I was so driven by infatuation that I disregarded their warnings.

"Then, when you were born shortly thereafter, and as you grew, bearing no resemblance to me whatsoever, they said you were not my son. But, even then, I refused to pay heed to that suspicion, the one that has plagued me in my fading years. And now, as you stand before me, there is nothing of which I am more certain. You are not my son, neither by blood nor in spirit."

Felkoth stammered as his prize became more distant. "I... I am your son. I have always been your sole heir."

"I have commanded Nottleforf to bring me the Goldshard," Fendon continued, noticing that Felkoth ceased blinking altogether as the words left his mouth. "I will use it to prolong my life, so that I can lead and protect Korindelf for decades to come."

Panic began to grip Felkoth as his delicately cultivated goal came closer to being thwarted. "You cannot do this, Father," he pleaded.

"You will never be king, Felkoth. I know that is the only end you have ever sought, and I know the horrors that Korindelf and all other lands would continue to face if you were to rule. And that is why it must never be."

"But Father"— Felkoth searched for any saving words—"all I've ever asked is that you do not strip away what I've earned. I love you, and always have."

The king laughed mockingly. "If only that were true," he lamented. "But I know you, Felkoth. You love only power." At that, he turned his back and walked away, the decision final.

Felkoth reeled from the blow, bitterly fathoming that he was to be denied what should have been given to him and no other. The numbness slowly melted, and he stood watching the king peer out over Korindelf on the wide balcony behind his chamber. Then, finally, he pivoted away and left without uttering a sound.

Pacing down the hallway, he knew what was rightfully his would be snatched away in mere moments. Soon he came upon his lieutenant, who awaited him near the stairwell.

"What news, my lord?" Nefandyr asked, his eyes bright with anticipation of good word.

What news indeed? With all the forces he had labored for years to amass, he could still be opposed, even defeated. There was only one way to seal his victory, and he could never let it slip away from reach. "Nefandyr," said Felkoth in a deep exhale, "alert the men to wait for my signal. And then," he trailed off, preparing for violent redemption, "take the city."

Nefandyr bowed his head obediently. Then he asked, "My lord, what signal?"

"You will know when it is given."

"Yes, my lord," Nefandyr replied, making haste for the lower levels.

Then Felkoth, alone in the long, quiet hallway, drew the Dark Blade from its sheath under his robes, and began to speak purposefully, letting each word reverberate off of its cold, unnatural metal.

"My beasts," he called to those that remained in hiding at the end of his lengthy underground passage, which opened up just a mile outside the city gate. "The time has arrived for you to return to Korindelf, to taste the blood of free men once more, to fill your aching bellies and forget the cruel sting of hunger. Come now to the city, as you did centuries ago, and none will be able to deter you." On hearing their new master's call, the shriekers emerged by the thousands and hurtled toward Korindelf, licking their fangs in anticipation of the bounty ahead.

Having delivered his orders, Felkoth marched back through the hallway until coming again to the royal chamber's closed door. He entered, and the king met him with a startled expression that turned to scorn. "Do not come to dissuade me now," he admonished.

But Felkoth approached him nonetheless, closer now than he'd been before. "You want to know exactly what I've done?" he hissed with a growing smile. "Do you want to know how I won your war so easily? I rode alone into the heart of the Dead Plains, where no man of Korindelf has ever set foot. I rode where Mother told me to go before she died, where she said I would find my true father, her very own brother—can you imagine? The king of the South, high in his ancient keep, not quite the formidable adversary that myths and lore have made him over the years, I must say. A greasy fellow, really—unkempt, soiled in his own filth, but so pleased to finally receive one from his own lineage.

"We spoke briefly, as you might guess, exchanging pleasantries, reminiscing about lost relatives. Then I took his sword from him and ran it through his gut, watching him slip and fall in a pool of blood while the word 'son' still echoed from wall to wall. After that, I doused him and the rest of his tower with the casks of siege oil he kept in such ample supply, and burned it all to the ground."

The king tried to make for the door, but Felkoth stepped

directly in front of him. "I know you met the shriekers in battle when you were young, insulated by your many swordsmen who took the brunt of their assault. But oh, if you could hear their cries all around you, rising for miles upon miles in every direction. You speak of horrors the world has faced—the world does not know horror, Father. Not yet."

"Guards!" the king yelled, voice brittle with fright, and Felkoth put a hand over his mouth, holding him as he trembled.

"Shhh," Felkoth whispered gently. "Your friends aren't coming, Father," he assured, kissing the old man's wrinkled, sweat-drenched brow while gazing past the balcony ahead. "Only mine."

Morlen's innards churned for a long while after being so close to Prince Felkoth, who undoubtedly went to claim the king's endorsement as successor. The rippling of a cloak in his periphery alerted him to Nottleforf's approach from the castle entrance, and the wizard's unsettled look only confirmed his suspicions.

"What's happening in there?" he asked, but before the wizard answered, one of Felkoth's soldiers rushed to the citadel, tethering his horse so loosely in the courtyard it seemed he intended to be in and out quickly.

"Felkoth is in the castle," Nottleforf said heavily. "Today King Feldon has decided to deny him succession to the throne."

At this, Morlen wondered what misdeed could have poisoned the king against recognizing Felkoth, even after the army's victory. "But the king is dying, isn't he?" he asked. "Who inherits the throne if not his son?"

Nottleforf glanced over at the Talking Tree, showing great reservation. "The king wishes to claim the Goldshard, though I strongly advised against doing so, to heal himself with its power so that he may hold death at bay while he reigns over Korindelf. That is why I've come. He sent me to obtain it for him."

With that said, Nottleforf reluctantly reached up into its boughs, and Morlen grieved when the wizard's ancient fingers wrapped around the elevated treasure, concealing its sheen. Many over the years had tried to pry the relic free, only to be near-deafened by the tree's unrelenting bellow as its grip tightened. Nottleforf, however, met no such resistance. "It was seen as a great triumph when the kings of old persevered through hardship without taking this for themselves, going to their graves with honor while still it remained for those who followed. This king means to use it to keep him from his own."

"But…" Morlen stumbled over the words, trying to stall him. "Are you certain you can do this? I thought only the king himself could…"

"The king has given his blessing and trusted me to obtain it strictly for him, and thus it shall be permitted." He plucked the Goldshard delicately from the gnarled grasp, and a forceful tremor shook the ground beneath them. Morlen's heart plummeted when the tree immediately withered and retracted back into the soil that had sprouted it, never to be seen or heard again.

But his focus was lured to the soldier who had entered the castle moments before, now hurrying to ride off toward the nearing battalions. The vicinity shook as dozens of horsemen joined with him, and some splintered off throughout other parts of the city. Stationed at the courtyard's edge, the warriors sat staring up at the castle in expectation.

Morlen absorbed his loss of the only thing that had ever brought hope while realizing how truly lacking he was. Any chance of a fresh start now felt utterly gone.

"Nottleforf," he said, as though holding down his own bile, "I have nothing. I've been nothing, my whole life."

The wizard, taken aback and remaining silent, lifted his regard away from the soldiers and slowly looked down, feeling Morlen's pain as if it were his own. And, he finally began to speak the words he'd tried to withhold for so long. "Morlen," he said, "you... you are—"

But suddenly, he was cut off by a scream of terror from the citadel's peak. All nearby looked up to see that the king had been hurled from his balcony overlooking Korindelf, flailing downward before he hit the stone base with a nauseating crash. Dreadful cries erupted on all sides, and Felkoth's soldiers, recognizing their signal, stampeded through the masses, trampling and beating all into submission.

Morlen felt immobilized—Felkoth was taking over Korindelf. "Nottleforf!" he yelled over the rising clamor, "Nottleforf, what do we do?"

But the wizard gave no reply, scanning between Felkoth's army that closed in around them and the newly-taken relic in his hand, soon to be demanded by the one orchestrating this massacre. Facing Morlen again, he grabbed him tightly by the shoulder, holding out the Goldshard.

"Morlen," he said urgently, "you must take this." Morlen kept still, and the wizard held the lustrous object closer while shouting, "Take it, Morlen! Felkoth is coming for it—you must keep it for yourself, away from him!"

Rattled by Nottleforf's command, Morlen shakily reached out and withdrew it from him, burying its jagged metal against his sweating palm.

Nottleforf calmed after this, yet his voice became grave as he added a warning. "But Morlen, you must not use it, do you understand?" Too shocked to protest, Morlen nodded. "Good." The wizard breathed a little more at ease. "Now I must get you out of here."

"But what about them?" Morlen panted, watching those around him trying in vain to flee.

"My abilities are limited, Morlen," Nottleforf grumbled, still clinging firmly to Morlen's shoulder. "Our best hope is your departure, now!" They scurried toward the courtyard's center, where the same soldier they had seen earlier charged at them on horseback, brandishing his sword. Quite unthreatened, Nottleforf raised his hand, and a flame shot from it into the man's face, blasting him off his horse as he bellowed in agony.

"Get on quickly!" Nottleforf ordered, and when Morlen mounted the fallen soldier's steed, he paused as Felkoth emerged with the Dark Blade held high.

Now the new king of Korindelf, Felkoth cut down all castle guards in his path and stomped to the spot where the Talking Tree had stood, to claim his prize. Finding both it and the tree already gone, he scowled, eyes darting madly about the chaotic scene before slowly tracking to Morlen, who sat ready to ride with the glittering object secure in his hand.

"Men!" he blared. "The boy! The boy on the horse! Kill him!"

Soldiers on all sides barreled toward Morlen with swords and bows raised. But as they came, Nottleforf squeezed his arm hard with one hand, placed his other on the horse, and the three lifted off.

Morlen's head swam while summoned winds bore them out of the tumultuous courtyard and away from the city. Then a spark of hope flared as he caught brief glimpses of the Eaglemasters on a rapid course to Korindelf's aid, though it would be long yet before they arrived.

They rematerialized just outside the channel leading to Korindelf's open gate, now manned by one of Felkoth's contingents. After landing with a painful thud, still in the saddle, Morlen looked ahead in fear as thousands of savage creatures bounded toward them with fangs bared, their front ranks only a dozen yards away and closing.

The shriekers lunged, pouncing as one gray wave, but Nottleforf stretched out his arms and thrust forth a wall of light that halted them in their tracks. Snapping viciously, the endless packs pushed harder as the barrier flickered more dimly against their advance, and the wizard groaned, a creaking dam to rushing waters.

"Ride, Morlen!" he thundered. "You know where to go." And Morlen looked due south, seeing the Forbidden Isle a few miles away.

Not daring to hesitate, Morlen tucked the Goldshard deep inside his inner chest pocket, grabbed the horse's reins, and kicked it into motion. With one last look at Nottleforf, he galloped off as the wizard called out a final command. "And Morlen, remember—Do not... use... the Goldshard!" His last words echoed like horn blasts, and Morlen sped out of harm's way, with the Isle lying directly ahead.

Tearing through an open field, he slowed and turned to look back at the city. What would happen to Nottleforf once he could no longer hold the pressing beasts at bay? He watched with cautious relief when the Eaglemasters reached Korindelf and swooped down into it like a bursting storm cloud. But then he gasped as they emerged in fewer numbers with each pass, descending so low that they made themselves open targets. And Felkoth's troops brought them down with precision, taking advantage of their fruitless attempt to distinguish friend from foe while the formation grew smaller, more disjointed with every minute.

Then suddenly, droves of men on horseback began to appear in the distance, pouring out of Korindelf behind countless shriekers that sprinted on hands and feet, no longer restrained from following his trail. He shot onward with double haste, knowing Felkoth's servants were coming for him.

His horse's breathing was becoming labored, and soon even the sharpest prod of his boots brought no change of pace. Looking back to see how close the enemies were, he realized with dismay they would be upon him in minutes. They had even commenced firing, hitting the ground only a few yards behind, and as his murky destination still lay far out of reach, he unslung the bow from his shoulder and gripped it tightly in one hand.

Gradually the archers gained enough to place him in range of their arrows, which fell like a deadly rain on all sides. Then, despite his carefully improvised swerves to deny them any fixed target, a well-placed shot pierced the horse's hind leg and sent it slamming into the ground with a cut-off scream. He was hurled forward, tumbling painfully through wet grass.

As he rolled to a stop, he looked up in a panicked daze to see that two shriekers had broken away from the rest of the pack and were careening toward him. Smelling the animal's spilt blood, they charged for the kill, drooling mouths agape. With all his arrows now loosely scattered, he scrambled to pick one up and frantically loaded it, firing at the bony assailant in front, which yelped shrilly with a punctured lung before falling. He had scarce time to prepare for the second that leapt over the fallen horse. Knifelike claws extended to impale and dissect him as he knocked its head back with a shot to the throat, and its dead weight flattened him.

With its sickeningly slick pelt stretched over a tall, nearly human frame, the putrid carcass sagged on top of him despite his furious struggling until, with a desperate gasp, he broke free. The others, equally menacing and disfigured, were closing from fifty yards at most, and the men on horseback followed. He had no choice but to run now, and though his only possible refuge was at least one mile away, he sprinted against every sore tendon and spreading stitch.

The lethal downpour was all around him, and failing muscles

begged him to submit to what only sheer chance could delay. What was the use of even trying to get beyond the Isle's dense vapors, when all others had found them to be impenetrable?

It was someplace new, he thought. And if he actually got there, no one could say he did not belong. He would be past the confines of what so many people had told him he was, and would finally get to explore the other side. Or die trying to get there.

With this fresh solace in mind, heavy limbs and depleted air were replenished tenfold, and his eyes lit up like embers. Felkoth's men pressed in, seconds away from shooting a thousand holes into him, and the lead shriekers were raring to devour his riddled corpse. They unleashed their volley, but then watched in confusion as every arrow pierced nothing but soil while he suddenly sprang out of reach, surpassing even their own rate of gain.

Morlen's extremities became blurred, and his rapidly moving feet seemed not to even touch earth. The blue mists for which he forged were close now, rising hundreds of feet high, and he could do no more than hope that once he reached them, he would be able to pass through. Bolting forth with one last surge of energy, he took a deep breath and then plunged headfirst, disappearing into the billowing bright fog.

The soldiers witnessed this with a shudder, and the shriekers nervously skidded to a halt a safe distance away. Those on horseback maintained full pursuit, thinking that they too would be able to breach the confounding borders, but it was as though they slammed into a rock wall, and all were thrown violently to the ground.

Screaming in disgrace, they cursed the boy who had eluded them, the boy who held what their master wanted. The thought of returning to him empty-handed filled them with dread, as his wrath would be terrible. But now, they had no other option.

Felkoth's boots sloshed in the reddened fields of Korindelf, littered with bodies of fallen Eaglemasters and their fearsome birds. He wished that Valdis could have been among the dead, but had watched him lead the airborne retreat, undoubtedly knowing the dire consequences that any future trespass would elicit.

Outside the city gate, he stood surrounded by many packs of shriekers whose stained jaws were briefly appeased, while the people of Korindelf who had not fallen prey to them were locked away, now enslaved to expand his realm. He awaited the return of his prize, as well as what little might be left of the thief who had stolen it, and cast hateful regard on the one standing before him bound in chains, who had helped the boy escape. Nottleforf was breathing heavily, greatly taxed from holding so many at bay until the soldiers had emerged and seized him.

"What shall I do, Nottleforf?" he said with playful disdain. "Now, when I am finally king, you give what is mine to a mere boy? I would relish cutting that meddlesome tongue in two, and watching the rest of you slowly wither. But look at what you did to poor Nefandyr. Surely he deserves his revenge as well, wouldn't you agree?"

Nottleforf glanced at the soldier he'd blasted with fire, whose horse Morlen had used to get away, holding his blistered face tenderly. The man's eyebrows were singed off, and his scalp was red and peeling beneath a hairline that seemed to have permanently receded. "I think the look suits him well," he answered.

Screaming in anger, the lieutenant leapt forth with sword raised, but Felkoth held him back upon seeing that the legions he'd sent out were finally returning. He strode swiftly to them, trying in vain to glimpse the Goldshard and the one who had taken it. "Where is it?" he demanded violently. "Where is the boy?"

One man dismounted and reluctantly approached, his

radiating fear needing little elaboration. "My lord," he whispered, "the boy escaped. Into the Isle."

Felkoth glared with disbelief. Tasting deprivation again, he released a grunt of outrage and took off the man's head, then spit in disdain as the lifeless body crumpled to the ground. Escaped? Where none but a select few had ever come and gone? He turned to Nottleforf, nostrils flared. "I swear to you—I will drain every drop of the slime that flows through your veins if you do not answer me. The boy... who is he?"

Nottleforf showed no hint of fear whatsoever, letting his body meld with the air, and the shackles binding him fell in a clanking heap as he began to drift weightlessly, carried on a gust toward the West. His voice resonated like the wind itself:

"The last son of Morthadus was mine to protect, and he goes where you cannot:

Where worldly snares have no effect, where wars are never fought.

So seek what spurns your reaching hand, and you may find no rest

Till he returns upon this land, from within the Isle of the Bless'd."

They stood and watched him vanish, and even Felkoth took in the spectacle with wonder. But with the wizard gone, he let his mind stray from thoughts of any who might challenge him now. Korindelf was his at last, and his prize lay somewhere in the Forbidden Isle, held by a runt who probably hadn't any understanding of how to use it. He would just have to wait for him to foolishly emerge, or, discover how to gain entrance himself. Either way, he intended to kill the boy and take back what was his.

And that was all he was, Felkoth assured himself. Just a boy, nothing more.

CHAPTER FOUR

IN THE FORBIDDEN ISLE

MORLEN GROPED AROUND as though immersed in water, his toes stretching to touch ground and finding none. He could hear by his pursuers' muffled shouts that they were unable to follow him through the boundary, and, remaining suspended in the mist, he was filled with peace. They may as well have been miles away.

Clasping his bow, he leaned forward to swipe at the thick vapors and fell face-first into a grassy floor on the other side, which was fragrant and soft. Then, flat on his stomach, he looked ahead at a sight that even hours without blinking would fail to fully capture. Colors he had never imagined were painted all across a broad forest, each tree a spectrum of dripping light, with swollen fruits that looked to have gone unclaimed for some time, until now.

Jumping to stand, he plunged into the shimmering grove and embarked on the daunting task of choosing among the apples that dangled above and on every side. Some were the blue of watery depths, and others the purple and pink of sunset, with a slew of mixtures in between, caressed by shades of indigo, emerald, turquoise, amber, and gold.

With the bow slung over his shoulder again, he reached up, wrapped his fingers around one fruit's smooth, almost glassy mauve surface, and plucked it from its branch, surprised at how dense it felt in his hand. Then he opened hungry jaws and crushed into the apple's side, blinking through a luminous splash as he took off a chunk so large it kept his lips apart, and chewed until his mouth became flooded with nectar that drove out pain and fear.

He enthusiastically bit again, letting his teeth bring out a cool wave that soothed even more, and potent juice dripped down his chin while he tried another apple, knowing he would grow old and gray before sampling them all. And as he devoured the Isle's fruit, his senses seemed to expand, detecting many life forms that sent warm vibrations through the soil.

Making his way south, he delved deeper into the woods, arms spilling over with apples he couldn't bear to leave unbitten. Beds of lavender decorated the forest floor like hundreds of purple carpets around the plentiful orchards, lifting fresh perfumes and stretching far in each direction. Sunlight filtered through a leafy canopy above, reflected by every branch's heavily strung orbs, and the air remained cool and fresh, unpolluted by the fires and stench that covered the adjacent lands.

The apples sustained him through hours of walking, and the resultant waves of heightened awareness brought with them the suspicion that he was being watched. Soon, he glimpsed bright movement in his periphery, like flames springing up on either side, and came to a halt. When he slowly turned to look between the trees, countless pairs of silver eyes under thick, flowing manes stared back, observing him carefully. Drawing a quick breath, he saw, concealed in the brush, that the Isle's fabled lions had gathered all around.

He felt no danger or threat from them, instead drawing comfort from their presence. One calmly pushed out of the bushes, shaking leaves from its fur in a graceful march toward him. The lion's stout head was as high as his chest, but he stood unafraid when it came closer to sniff him curiously. Seeming to decide he was no intruder, the creature withdrew its inspecting prod and affectionately nuzzled his arm. To Morlen's astonishment, the others emerged and followed suit, taking a closer glance at him while pressing moist noses against his hands.

Then, they bowed their heads around him, permitting his passage, and he stood in awe of their unwarranted show of respect. Often he'd felt a strong kinship with beasts of the wild, as if he could somehow empathize with them and they with him. But he had never experienced anything like this, almost able to inhale their bravery and resilience. Pulsing with humility, he moved through their ranks and knew without looking back that they were following him. He was glad to have their company, unsure of what or whom he would encounter as he journeyed farther.

He had always been fascinated by stories of the Isle's people, reclusive warriors whose strength and speed were said to be extraordinary, noted to emerge only when Korindelf was under attack. But why had none shown themselves this time? No tale he'd ever heard suggested they were prolific, but some could very well still reside here. And, if any did, he wondered how long it would be before they found him, since his presence was already quite conspicuous.

Eventually the sound of water tickled his ears, and parting trees yielded to an open strip that sloped down toward a river. Its current was gentle, and it wound for miles past his vision east and west. He eagerly strode to it, convinced there could be no purer water anywhere, and got down on fertile soil that dampened hand and knee, drinking deeply. He dunked his entire head, scrubbing away all grime he had carried with him, not for the last few days, but years. After minutes of washing up for the first time in too long, he looked down at his reflection through dripping hair that clung to bruises and scars soon to be forgotten, and was clean.

Purple hues painted the sky as night fell, and he decided to travel no farther until morning. He would rest within the woods, and rise at first light to follow the river east, though what compelled him to go in that particular direction he could not precisely say. Above all else, some inner part of him was being pulled that way.

He reclined underneath the trees, and the lions keeping to his trail bedded down in a semicircle behind, where they seemed content to remain all through the night. Surrounded by his willing protectors, he lay in complete relaxation, and despite the horrors that had transpired that day, he could not help but feel happy, happier than he recalled ever having been in his sixteen years. He did not even remember that the Goldshard, which he had coveted for so long, sat in the pocket over his beating heart.

He let all worries melt away, and sleep swept over him while the apples twinkled above, uncharted constellations within the forest. He needed no bed, no pillow, no fire; the Isle's soil was soft, and its shelter warm.

Morlen's eyelids were slowly pried open by sunlight, and he awoke like he'd slept for years until this day. He could tell the lions were still close, feeling the air buzz with their focused interest in him. But, there was something else, *someone* else, a presence charged with loneliness built up over years of unbroken solitude, though it exuded great power as well. He gingerly rolled to his other side, and saw that a man stood a few paces off with his back turned, facing the river.

"I envy you," the stranger said. "Tasting the Isle's divine fruit, feeling its unequaled comfort for the very first time. I myself was born here, and I took this place for granted until I left its shelter, long ago. When I came back, I was as you are now—alone, afraid of the world outside, immersing myself in the Isle's pleasures and vowing never to leave again."

Then, the man turned around and looked down at him. At his side shone the steel grip of a large sword sheathed under his brown cloak. He folded both thick arms across his chest, which puffed out beneath light furs stitched together. His face and long hair were rugged, but his eyes were cool and relaxed.

Morlen regarded him almost as an apparition brought on by the Isle. "You're one of the people the stories are about," he marveled.

A grin opened up through the man's dark beard, further diminishing his wild look. "Before your entrance I was the only one left, and had been for quite some time. But now, I am glad to say that we are two."

"Glad?" Morlen laughed skeptically, propping up on his elbows. "Hardly anyone has ever cared where I go, as long as it's away from them."

"Those horsemen cared very much. So did the shriekers. Yet, though they were at your heels you eluded them on foot. Is that something you dismiss as an ordinary feat? Something any man could have survived?"

"I was afraid," said Morlen, "desperate, really. I didn't have time to understand it. Anyone being threatened like that would have run just as hard."

"Just like anyone with a mind to enter the Forbidden Isle could do so at will?" the man retorted. "Those fellows looked determined to follow you to the ends of the earth. But you are here, Morlen, and they are not."

Taken aback, Morlen sat up with arms around his knees. "How do you know—?"

"What I know matters little. And what the people of Korindelf knew is far less. You place such great value on what others think of you. But what do *you* know, Morlen? Who are you?"

Morlen stared at him in bewilderment. "I…" He fell silent, grasping at nothing.

"You do not know?" the man asked glumly.

"Who are *you,* then?" Morlen said in frustration. "Is it easy for you to understand?"

"It is never easy. For me, there are moments when, like you, I am at a loss. But at this moment, I know with complete certainty. I am Matufinn of the Blessed Ones."

Morlen raised his brows at the answer. Straightening stiffly while remaining seated, he said, "The Blessed Ones are dead."

"Yet look at us, the two remaining sons of Morthadus, in good health," said Matufinn. "Separated by a world that would see his line extinguished, now together in the place where it began."

"I've never heard of him before," Morlen cut in.

"You have," Matufinn answered, "though not by name. He led the lions into the Battle of Korindelf centuries ago, against those that cast down the rest of his order. That strength endures in his blood, strength that has undoubtedly manifested itself in you, though you refuse to acknowledge it. But soon enough, you will." He bent forward, stretching out his arm.

Though utterly unsure what to make of the man's claims, Morlen felt no reason to fear him, and saw danger now as something foreign while taking his extended hand. And Matufinn effortlessly lifted him to stand, his grip lingering slightly longer than necessary as though to savor the first human contact he'd had in many years. Then he abruptly let go and turned to walk beside the river.

Morlen followed, silently in awe as Matufinn appeared something more than human. His mind ached trying to comprehend this paradise that had for centuries stood uncorrupted by the world. "What is this place?" he asked. "How could it have stayed so pure for all this time?"

Matufinn replied, "When Morthadus escaped the massacre that ensnared his brothers, Korine the Ancient gave him this realm, so that the Blessed Ones would always live on within its borders. The river that flows from beneath the high mountain, the fruits that never wither—these are gifts to only us, to be touched by no other, except those we invite inside. And the children of Morthadus have kept it for him ever since he departed, some looking to his return."

"You're saying this... Morthadus... is immortal?" asked Morlen.

"Yes," said Matufinn. "The original One Hundred all were. The Blessed Ones, chosen for their bravery, endowed with the powers to protect Korine's city through the ages. But after they fell, ambushed by the shriekers, their tradition lived on in Morthadus, and it is said that as his sons grew old and died, he remained young. We have carried on his legacy ever since, fighting for Korindelf as he did."

"Then, if this is true," Morlen replied, having difficulty accepting it, "you're telling me that makes us ... brothers?"

Matufinn chuckled at the question. "What it makes us is ours to find, in time. What remains to be found is in you, and always has been. You must decide whether or not you are ready to face it."

They traveled for miles through woods that receded to reveal wild grasslands, down green hills and quiet glens that opened into valleys of violet and jade. When Morlen passed under more enticing apples, he eagerly gathered two, relishing them both. Matufinn, however, hardly even glanced at the overhanging bounty.

"The apples," Morlen sputtered through a mouthful. "I've never had anything that made me feel so... free. Why are you not eating them?"

Matufinn smiled. "The apples are beyond your world, but they have always been an ordinary part of my own, from the moment I left my mother's womb and opened new eyes to see them around me. It is through knowing the vastness outside of what we've known that we find real freedom."

Morlen cautiously pressed, uncertain whether he should question Matufinn's decision to live here in seclusion. "And did you find that, when you left this place?"

Holding quiet at first, the man led Morlen to think he'd struck a nerve. Before long he replied, "I found a great many things when I left, when I was not much older than you are now. Death and suffering, more than anything else. I lost... people, out there... one in battle, and the other later, in Korindelf."

"You did battle with the shriekers?" Morlen asked intently.

"Oh yes," said Matufinn. "Along with the only other of my kind who dwelt here, years ago. We charged into the fray with Korindelf's army—men who served long before those treacherous fools currently in power, mind you. We moved like water and wind," he boasted, drawing his sword to swiftly cut two apples from a nearby branch, slicing them both cleanly in half with a single stroke before they hit the ground. "We shattered scores of foes by the minute, letting none land a single blow.

"Until"—Matufinn's voice became grave—"the two of us were separated. And I, engrossed in the task of keeping them off of me, saw that they had overpowered him... biting, ripping, pulling him deeper into their fold where even the strongest bones are crushed, and thickest skin devoured.

"I drove them back in rage," he continued, "lifting one after another as shields against the rest, hoping that as they withdrew, they would leave something of him to recover. But they leave nothing of what they take."

Matufinn stopped from time to time as though basking in the atmosphere, guided by every energy that Morlen was only beginning to feel, near and far. Such an odd mannerism led Morlen to suspect that if Matufinn had ventured to Korindelf during his upbringing, perhaps his own uncommon features would have met more acceptance than distaste.

"When you first went to Korindelf," said Morlen, "did you feel—"

"Overwhelmed?" finished Matufinn, laughing under his breath. "Dazed by the thousands who knew not whether to fear or accept me?"

"Like you would drown under the way they looked at you every day?"

"Ha!" Matufinn laughed aloud this time. "I had a special spot picked out to escape them, where I'd often go just to remember which feelings were my own."

"Till it became more difficult each time."

"Much more. That is, until I let in someone different than the rest, someone who wanted nothing from me except what I wished to freely give."

Morlen's interest rose, this time unable to share from his own experience. "What was it you gave this person?"

Matufinn's steps scuffed more against the ground as his expression became nostalgic. "Everything," he answered.

"And they took it from you? And left you worse off?"

"She? No. She made me better for it, far better. But, when she died, a great deal left me as well."

Beginning to uncover how deep Matufinn's wound was, and

how it had kept him here unhealed for so long, Morlen realized they were equally alone. "And you've been here ever since? With no desire to venture out again?"

Matufinn's expression remained pleasant, though it seemed to require too much effort. "The desire arose at times," he replied. "Some nights I told myself I would again. But when tomorrow became the day after, and months soon turned to years, I knew the part of me that had so readily left these borders was gone."

Morlen recalled the countless times he'd wanted to shut himself in rather than struggle to improve his daily life. He could understand someone else's submission to that fear, when his own resistance had never gained him much. "But what about your people's tradition?" he asked. "Going out there when oppression is at its worst? I thought you meant to carry on their legacy."

Matufinn nodded. "That's where you come in."

Morlen scoffed, shaking his head. "I'm sure my ability to enter this place can be explained," he began. "But I doubt it has any connection to some warrior who's lived for over nine hundred years. If my father was alive all along, where was he when I spent most days getting beaten into the ground? If I have the same qualities he does, why couldn't I ever keep myself from harm? If he's powerful, why am I weak?"

"Maybe he wanted you to have a life different than his own," said Matufinn. "To be born outside the confines that held him too long. For comfort and shelter to be so scarce that you would develop strengths he never possessed."

"How can you be so convinced?" Morlen asked. "You said yourself that anyone invited to the Isle can freely pass. I would never have thought to come here if I hadn't been told."

"Nottleforf merely suggested the path. You are the one who found it."

The familiarity in Matufinn's reference to the wizard confirmed what Morlen had begun to suspect. "You knew him too," he realized aloud.

Matufinn answered halfheartedly, "Knowing Nottleforf is like knowing the weather. Hope for what it's going to bring, and be devastated. Or open yourself to the unexpected, and be uplifted. Either way, there's no telling what's in store for you."

At this talk of Nottleforf, Morlen felt a pang of worry. Could he still have had power left to reach safety after helping him escape the shriekers? Or could he be languishing now at Korindelf, held captive by Felkoth in a putrid dungeon? Or worse?

No, he told himself. Nottleforf was strong, cleverer than anyone. Somehow, he felt certain they would meet again. And despite the distance the wizard had made a point of keeping from him in recent years, he was comforted by that thought.

"He never told me anything," said Morlen. "Nothing about my father. Nothing about what it was that made me seem so out of place to everyone, even though he saw me suffer because of it. He could have just sent me here all along, years before now."

"So you could be brought up hiding from the world, like the rest of us?" Matufinn asked. "For generations we were born into pleasure and safety, never having to earn it, never having to do without it so long that we could appreciate its value. All the treasures to unearth out there were too far beyond our reach, when all we knew was abundance… permanence.

"But you," he continued, "unspoiled, gaining nothing without hardship, have been immersed in everything our people feared, conditioned by it as we were not. You could be the best of us. The best of both worlds."

"What about the woman in Korindelf?" asked Morlen. "Did losing her make you wish you'd never found her in the first place?"

Matufinn turned solemn, and he was silent for a long moment as they walked beside each other. "I begged Nottleforf to save her," he finally replied. "To keep her as I had known her, not to let her slip away while still in the young bloom of life. He told me we cannot halt death, only be gladdened by the life it leaves behind. So I returned to the life I'd left in here, where the creep of death is slow, and no beauty ever wilts."

Morlen asked no more after this, thinking it wise to leave the subject alone. He began to notice that the same force pulling him from afar the day before was stronger now, and felt they'd reached its source when the river led to a wide open meadow, flowing into a lake at the opposite end.

"The lake." Its energy was too bright to fully grasp, as if it were the Isle's pulsing heart. "There's something inside it. Something powerful." Morlen squinted at the surface.

"Yes," Matufinn replied. "The lake holds a doorway."

"To what?" asked Morlen.

Matufinn looked out with a slightly furrowed brow. "The lake is fed by the eternal river, but its waters do not flow out," he said. "Instead, it deepens to where the physical world no longer exists, where space itself can be bent and torn. And rising from within this distorted plane are pockets, like windows through which one can crawl to other locations."

Morlen's eyes sharpened with interest at this.

"But," Matufinn added, "it is only an aid for those who wish to venture outside."

"You mean," Morlen pressed, "it can take us anywhere we wish to go, if we ever want to leave?"

Matufinn gave half a smile, led him toward a small boat that sat at the lake's edge, and pushed it down the pebbled bank until it became adrift in the shallows. "Don't be concerned with that just yet," he said, stepping inside the vessel with a gesture for Morlen to follow. "Leave those weapons for the moment. Right now it's time you see what you have thus far turned away from."

Morlen hesitated at first, unsure what Matufinn could possibly mean for him to find out in the water. But, reluctantly casting any misgivings aside, he removed his bow and quiver, setting them on the ground. Then he sloshed forward clumsily, and his boots sank through the mud before he wrenched them free with two loud slurps, hoisting himself aboard.

Oars in hand, Matufinn pushed into the smooth, open calm, and Morlen felt like they were floating on liquid light as they rowed farther. Eventually they approached a large rock not far from the opposite shore, its tip protruding from the water like an iceberg, and Matufinn turned the boat to glide against it with a gentle thud.

Nodding toward the rock, he said, "Up you go."

"For what?" Morlen protested, brows raised suspiciously.

Face hardening, Matufinn said, "An important lesson."

Morlen stared, arms crossed in skepticism, until Matufinn's expression turned stern enough to make all hesitation flee. Careful to balance his weight, he rose and stepped out upon the uneven island, wide enough for only one person to stand. Matufinn then swung the boat around and rowed away with great strokes, stopping about twenty yards off to face back again.

"Are you ready to meet what you've locked away for so long?" called Matufinn.

Morlen furtively glanced over both shoulders, making sure the question was not posed to someone else. With as much seriousness as he could muster, he nodded.

"Good," replied Matufinn. "Now run to the boat."

"Do what?"

"Run to the boat," Matufinn repeated, with stronger authority this time.

Morlen looked around again in all directions.

"The one in which I sit, Morlen. Run to it, now."

He let his adjusting vision take in the space between himself and Matufinn's skiff, feeling absurd for even trying to gauge the distance. Slowly he bent to look down at the water, seeing a helplessly lost boy staring back at him. Aiming for his face, he lifted one foot and stepped out only to fall forward with a pitiful splash.

Half amused, he swam beneath the crystalline water for a few seconds, tempted to summon one of the lake's distorted pockets to see if it could take him directly to Matufinn's side. But, thinking such a trick would not be well received, his better judgment took hold.

"Are you ready to learn or not?" Matufinn's voice bubbled through his ears as he resurfaced. "This time put your heart into the task."

Aware how foolish he looked climbing up to attempt the feat a second time, Morlen shook the water from his hair and set himself firmly again, fighting to muster a shred of the confidence Matufinn demanded. There was no way that this could be achieved by any man or creature.

"Have you done this yourself?" he yelled out in frustration.

"You have bigger worries than what I've done. What have *you* done?"

Morlen hid his enjoyment of the man's wit and leapt out, feet scurrying as though their speed would carry him across, only to sink once more. Could this be some kind of mental test, to teach him that one must sometimes accept failure? If so, he was learning quickly.

Nevertheless, he persisted in the most creative ways he could devise: hitting the water on all fours in an effort to run like an animal, flapping his arms as though to fly. An hour whittled away, minute by minute, while he tried in vain again and again, until finally, one plunge sent an encouraging flash of gold through his mind. At this, he urgently clutched his inner chest pocket, relieved to feel the flat metallic object he'd almost forgotten, safely concealed.

Rising soaked again upon the rock, he faced down the open blue that chided him as it remained untrodden. He was simply not fast enough, not strong enough. But... he could be. His strength and speed could be unsurpassed, as the Talking Tree had promised. He merely had to take out the treasure in his possession, and ask it to make him the way he'd always wanted to be.

"Have you given up already?" Matufinn asked. "Do not think about what you know. You can hold firm to it for the rest of your life, but there you will be stranded. So, step out, and leave it behind." Then he seemed to whisper something else under his breath.

Don't think... don't think. Morlen could not help but disobey the command, springing off once more with his hand cradling the Goldshard to prevent it slipping out, and made another miserable splash. He partly expected to be scolded as he came up for air, hearing instead the same rapid whispering that could only be Matufinn's way of venting frustration.

Clinging to the rock while still half-immersed, he questioned whether he could climb one more time, let alone give this fruitless exercise another attempt. But, Matufinn expected him to carry on, and the thought of letting him down was strangely dispiriting.

Despite the soggy chill that numbed his fingers, he dug hard to pull himself up again. He crouched with hands upon his knees, deliriously trying to form a new approach to this obstacle, but none remained. Every strategy had resulted in the same failure. There must be some obvious solution Matufinn wanted him to see.

As he searched for the answer, a curious dark cloud gathered above the lake's bordering trees and descended toward the water. Then it scattered, revealing hundreds of ravens that screeched in unison while they swarmed the boat to attack Matufinn. Before long he disappeared from sight, and Morlen could only listen to his frightful screams.

"Aghhhh, get away! GET AWAY!" Matufinn yelled painfully. "AGHHHHH!" he wailed. "STOP! AGHHHHHH, MORLEN! MORLEN, HELP ME!"

Morlen lunged out, leaving all deliberation behind, neither watching the water that barely rippled beneath his feet nor looking back at the rock that was now a speck. He saw only the black cloud that swelled and tightened as he drew nearer. Leaping with all his might, he dove straight through their swarm and arched into the water, and they noisily dispersed back to their perches in the forest.

He shot up to the surface and found, to his slight irritation, that Matufinn stood inside the boat completely unscathed, beaming at him while kneeling down to offer his hand.

"We can walk on water," said Matufinn, "if we just forget how to walk."

Morlen sputtered, clasping his forearm, which pulled him up over the side of the vessel. "You tricked me! You made the birds attack you? And what is that supposed to mean, 'forget how to walk'?"

"I called the ravens, yes," Matufinn replied. "But they did not actually harm me, as you can see." He lifted a large brown blanket from behind his legs and wrapped it around Morlen's shivering back. "When you thought about the step, you fell; when you thought about the water, you sank. But when you forgot about them both, and walked, what else did you forget?"

It had all happened so quickly, he hadn't had time to think like in the previous attempts. Each of those had taken fierce concentration, and resulted in disappointment. "I forgot that I couldn't," he answered finally.

They shared a comfortable silence after this, one that held

understanding, and needed no distraction. Then Matufinn rowed back the way they had come. And though Morlen was soaked, he drank in the evening breeze, open to whatever lessons the day still held.

After making their way back to shore, they pushed the boat to rest upon the lake's gravelly bank. Seeing Morlen's bow on the ground nearby, Matufinn picked it up and gave it a long look of appraisal. "A fine weapon," he said, drawing back hard on its string while the pliant arc bent without a creak. "So light and lean that you could fire off two shots before your targets knew what was coming. I'm sure it's served you well," he added, handing it over.

Morlen nodded as he took it, gripping the blurred outline of a hand imprinted upon it years before. "It's all I've ever had," he said, restrapping the quiver as well. "All that's ever been mine."

"What about a sword?" asked Matufinn, glad to see the spark in Morlen's eyes at the question. "You've never had one?"

"Just this," Morlen answered as he drew his small hunting knife, its rusty blade too dull and dented to pose even a modest threat to an apple.

Matufinn laughed, taking it in his palm to examine its decay, and then tossed it far into the lake without a second glance. "Come," he said. "We'll find something more suitable for you." He turned to walk back toward the woods, and Morlen ran lightly to keep up.

The sun was sinking low when they entered a small clearing, and Matufinn went to a large round stone sitting at its edge. Prying it up, he flipped it to the side and brushed away the undergrowth, revealing an old, worn cover that he pulled away to expose a rectangular hole.

Morlen crouched to look within, seeing many shapes of

various sizes, overall similarly long and narrow, wrapped in cloth. Swords. Dozens of them. Some were old, rusted, from long before his time; others were in fair condition; and all had surely seen battle. Matufinn extracted the freshest one of the batch, took its grip firmly in hand, and then held it out for Morlen.

"My first sword," he said. "The one I wielded against the shriekers. I set it aside after my brief travels led me to befriend one of the Freelands' finest sword smiths, a fellow by the name of Edrik, who forged one that has maintained a cleaner history." He tapped the hilt of the weapon at his hip.

Its blade still had a subtle luster, though chipped in some places, and Morlen's expression was bright as he studied it. "This is to be mine?" he asked, taking it from Matufinn's hand.

Matufinn nodded. "For now, at least. Until you obtain your true sword." Then, with his chin raised boldly, he added, "But first, you must get acquainted with it."

Unsure what to anticipate, Morlen rose and followed Matufinn to the clearing's center, setting his bow and quiver aside again. The air rang as Matufinn smoothly drew his own weapon and faced him a few paces away.

"Though you've had little experience with a blade, not to worry," he said. "Much more than mere swordsmanship will be tested here. Stand ready now."

Morlen dug in his heels, clinging to the steel with both hands as if it were timber in a flood. Matufinn swung down vertically, and he quickly raised it above his head to parry a blow that shook him to his core. The sword swung again at his left this time, and he stopped it just a few inches from his head with a deafening note. Then Matufinn's blade swept toward his right leg, and his tattered garb narrowly escaped a new shred as he swung dangerously close to defend.

"Faster!" Matufinn urged as their blades met, thrusting

forward to stab. Sweeping across his front, Morlen knocked the strike aside and opened Matufinn's guard.

"Good. Attack!"

Morlen swung diagonally, connecting with nothing as Matufinn dodged so quickly he nearly vanished, coming at him again as though to fell a tree with an axe, and it took all his might to repel the blow, which staggered him back several feet.

"Again." Matufinn spurred him on. "Attack."

Morlen's enjoyment of their amicable exchange faded as the exercise grew more heated. He charged forward, aiming the point of his blade at Matufinn, but hit only air while a kick to his backside sent him stumbling. Then he turned around in frustration and saw Matufinn staring at him with the look he began to despise, as though to make him feel an inherent strength that he found quite elusive.

"Are you trying to fight me with your sword? With your arms?" Matufinn mocked. "These alone will not help you. Must I trick you again so you may forget them?"

Morlen grunted stubbornly through another advance, swinging as Matufinn flowed around his guard and jeered.

"Do you think your blade is a threat to me? I am already gone before it's thrown."

Anger building, Morlen thrust his elbow upward at Matufinn's voice, missing again as a painful kick to the small of his back scuttled him forward. Whatever speed Matufinn demanded, he couldn't summon it. Every boy who had pummeled him into the dirt came rushing back with each clash of steel on steel, punching, kicking, laughing at his weakness. He felt the Goldshard against his heart, offering hope and refuge.

"Morlen!"

He ducked Matufinn's blade and barely kept his ear unscathed. Lunging forward again on the offensive, he held his weapon close to his body this time, anticipating Matufinn's quick evasion. He reared back as though to execute, and Matufinn took the bait, moving sideways in the path of his deliberate strike. Stumbling slightly to block, Matufinn tried to pass it off as a misstep, but Morlen was not fooled.

Matufinn gave him the faintest look of approval. "Good. Now, faster!" he bade, and struck high as Morlen ducked with a low swing. He grimaced when Matufinn hurdled easily over the jab to whip him between the shoulders, and quickly spun around only to be shoved aside. Turning once more, he sent sparks through the air as metal met metal with a sonorous clang, and then slammed his shoulder into Matufinn's chest, throwing an upward slice that took off the bottom inch of his beard.

Brows arched in surprise, Matufinn's eyes lowered furtively toward a less-covered chin, his free hand twitching a few inches up and stopping, as though he willed himself not to touch it. Looking at Morlen, he fought to keep the corners of his mouth low.

Morlen held his position for the next attack, and it came swiftly as Matufinn leapt forward, bombarding him with a flurry of blows that demanded all he could muster to deflect. Their blades tore through the air as each tried to drive the other back, neither one budging.

Morlen pushed against the weapon bearing down on him and wheezed. "What did you mean... urgh... when you said... I would obtain... my 'true sword'?"

Matufinn let up and quickly batted his thrust away, forcing him back again, and saw that he was not inclined to resume until the question was answered. Grateful for a chance to rest while under the guise of obliging this, he took a few paces back of his own.

"There is a sword, unlike any other," said Matufinn. "It has been waiting to be claimed by one of us for centuries. But, all have tried, including myself, and all have failed."

"Where is it?" Morlen asked.

Trying subtly to catch his breath, Matufinn continued. "Beyond the Dead Plains, high in the Dark Mountains, where Morthadus saw the rest of his order fall into mists of black. It is said that Korine the Ancient helped him escape, and left the Crystal Blade for our bloodline to obtain, just as he gave the Crystal Spear to the Eaglemasters. And it sits before the black mists to this day, for one who is worthy of it."

"Then I could also go to the Dark Mountains, and try to claim it?"

Matufinn nodded. "When it is your time."

Daring to tread where he knew Matufinn wished to avoid, Morlen asked, "And, you will lead me to the mountains? You will go out, and take me to the sword's path?"

Matufinn's nostrils widened. "Enough rest. It is time to resume." And he raised his blade, Morlen doing the same.

They stared one another down, each waiting for some sign to make a move, until both finally lunged at the same time, and their colliding swords sent tremors through the ground. "Why are you so afraid?" Morlen steamed, probing for weakness. "What am I supposed to learn from you, when you test my limits while hiding behind your own?" He swiveled and struck again, only for his attack to be negated.

"Learn not to be like me," Matufinn replied, dodging his counter jab. "Be better than I am."

Morlen pivoted to thrust out again. "That won't be difficult. I just won't surrender as easily as you." He missed as Matufinn forced him back with a kick to the chest. Stunned from the blow, it was all he could do to stand rooted and lift his sword to absorb

Matufinn's next strike, which stamped a deep imprint of his feet into the grass.

"I didn't surrender—I lost." Matufinn seethed as they stood blade to blade. "I lost my father to the shriekers... I lost Dirona."

"Dirona," Morlen whispered. "I know that name. She was my... mother."

Matufinn broke eye contact, and, feeling him ease back, Morlen pushed with all he had left, creating a gap that neither one immediately breached. His glare burned Matufinn, who made him wait long before finally meeting it. And more was told now than all they'd spoken before.

Then Morlen swung hard, and their blades hit with an echoing blast. But this time, when Matufinn darted to elude him, he followed. They became two swirling leaves in a gust, striking with tremendous speed. Sparks ricocheted left and right while they battled, neither of them yielding.

"You're doing it, Morlen!"

But Matufinn was faster, stronger, and as Morlen struggled to keep up, the familiar jagged touch from his inner chest pocket comforted and reassured.

"Morlen!" shouted Matufinn, seeing him falter.

Why not use it as he wished? It could make him strong... invulnerable, even. He wouldn't have to fear or hurt again as long as he relied on it.

"Morlen!" Matufinn bellowed louder.

His stance slackened, and Matufinn swept in before he could deflect, knocking him to the ground. He lay motionless, his entire body completely drained. Then, looking up at the sky, he began to laugh. "When you called us sons of Morthadus, you didn't mean we were brothers."

Matufinn stepped closer, broad shoulders and long cloak

casting a shadow over him as he lay flat on his back. "Who are you, Morlen?"

Morlen struggled to prop himself up, sitting ashamed while Matufinn sought an answer he could not even pretend to have.

Matufinn let out a heavy sigh. "If you cannot look inward and know now, then you must when you stand before the enemy out there, and the thousands that march behind him. If you are weak from within, like they think you are, they will have already beaten you." Then he bent down and held out his arm for Morlen, who took it loosely, and gripped harder than necessary while hauling him up.

"The answer," Matufinn finished, "will not be in your words, but in what you feel when you say them, in the truth that shatters all barriers. Feel it, and know it."

Matufinn looked at him for one last moment. Then, with night beginning to fall, he turned and strode back through the trees.

Alone in the clearing, Morlen limped to gather his belongings, and gingerly picked up the old sword. He used his sleeve to polish off any dirt, and then followed the sound of Matufinn's efforts to spark a campfire, ready for the day's end.

They sat opposite each other across the fire, immersed in a tensionless quiet, and Morlen thought of how different tomorrow would be than any day he had ever experienced. Unable to spare the energy to speak, he rolled onto his side and faced away from the flames as Matufinn seemed to pay no heed. He reclined on the grass and stretched his throbbing tendons as far as they would permit, drinking in the heat at his back.

Matufinn remained seated, tracing every form within the orange glow while Morlen became a silhouette in his periphery. "My mother was an Eaglemaster." His voice suddenly filled the surrounding calm. And Morlen lay still, careful to maintain the impression that he was asleep, though he kept eyes and ears wide open.

"One of the only common women in history to be counted among those warriors," Matufinn continued. "Often she would fly over the Isle, singing a sweet song, and my father would watch her from the trees, thinking her fair beyond measure.

"One day, she flew close enough that he called out to her, inviting her to see the marvels held inside, and so she came." His sight did not stray from the fire while he spoke, and Morlen dared not twitch a muscle, listening closely.

"From then on, she would fly here and sit atop her eagle, perched in the trees above where my father slept, soothing him with her melodies. Every night, as he lay waiting for her song, she came and sang it lovingly. And when she took it away with her each time, she hoped that he would follow so they could be together. But, as her song trailed off beyond the Isle's borders, he remained within, afraid of the world outside.

"So she chose to give up her eagle and her station, binding herself to him in the Isle instead. They lived together in happiness for years, and eventually she bore me to him. But, even as a small child, I began to sense a deep sadness within her."

Unable to conceal his interest any longer, Morlen rolled over to face him. "Why?" he asked. "Why was she sad?"

Matufinn turned his eyes from the flames to meet him head-on, smiling. "Because she'd climbed into his cage with him. I would often see her crying all alone, and I knew she despaired because she did not want to stay here forever, as he did."

Scratching a nervous itch on his cheek, he resumed. "When I was grown, I wanted to help her, but I didn't know how. Her prime was long past, and her body too frail to ever fly atop an eagle again.

"That is when I met Nottleforf for the first time. He visited the Isle, warning that the shriekers were marching out from the South. But, it seemed he came for another reason, as though he knew my mother's pain. He offered her a solution, a chance to be free again, and she took it."

"What was it?" Morlen asked.

Matufinn cleared his throat. "Nottleforf could not bring back the youth she'd lost over the years. So, he transformed her. Into a bird. A songbird. And, pouring out her melodies once more, she took flight and left the Isle, never to return." He wiped a tear from the corner of his eye.

Voice heavier, he continued. "My father's grief at her departure turned him cold, and I told him that I, too, would be leaving to stand and fight against the coming enemies. I said that if he chose to stay here forever, he would never see me again. And, on the day of the battle, as I stood alone within the edge of the Isle, preparing to emerge for the first time into a world I had never before seen, he came to me, and we set out together."

His glistening eyes returned to Morlen now. "The greatest comfort I took was just before the battle commenced, hearing, in the dead of night, the sweetest chirping. And I knew he heard it too, as clear as could be, before he met his end."

The fire crackled louder between them, and both fell silent. Morlen lay propped on his elbow with full focus still on Matufinn, wishing for him to go on though there was no more to tell. Finally though, he rolled over onto his other side.

"Good night, Father," he said.

Matufinn's expression became a thousand times more alert. Observing Morlen intently, he barely exhaled, listening to find if he had misheard. Unable to move, he looked over him as he rested, and when his heart gradually eased its rapid pace, he found the strength to stand.

He forged through the woods until the fire vanished miles behind his trail. Apprehension slowed him, but he pressed forward nonetheless. He would face it head-on; he would not hide another day.

The sea of trees parted as he went on, his pulse rapidly hammering, and then, the wall was there before him, rising high above the Isle, its dense blue mists still brightly discernible through the night.

Sixteen years, he thought. *Far too long.*

He took one step closer, and then another, inching toward it as though pulling a boulder with rope until it was but a hair's width from his face. He lifted his right hand and pressed it flat against the contracting fog, and saw it vanish before his eyes. Then, he followed with his left, both arms becoming immersed. Finally, he gulped the largest breath his lungs had ever drawn, and plunged forth, swimming, floating, leaping, and then...

His feet touched down on earth that was hard, cold. And, opening his eyes, he quickly realized, he had never seen land more beautiful. It stretched on for miles and miles, clear in all directions. But, there were people being enslaved, oppressed, tortured. He felt their distress as his mind reached out. Their captor was ruthless, as were those who followed him.

He would go to them, he decided. He would go to Korindelf and its suffering people, be as one of them, help as many as he could to escape. And he would return to Morlen often as well, to see him grow strong.

An eruption of growls broke out as a throng of shriekers came rushing toward him along the Isle's edge, no doubt stationed there by their master. Standing exposed, he felt no need to reach for his sword while they swarmed all around, and soon, they halted yards away, emitting high-pitched whines when they saw him. And as he slowly walked nearer, pacing before them without pause, they inched back.

"Now," he began, "I know you remember me. And I remember you. Do not fear, though—I am not going to kill you tonight. But, be careful, because"—and at this, he grinned to himself—"I think I shall be coming and going through here quite frequently now, and if I ever see you near these borders again…" He abruptly scraped the silence with a swift draw of his sword, needing not to even brandish it as they scattered away, yelping into the night.

Laughing with a swell of pride as they dispersed, he kept a satisfied smile on his face. He peered off toward Korindelf, not knowing the struggles he would face there, and found peace in that uncertainty. He would see, and be seen. And nothing would shut his eyes again.

Morlen lay by the fire, sleep eluding him despite his exhaustion. He turned to his other side, and saw that he was alone. Sitting up, he focused on the flames, and their light danced all about the trees to the area in which he and Matufinn had sparred.

With rest seeming a futile effort, he got to his feet and strode out. Scanning the clearing's perimeter, he went to the large hole that held the old swords and stared into it, hoping dearly that it would be deep enough. Then, he reached into the pocket within the folds of his clothes, and the Goldshard's jagged edges were sharp against his fingers as he withdrew it.

He looked at it with starving eyes and could think of nothing but what it offered, for which he had longed so desperately. But now, things would be different, he repeated to himself.

He extended his left arm and grabbed the ripped sleeve, stripping away a sizable length upon which he laid the Goldshard. Taking in its sheen for one last moment, he folded the cloth tightly, kneeled to place it deep inside the recess, and covered it with the worn blanket that blended so well into the ground. Then he went to the large flat rock that had guarded the secret spot, and flipped it forward onto its rightful place.

Standing still for a moment, he suddenly felt the sweetest breath of relief, as though an insect knifing into the back of his neck had just been swatted away. He returned to the fire lighter than ever, and bedded down again. When he sank into the grass, he allowed his mind the comfort of knowing that it could look where he hadn't permitted it to look before. And, this time, rest came to him on quick wings.

CHAPTER FIVE
LADY VALEINE

A DOZEN SUN-BLEACHED skulls with long, curved horns sat atop the walls of the Eaglemasters' southernmost city, Veleseor. Their vacant sockets stared across the Silver River toward the Ferotaur Wildlands, silently warning all others that wished to trespass.

In the city's outer training grounds, hundreds of bright-faced youths clasping untested spears gazed upward at the woman who stood on the wall. Her milky white garments beneath blonde hair distracted no one from the spear she gripped firmly in hand, its blade and shaft chipped and reddened, the weapon of a seasoned warrior who had defied death. Surveying the crowd with pride, she addressed them with a melodic voice.

"You stand here today, no longer boys of twelve, swept from your mothers to snivel under harsh elements and trials of physical aptitude, but a grown, ready crop, scraped from the weeds. You stand at the city named for the grandfather of our king, because his spear and sword carved a place for you here, and because this realm's true defenders hold it for you still. To one day be counted among our honorable ranks, you must first see what we have seen, taste, smell, as we have, and bleed, too, as we have bled.

"You have endured several assaults over the last year, firing beside your friends to halt clumsy handfuls of enemy ships, striking down those few that we allowed through our defenses. You may have even seen a skirmish or two as you progressed through our sister cities.

"But have you seen a hundred ferotaurs up close, all in the best health that such creatures can be? Have you felt their rough, pale skin on yours, or looked into their ghoulish faces? Have you taken in their rancid breath, billowing out through teeth laced with flesh?"

Mounted on their eagles that perched conspicuously just behind the captivated soldiers-to-be, her three older brothers observed the address with the good humor of sibling rivalry.

"She's doing well," Ivrild said with a smirk. "Very inspiring of confidence."

Verald, the eldest, replied, "I'd rather have her at my side than you against that many."

"As would I," said Ondrel. "And besides, if combat were to fail, I at least could escape if they found her more appealing." They snickered together, listening in.

"Four years' diligence, excellence under controlled conditions, may be forgotten in two breaths out there," she cautioned, pointing to the hostile territory beyond the river. "Which is why you must all go, very soon, and know the true force that swells constantly over our tenuous border, that will spread and drown you all, if you do not remember.

"And now," she continued, "we can no longer say that only the ferotaurs threaten us here in the West, and that the shriekers cannot reach us. Now, there is a greater enemy, and he will march both hordes against us if given the chance; a great many already follow behind his sword, which he points in our direction.

"The people of Korindelf, our friends and allies, have sat chained under his rule for a full year now, tortured into obedience and fed to his pets for mere sport. His threats of further action against them have hindered our ability to face him head-on, but make no mistake: A great battle is approaching. Whether on his ground, or ours, I care not. All that matters is that however arduous these final weeks prove, you push yourselves harder than I demand, so that when the day of war arrives, and we meet Felkoth along with all his gathered forces, you will have strength enough when it is over to spit on his corpse!"

Thunderous cheers erupted from all who stood below, accompanied by the clattering of weapons against chest plates, in a loyal chorus.

"Our spears are yours, Lady Valeine!" one shouted proudly, those beside him quick to repeat even louder.

Still watching behind the trainees, Ivrild jabbed his older brother. "It seems your position as future king may not be so secure after all."

Verald grinned. "As though you haven't held me in your sights every time we've gone to battle, thinking you could put an arrow in my back with none being the wiser. I always thought the crown was to be yours, anyway. Isn't it meant to go to the best-looking heir?"

"Then both of you will be spit-shining the castle floors while I sit on the throne," gloated Ondrel, unaware that their father descended briskly toward them.

"What is this conspiracy I hear?" King Valdis asked, joining his sons. "As if any of you could take my place."

Pleased to hear his voice, the brothers directed their huddled eagles to part and let him take his position in between, all four now looking directly at Valeine, who stood more than aware of their close attention.

"There was no morbid plot in my words, Father," Ivrild joked. "I only presumed that one day soon, you would pass the crown to me when you grew tired of your kingly duties."

"I grew tired of my kingly duties before you were born," Valdis replied. "And my fatherly duties soon after."

Trying to avoid the scrutiny of her father and brothers, Valeine focused on the devoted host as their raucous support quieted down. "My spear is for all people of the realm. And so too shall be yours. An Eaglemaster is deadlier on the ground than in the sky. If you are to rise as one of us, then first, you must be deadly. Be deadly here. Be deadly wherever swords, arrows, horns or fangs aim to rip you open. Then, you will be counted as true protectors of this kingdom, and the sky will be yours for the taking."

The enthusiastic group stared up in admiration, finally breaking off as other instructors began conducting the day's training exercises. Waving a smooth hand at her nearby eagle, which fluttered down and waited for her to mount, she wondered fondly what scheming she'd soon come upon as she flew toward her ascending family.

"Not bad for a girl of, what is it now, fourteen, fifteen…?" Ondrel greeted her playfully as she joined them in the air.

"Well now," replied Valdis, "I don't recall any of you having command of a city at seventeen. You were all too occupied giving flying lessons to every girl in sight."

"Is that what they called it back when you were a lad?" Ivrild laughed, his brothers and sister quick to join.

With his children all around, gliding to land atop the tall hill that offered a quiet vantage point, Valdis released much of the weight that lately had sunk him. He hoped to steer conversation away from deteriorating campaigns in the East for as long as possible. Felkoth's hand reached nearer every day, and they could ill-afford to lose any more men trying to halt it while other threats closed in.

"You've done well with them," he praised his daughter. "They seem eager to fight, eager for honor. Perhaps the Wildland Test will take some of that wind out of their sails, as it did for most of us."

"They're ready for it," she assured him. "I'll take them over the river before month's end, and they'll earn their horns as we've all done." She proudly glanced at the scythe of sharpened bone fixed into her spear's base, a trophy as lethal as the ones that her brothers and father each had fastened to theirs.

"You may not need to," said Ondrel. "The ferotaurs may come to you in droves before you send your students onto their final task."

"Perhaps if you traveled more often down to the kingdom's most dangerous corner, you'd see the droves we frequently repel," she replied.

"Aye," said Ivrild, "but when your boys get their first glimpse of what it's like not to have the river between them and what's out there, they'll lose half their body weight through their trousers. Do you remember your first time, big brother?"

Verald nodded. "One never forgets." He gazed off in silence for a moment, not eager to dredge up the memory. "We were dropped about twenty miles in. And on the journey over you finally grasp how few we all are, next to the packs that cover the land like insects. But I still felt separated from that place, safe somehow, until the instructors ordered us to dismount. After all the ugly things I'd seen, watching them fly away was by far the worst. You're never deadlier than when you hear those first snarls closing in to welcome you."

With a chuckle, Ivrild chimed in. "Even though they didn't drop my group near the biggest clusters, and they seemed confident they'd return for us before we got overrun, we thought we were as good as dead. We ran more that day than in the four years leading up to it. All those exercises they make you do when you're just starting out, not a single hair on you from knees to nose—scaling walls, crawling on your elbows through mud. It'd be more authentic if they sicced the dogs on you while you're at it, and you had to bash their heads in every time you stopped to breathe."

"We emptied our quivers in the first half hour," said Ondrel. "There must have been four hundred of them littering the fields when we fired our last shots, and that was barely a fraction of what came after."

The three glanced at Valeine, waiting for her to give a similarly suspenseful account. Their father, though, knew that she was never one to conform.

Instead, she turned her head to look out over the distant Wildlands that stretched fallow and brown to mountains that concealed a vast network of caverns, which crawled with enough vermin to make the ones they fought in the open seem like barely a trickle. "I felt strangely alive there," she said, and her brothers scoffed as though it were nothing but false bravado to shame them.

"Not because I wasn't afraid," she added. "We all were. But because I was outside the world we were born into, back to the way everything was in the beginning, when there were only monsters and chaos. And I realized we've been in their world all along. We're just a patch of moss on their rock, and we're on borrowed time."

"What are you saying?" asked Ondrel. "That we should stop patrolling the river, abandon our garrisons, and let them pour in? Make it like it was centuries ago, when there were no Eaglemasters, and a good day for a man was not getting his leg chewed off?"

Valeine shook her head. "I'm saying it's easy to think that this way of life is what's meant to be. But when I stood in that chaos, I saw so much more that could have been, so much that *can* be.

Our tradition that demands devotion is just a stepping-stone to greater knowledge and freedom. And I'll gladly man the defenses while you three do whatever it is you do, so that some of us can be around to find it."

Her brothers quieted down at this, and their expressions gradually abandoned the ridicule they often showed. Her father, too, looked at her as though having forgotten she was his youngest born.

Valdis wished that matters of war and governing did not have to intrude on time spent with his children. But he knew their remaining days together would be few indeed unless he kept firmly to his role as king, saving that of father for rare moments of peace. "I've been hearing reports," he reluctantly began, "like before. More people showing up in the realm, with whispers that they came from Korindelf."

"Spies?" Verald asked with a less jovial tone.

Valdis shook his head. "No, I don't think so. The accounts I've heard suggest families, mostly. Mothers with children."

"But how could they manage to reach us from there?" asked Valeine.

Valdis breathed against a gnawing fear. "Someone is smuggling them in," he answered plainly.

"Going back and forth, without being seen by either side?" Ivrild asked. "Can we recruit him?" Valeine arched a brow at him, "Or her?" He bowed apologetically.

"I'd say the wizard is out of the question, or he'd have told us," suggested Ondrel.

Valdis nodded. "Agreed. I've not yet been able to produce someone we could question. But if these rumors are true, then, I am at a loss to say who is responsible, though my instinct says friend over foe. Still, with such a feat being possible, the capital may no longer be safe. If the reports continue and I ascertain their source, evacuation may be prudent."

"Evacuate?" Verald looked over in alarm. Then, understanding the real danger at root, he said, "You think Felkoth would dare follow them here?"

"I know," Valdis said sternly. "He means to conquer us at all costs. He would spend every last drop of his men's blood just to stand, for a few thrilling moments, unopposed. And he would gladly see all of us ripped and burnt, and leave our cities fodder for the ferotaurs."

"And what about Korindelf's people?" asked Valeine. "While we take these precautions they're trampled and whipped, now, and every day. He laughs at us, too, knowing what fools we are for thinking our inaction will spare any of them."

"If we breach the border he'll slaughter prisoners at every camp just to spite us," Valdis answered with a stern look, finding that its effect on her had diminished over the years. "He'll mingle them with his troops as he did when we last challenged him… use them as human shields. Either we'll get their blood on our hands, or lose more of our own while we're nearly bled dry already!"

"No matter how quickly his alarms sound, we could fly faster, save as many as can be carried, before it's too late," she implored, unfazed. "Whoever has been bringing them here, maybe it's a desperate call for us to follow suit, because soon there'll be none left alive."

She sympathetically studied her brothers, who worked hard to conceal their underlying scars, like their father. "We've all seen friends die this last year," she said. "And I know we're in more peril now than we've ever been before. But those people look to the skies hoping we'll come end their suffering. We can let Felkoth have his way as he inches closer to us, or show him that we're not so easily manipulated."

But, she knew she was alone in her estimation, lowering her head in disappointment. Then she straightened up again, and tightened both legs around her eagle to depart. "We should be helping them," she said scornfully, and turned away, flying back toward the city in their wake, *her* city. It sat at the edge of a storm that was unlikely to abate, and she would hold it every day, the first shield to be struck and last to break.

The king and three princes knew better than to go after her. They had enough battles to anticipate as it was, the worst of which could soon be fought in the very heart of their kingdom, against a force they may never see coming. A door to the realm was open, allowing many to pass unchecked, and they could neither find nor close it—only wait patiently for those it brought.

Chapter Six

The Missing Prisoner

THREE LARGE WAGONS rolled in single file across the Quiet Waste, each one pulled by ten sullen-faced prisoners where horses ought to have been, and pushed by ten more behind. Having begun two days earlier at the ford of the Freeland River, they carried crates of steel arrowheads and pikes toward Korindelf and were flanked on every side by mounted soldiers who rode with whips at the ready.

Behind the lead wagon, one prisoner with a dark beard uneasily eyed the faltering, sick man beside him. Turning to the rest, he whispered, "This could be trouble... did you hear him coughing all night? He's not going to make it."

"None of us may," answered one whose cloak was shredded open at the back, dried blood staining tattered threads around a wound. And those next to him bore marks as well. They all wore meager coverings and stiff leather boots that crackled in the cold, and their sweat-beaded faces burned terribly under frigid air. Snow would soon fall, and this spurred them on faster than their captors' lashes ever could. Still, all thoughts of getting to Korindelf before winter turned harsh did little to bolster their hopes.

"Save your strength," an older man among them spoke dismally, legs and back quivering. "After this job is done they'll only ship us out again, probably on the day we unload these weapons. Reorganize us into different camps when the snow hits."

The only woman in the group sighed beside him. "I doubt we'll see each other again. Not until they've pooled us into so many camps that we've lost track of every name and face."

"All a part of the Tyrant Prince's plan," rumbled a gruff man who was strongly built. "Never teaming us again with the same people after a job. He means to weed out companionship. Kill an uprising before it even has a chance to spring. Same with making us cart supplies like animals, when a few men with horses could bring this load to the city in a day. Wear us down till we have no choice but to accept his rule."

A tall man added glumly, "And our families soon forget us. I've not seen mine in almost six months, and before that, hardly at all since he took control. A year already, and the last I saw my wife, she told me that all children are instructed to follow him... even love him. That his new order is necessary to lead a dying realm to prosperity."

"And the Eaglemasters sit idle as his power grows," the gruff one continued. "I was a farmer at the Freelands, and they came telling us to abandon our fields, our forges, because he was coming. And many fled across the bridge into their realm, leaving it all behind, but not I. I stayed to fight for what I'd worked so many years to build, and his army marched in with hundreds of Korindelf's people chained in lines among them, with the shriekers all around. I saw a hundred Eaglemasters fall before they finally pulled back, destroying all they could so that Felkoth couldn't have it, destroying the bridge too. And those few of us who stayed lost everything."

"The Eaglemasters will do something," the woman replied.

"They will. They have to. King Valdis has always been true to Korindelf. He'll not simply leave us to die."

The sick man groaned, convulsing as his limp arms merely rested upon the wagon, and the darkly bearded fellow beside him gave the others an apprehensive look, watching the soldiers as they appeared so far not to notice. "The Eaglemasters can do nothing for us," he said. "We are going to have to help ourselves."

"Besides," said a man whose face was scarred, positioned on the other side of the sick one, "the Eaglemasters have the ferotaurs in the West to ward off as well. And, if Felkoth invades their territory, they may not be around much longer."

"Would he really strike out that far?" asked the tall one anxiously.

The farmer answered, though keeping his voice low, "Why such a steady flow of weapons to the army? They have the shriekers and whips for us, no need for arrows or pikes."

"Maybe we should wish him to invade," the woman broke in hopefully. "Trying to take the Eaglemasters on foot, in their own land. How could he stand a chance?"

"Quiet, you crawlers!" a soldier bellowed from behind, and a whip cracked against the air.

Driving the caravan on for miles more, the prisoners felt their muscles scream out for rest that was ages away, nourished only by scraps of food each was allotted in a small pack. Soon, the eastern woods appeared on the horizon, marking the end of a thirty-mile stretch, and the start of one far longer.

With a brief backward glance, the bearded man took note of the fiery mountain that towered ominously in the center of the Waste. Its silence disturbed him, as though it were capable of shaking the entire earth to pieces, but only waiting for the opportune moment.

Seeing how it drew his attention, the woman stealthily glanced at all nearby soldiers before speaking, hoping they would pay no mind. "Do you know the story of the mountain?" she asked.

He looked diligently from side to side, and after determining it was safe to resume conversation, his eyes asked her to go on.

Relieved to bring an end to the chilling quiet, she said, "According to legend, a terrible winged serpent sprang from these lands long ago. Its hide was forged from molten rock, they say, invulnerable to the devices of men, and the wretched sound preceding its fiery breath was the last thing men heard before death. So the creature came to be called Bloodsong. But, it was no match for the Blessed Ones, who sealed it within the mountain, where it is fabled to slumber to this day. And only he who has killed one of them can break the seal."

The man glanced uneasily back at the mountain. "Well, I'm glad that is no longer possible."

At this, the farmer beside them scoffed. "Listen to the two of you, talking as though it were true. That is nothing but a mindless children's tale." He chuckled. "Pure farce, like the Missing Prisoner."

Another quickly interjected, "He is not farce—have you not heard the stories?"

"I have," said the man whose face was scarred. "Many have said that he turns up in different prison camps."

"Yes, I've heard this too," the woman whispered. "He blends in with the rest of the prisoners. Then, after a few days, a small group escapes in the night, and he always shows up again somewhere else."

"The guards know of his efforts too," said the bearded one. "But they don't deter him."

A whip split the air again, this time snapping but a foot away, and the man's heart sank at the sound of fast-approaching hooves.

Throwing all strength forward, he pushed on, and hoped his conspicuous effort would be enough to defuse any danger.

"You there!" the soldier shouted, riding up close on the wagon's right side with his weapon brandished high. "If I have to silence you again, it will be permanently! And that goes for the lot of you! Understood?"

All nodded in unison, except for the sick man, whose head hung low as he struggled to keep up, hardly exerting any weight against the wagon. The bearded fellow discreetly opened posture to obscure him, and to his well-hidden relief, the soldier slowly withdrew, eyes still burning them while he formed up with the others.

Keeping his face forward under such hostile surveillance, he moved his lips just barely to say, "You, with the scars. We can't let them see him like this. We can't let him fall back. It could mean death for all of us—do you understand?"

Silence followed, broken only as the scarred man to the left of the sick one gave a slight cough, which seemed to indicate his affirmation.

Finally they reached the White River, crossing its bridge into welcoming trees, and found the first shelter from wind in what seemed an eternity. With trees standing close against the cleared path, all seventy soldiers were forced away from the caravan's sides, splitting off so that half rode out in front and half behind. Every prisoner breathed a little easier at this altered formation, less vulnerable now to prying eyes.

But, as the bearded man closely watched the worsening fellow at his left, he could not yet enjoy this newfound comfort. Noticing his worry, the nearby woman whispered, "They even say that he takes shelter within these woods."

His focus stayed fixed upon the sick man, whose face appeared devoid of all hope, all lucidity, merely a mask around eyes that barely left the ground. Suspecting that the man could fall limp at any moment, he reluctantly turned away and replied, "Who?"

"Him," she answered. "The Missing Prisoner."

"Ahh," the farmer beside them broke in, chiding again. "Enough about him. Why would he be in the woods, of all places, when he should be out performing more miraculous rescues?" he scoffed. "It is a mere tale, born from fear and helplessness."

"Perhaps," she rebuked, "he's waiting for the right opportunity."

As the two of them disputed, the reins beside the bearded man lost their slack, and the one they bound now lagged behind aimlessly. Grabbing the scarred man's arm, he directed his attention toward the problem at hand. "Help me. Before they see!" he urged, and hoped that the rest of the caravan would be enough to conceal them from view if they worked quickly.

The two fell back together, nearly stretching their own reins to the limit while they both held the sick man, having grabbed him just as he seemed about to lose his footing, and scurried forward until they brought him against the wagon. Finally realizing the peril these circumstances posed, the seven others strained to make up for their loss of momentum.

"That's slowing us down!" the farmer grumbled as they assumed their positions. "One man is more than we can spare as it is—we can't lose the both of you pushing just to go after him. It'll stop us!"

"We can't afford to give them any reason to raise their whips, either!" the bearded man seethed in reply. "You know they never stop after just one—when they rip into him, they rip into those beside him next, then the ones beside those!"

The sick one groaned more loudly next to him, suddenly twitched, and sagged low as his hands tried in vain to touch the wagon. "I... I can't hang on," he muttered.

"Please, you must! For all of us!" urged the bearded man. But the poor wretch lagged again, and suddenly fell to the ground before they could bring him forward. "No!" he fretted, seeing him now being dragged along behind them. "Come on!" he pleaded to the scarred man, who darted back again, and the others heaved desperately in their absence. "Get up!" he said frantically, and struggled to lift him to his feet while scanning to see if the soldiers had yet taken notice.

Their wagon lost more speed, and the ten who pulled protested loudly, unaware that those who pushed had been reduced to seven. Soon, this imbalance caused them to veer off course, wobbling to the path's edge until the front left wheel slammed down into a rut, stopping them in their tracks.

The bearded man scuttled forward clumsily, left arm linking with the scarred man's right as they both hoisted the sick prisoner back to his place. The incensed guards swarmed around the disabled wagon, inspecting each person, none of whom dared look back. Then slowly, the back of his neck tingled from their stares as they found good reason to focus in.

"You!" a harsh voice rang, and he immediately knew it belonged to the soldier who had threatened him before. A long quiet followed, and even the other prisoners soon turned his way.

"You!" the voice boomed angrily again. "You abandoned your post. I know it."

His heart plunged through ice, sinking lower while the guard considered him more closely. And the sick man seemed barely within the threshold of consciousness, sputtering against their tight support.

"That filth you hold, drop him," the soldier ordered with a satisfied tone.

But his arms stiffened around the one he'd surely condemn to die by obeying the command.

"Now!" The word barely resonated over his own crying out

as the soldier's whip tore into his back, sending blood to hit the ground before the sick man did.

"Ah," the guard smiled sadistically, looking down at the helpless captive who trembled upon the dirt. "Here lies our true culprit." Then, tilting his head with mock inquisitiveness, the soldier laughed. "You're tired, is that it? You need to rest?"

The man coughed in a terrible fit, barely able to move.

"Or perhaps this work bores you. Do you need something to take your mind off it?" the soldier taunted. Then, dismounting, he lifted his whip. "I can certainly oblige."

"Please, he's ill!" the bearded man begged. "Please, don't!"

"Quiet!" the guard spat, slicing his arm this time with another excruciating lash. "You're next after I finish this one."

Blood slowly filled his sleeve below the gash, which throbbed like an execution drum while the man he had tried to help waited to be destroyed.

"You think you've suffered thus far?" the soldier hissed over his victim, wrapping several inches of the whip around his wrist for better leverage. "You know nothing of pain."

The prisoners watched, paralyzed with fear while they began to hear the slightest rustling in the nearby brush, too soft for their cackling enemies to detect.

Clearly savoring every second, with all eyes on him, the guard brandished his whip high, rearing back with deadly purpose, and cast it forth.

But suddenly, the sick man caught the whip in hand. Then, wrenching the soldier through the air like a ragdoll, he stood up quite easily and appeared to be in more than perfect health as his would-be killer skidded across the ground to his feet. Snapping off the reins that bound him to the wagon, he bent down to face the visibly confounded soldier, and said, unafraid, "Do you think your whip is a threat to me?"

All prisoners watched with awe, and as the guards frantically reached for their bows to shoot him down a great uproar broke out in the surrounding woods. Unseen archers around the caravan's perimeter sent a flurry of arrows from every side, dropping many soldiers in but a few seconds. Thunderous shouts rocked the air from all over while the prisoners crouched low, watching the exposed battalion fire haphazardly into the trees, their obscured attackers quick to counter and lethally accurate.

One soldier carrying a battle horn around his neck blew just one echoing note before a well-placed shot hastily shattered it, and a second threw him from his horse. The deadly rain pressed in, striking down the captors by the dozens. A mere minute or so after the first shots were fired, all noise ceased, and every horse around the caravan was left with an empty saddle.

Reluctant to move, the prisoners stayed huddled in utter confusion, bound to the wagons. Then quietly, the hidden archers—both male and female—emerged from their places of concealment along the perimeter, numbering roughly thirty in all. A sturdy man with grayish black hair appeared to be their leader, who stepped up to address the one who, up until a few moments before, had looked to be on the verge of death.

"The horn, Matufinn," he said apprehensively, tossing him a sheathed sword.

As the fighters spread out to cut them all loose, they rose, none now doubting the legend that had ignited hope within so many. Now he had a face, a name.

"Yes," said Matufinn, strapping the sword around his waist. "We'll leave at once. And, I'm afraid this will have to be the first and last time you help me, Edrik."

Seeming to take issue with this, the archer protested. "I don't understand."

Matufinn replied, "Felkoth has let me carry on for a full year, unabated. Whatever he's planning, I fear it will not be safe for you or the others to return." Then, mounting the nearest horse, he said confidently, "Morlen and I will take it from here."

The female prisoner asked, "How did you all manage to stay within the woods unnoticed, with the shriekers patrolling night and day?"

Edrik answered her pleasantly, "We only just arrived." Then, turning toward his group that brought in the scattered horses, he called out, "Forty must ride double."

Climbing into one of the unmanned saddles, the gruff farmer studied the bowmen's leader with great interest. "Edrik the sword smith?" he asked tentatively. "I stood with you when the Freelands fell. I heard you disappeared from the forges a month ago."

Nodding toward Matufinn, Edrik replied proudly, "With a little help."

Matufinn grinned, preparing to spur his horse on. "More than a few will go missing today." Then finally, with all seventy horses occupied, he led them off the road, heading southeast through the woods. "We ride to the Isle!"

And, as quickly as they could, they wove with great care around trees and brush, knowing the shriekers would rapidly be approaching.

Daylight had receded when they broke out into the open fields, where, to their relief, no enemies were yet in sight. Still, their destination was two hours' ride away, ample time for a patrol to gain on them.

"Form up on our left flank!" Edrik bellowed to his archers over the trampling hooves. "By nightfall, we'll be easy game, and they'll catch up before we make it through these parts, you can count on it!" Heeding his command, all thirty fighters spread out along the party's side, holding their bows tightly.

As each bounce sent flames through the gash on his back, the bearded man noticed the scarred fellow riding close by. Everything had happened so quickly, he hadn't yet been able to show gratitude for the man's aid during their predicament. Graciously, he said, "Thank you for helping me," and laughed, gesturing at Matufinn, "though, ultimately, he could take care of himself."

The scarred man smiled, and as they looked on, Matufinn rode out in front, glancing neither left nor right.

"Three packs following our trail," he called to Edrik. "A few miles behind."

The group pushed on for a great distance, seeing the Forbidden Isle under falling night. Soon, with visibility limited, unable to hear anything but the cacophony of horses, they felt naked out in the open, vulnerable to any predator with a mind to attack.

"Keep close together!" Edrik bellowed.

But as they pressed in tightly, they found little comfort, and one archer cried out, sending an arrow to a spot behind them with a short volley from his nearest companions.

"What?" Edrik shouted as they galloped on, trying not to slow. "What did you see?"

The bowman looked troubled by the dark that concealed whatever crept closer. "It was one of them. I'm sure of it."

The others, now fully alarmed, turned their heads to look all around, and the lightless surroundings haunted them.

"Matufinn?" Edrik called, unsettled by the jarring silence.

Holding his position out in front, Matufinn glanced back at the rest of the group. "They're close," he answered cautiously. "Be ready."

Wasting no time, the archers fitted their bows, each of them nervously staying mounted by knee pressure only. Their spirits lifted slightly when the Isle's blue vapors rose high before them, less than two miles ahead. But they were quickly deflated by shaking cries from the rear horses, whose riders struggled to keep control as they seemed to sense danger pouncing.

"Steady!" bellowed Edrik, who swept a handful of bowmen around the group's perimeter, firing into the air behind them.

"Edrik, keep up!" Matufinn yelled from the front. "We cannot fall back if you get separated."

The archers lingered for another moment before bolting to rejoin the group. "Show yourselves, you wretched dogs!" Edrik cursed. "I am in need of a winter pelt!"

Spurring the horses urgently, they rode on, finding the short stretch between themselves and freedom more unpleasant than any of the countless miles covered in captivity. Then, a sinister growl rang out, followed by many more in a bloodthirsty eruption all around.

"Hold your fire!" Edrik commanded as the group turned frantic, their enemies still unseen. "Watch all directions. Wait until they come in for the attack. Ride! Ride!" The screams closed in on every side except the open area before them, which was diminishing, with the Isle at its end.

"Ride!" Edrik urged. "Almost there—" But a wild bark cut him off, and the pair of jaws it came from quickly lunged on his right side, about to strike for the kill. Then an arrow flew from far ahead, darting over his shoulder directly into what could only be the creature's body, still veiled by the dark as it gave a shrill whine.

Looking up front, Edrik soon understood where the arrow had come from when another flew out from behind the mists, followed by one more, hitting targets that even he could not see. Then, the disembodied onslaught abruptly halted, pulling back in retreat when they finally reached the Isle's border.

"Quickly, into the mists," commanded Matufinn, who held

back beside Edrik, standing guard while the others rode through. They kept eyes and ears open for any sign of the beasts' return, and watched as the former slaves made safe passage. Then, when the entire group had gone through, both pushed forward to follow.

"Extraordinary," Edrik marveled, slowly becoming immersed as they went on. "He can see through the mists, in the dark no less?"

Matufinn smiled in reply, gladdened by the thought of seeing the one on the other side. "He doesn't need to."

Morlen leapt with tremendous speed through the moonlight, his brown cloak a canvas for the reflected colors of apples that blurred as he moved. It whipped against the wind, but didn't slow him in the least while he sprinted up a grassy hill, breaking out into open air. Four lions curved around its wide bend while he ran along the top, skidding down to head them off.

"You think I can't see you?" he called, and lunged through the trees again. He felt them like brilliant rays when his eyes closed, illuminating the paths that wound ahead in all directions. Obstacles were mere illusions now, the curtain of darkness a friendly backdrop to his mind's radiant torch. The woods thinned out and gave way to rocky cliffs. He was almost there... he would beat them for certain... just a little farther.

Their paws shook the earth beneath his feet, stomping with fierce determination to outrun, to overtake. He saw the edge, jutting out high over the water like a perfect platform from which he sprang, soaring without fear and plummeting, breaking the surface with a spectacular splash.

Spewing a laugh through the water, he was soon joined by an even heavier plunge, followed consecutively by three more. Then, muffled roars ascended from below as four stout heads shattered the epicenters of each rippling circle, assaulting him with volleys shaken from their manes.

Morlen drank deeply of their bright presence before they swam to shore, leaving him in the current. Feeling content, he gave in and drifted downriver comfortably on his back, toward the far-off lake. He would reach it near the same time his father led the others to it. The rescued prisoners were undoubtedly enjoying many forgotten comforts within the forest, their stomachs full of the meat he had helped provide before setting out ahead.

He was unsure how many had come and gone over the last year, and contemplated the prospect of setting out soon to help his father, who had faced more than his fair share of danger rescuing them alone. Soothed by the river's cool embrace, he was reluctant to leave this place behind when it felt as though he had only just entered.

But, he was ready. Well, nearly ready. There was still one task that lay ahead before he could join the struggle against Felkoth's oppression. One that many before him had attempted, only to fail.

But, the moment in which he would come to that trial still seemed ages away. Now, while the eternal river cradled him, there was only peace.

Matufinn led the group of freed men and women onward, carrying Morlen's bow and quiver that had once been his own as a young man. Beside him walked the two men who had tried to help him in the prisoner caravan, while Edrik and the rest of the party kept close behind.

With a strip of cloth now bandaging his back, the darkly bearded man reveled in the Isle's beauty. "You truly gave up this place to come live in squalor with the rest of us?" he marveled.

"I found more opportunity in a year out there than a life in here ever brought me," Matufinn replied. "And I resolved to help others find the same freedom."

"The others," the man said hopefully, "who were they?"

Struggling to remember all he had brought to safety over time, Matufinn said, "First, it was remnants of shattered families inside Korindelf. But, with the shriekers so alerted to my scent, attempts at rescue soon became too dangerous for those I wished to help. But there were many," he assured, "before I could finally do no more alone in the city. Then, as you know, I moved on to the different prison camps, infiltrating, extracting with care, and to that course I held, till today."

"Are they still here, then?" asked the man whose face was scarred, walking on his other side.

Matufinn grinned. "No," he answered. "Most of those I rescued departed to Veldere, while select others chose to stay, forming the band that helped carry out this latest campaign."

Intrigued, the scarred man pressed him. "But none can cross the border between the two kingdoms unseen. How could they possibly reach Veldere from here?"

Pleased to relive the joy of introducing distressed, hungry minds to wonders he'd come to take for granted, Matufinn replied, "You'll see, my friend. You're all about to join them."

Morlen waited in the lake meadow as the group filed through the trees, and they greeted him with appreciation one by one. Glad to absorb their outpourings of friendship, he could not help but wonder if any recognized him from Korindelf, from his old life, when every collection of energies had all but stung him to death.

"Here," said Matufinn, taking the bow and quiver from his shoulder, handing both to him. "I trust you moved quickly without these on your back. Though, sometimes we must learn to run with our burdens, till we feel them no longer."

Morlen had grown somewhat taller over the last year, now almost the same height as his father while they walked together. They came to the lake, a diamond carpet sprawling in the moonlight, and he stood aside while Matufinn prepared to address the rest.

All seemed to brim with interest as Matufinn began to answer what most were undoubtedly wondering. "The lake is a nexus between our world and a plane beyond distance and time," he projected loudly. "It bends the miles of stretching space around us into a mere stride that will take you anywhere in these lands you wish to go. It is what enabled me to reach the scattered camps undetected, and you can take it, like the others before you, to Veldere. There, you will find friends old and new in civilization once again.

"By bringing you into the Isle, I have committed a sacred act, one that empowers each of you to return here whenever you wish, with whomever you choose. For having been shown the way, you may now show it to others."

"Then let us hope we are all trustworthy," Edrik joked, laughing with the others, and Morlen realized that the scarred man was studying him intently, with eyes that quickly darted away upon being noticed.

Opening his arms to bid the group farewell, Matufinn said, "Go now, one by one, so your arrival draws no suspicion. Swim down into the lake as its doorway opens for you, and find life on the other side."

They slowly came forward, dozens offering their final thanks before wading through the shallows, and swam down toward bright pulses in the depths that suddenly whisked them away, leaving behind only faint ripples on the surface.

Coming face to face with the two men from the caravan,

Matufinn said, "I wish to express my gratitude to both of you for the good will you showed, thinking me to be on the verge of death. You," he spoke kindly to the darkly bearded man, "were bold in the face of certain doom, and I only hope the marks left by your lashes remind you of that bravery."

With a wide smile, he clasped Matufinn's arm.

"Brave indeed," said the man whose face was scarred, grinning at the bearded one. "I was convinced *you* were the Missing Prisoner. How very surprised I was."

"And you," Matufinn replied. "You too will always be welcome here in the Isle."

The scarred fellow smiled thinly, and Morlen sensed a strong surge of excitement in him. "Thank you," he said quietly. "I think I should like to return, someday." Then, the two men went into the water after most had already departed. Finally, being one of the few remaining, Edrik approached them.

"My old friend," Matufinn said gratefully as they clasped arms, "Remember always that you have strong allies in the two of us."

Bowing his head in appreciation, Edrik smiled. "I shall remember it." Then, looking at Morlen, he said, "I understand you will soon be claiming a new sword. I'll certainly be putting my skills to better use now. Come find my smithy, and I'll craft a fine sheath for the blade." Nodding in return, Morlen shook his extended arm, and Edrik followed his band's last members down the bank.

Morlen watched the party gradually disperse, and glimpsed the scarred man whose eyes were on him again from afar. Wading chest-deep, the fellow seemed to give him the strangest look, one that felt almost familiar, though lost in some distant memory. Finally, diving down, the man vanished with all others, and the lake's surface calmed once more.

*

Rematerializing one at a time in the quiet streets of Veldere, where most had closed their doors to the cold night, the liberated prisoners passed by one another inconspicuously with lifted spirits. Thoughts of bruising ropes and harsh lashes faded, and each of them stood marked by the shared memory of one who had cultivated hope in despair.

They would intermingle with the unsuspecting townspeople, find work in the same trades they'd practiced before, and continue their lives as best they could, though never fully healing. Feeling light and content, they went forward with such enthusiasm that the absence in their group went quite unnoticed. All had naturally assumed that each person going into the mystic doorway would choose the destination they were told.

They spread through the Eaglemasters' capital, admiring its high stone towers and its many defenders who passed deftly overhead. And none of them stopped long enough to realize that the man whose face was scarred had never arrived.

CHAPTER SEVEN

THE CRYSTAL BLADE IN THE DARK MOUNTAINS

DAYS PASSED FAR too quickly in the Isle as Morlen wished for each to halt in motion, delaying the inevitable moment that no longer lay down the road, but at his feet. Now, it was an icy plunge from which he feared he might never surface.

As he stained his lips with the juice of an indigo apple, he began to wonder if this would be the last he ever tasted of the Isle's fruit. Even if he had enough strength to make it back from the dark task ahead, would their sweetness be forever lost to him?

For a full year he'd called this place home, forgetting much of the cruelty that would soon try to choke him again as it had when he was younger. He had left that world behind, assuring himself in the passing months that he was able to face it once more. But first he must brave a place much worse, the place to which many before him had gone and turned back in shame.

Sensing his father, for the first time he did not welcome his presence, instead willing Matufinn to turn around, to go back, to leave him here for a little longer. But, coming into the meadow, Matufinn stood patiently as Morlen fidgeted under his watch. *Just one more day... one more hour... please.*

"Morlen," Matufinn's voice was hard, but not without sympathy, calling him out of safe ground, into the cold. "It is time."

Morlen tried to hold this image in his mind, and after savoring it for a long breath, he cast it away completely, certain that if he recalled it on the path that beckoned, he would likely stumble. Getting up, he took the tied skins that held rations of food and water for his journey back, and they walked together down the lake's pebbled bank, into the shallows.

Never having traveled through the lake's doorway before, Morlen kept his eyes hungrily open when they dove in side by side. As they swam deeper, Matufinn's hand gripped his arm, and a bright bubble suddenly rose in their path. It stretched into a wide nebula of light, and they propelled themselves closer while it curved around them, until they were no longer in water or any other substance. He saw distant reaches of terrain curve toward one another as though merely fabric through which he was a needle and thread, and drifted weightlessly, neither pulled nor pushed. Then, his feet stamped into barren earth, kicking up a thick cloud of dust.

He realized that they were far within the Dead Plains, seeing the Isle as a lean strip many miles behind. Marveling that they were both completely dry, he quickly strode to catch up with his father. And though he felt newfound exhilaration at being outside the shelter he'd grown so accustomed to, he could not shake the sense of doom that gripped him at the sight of the Dark Mountains, which towered a short space ahead. The air was frigid, and the first snows were likely to arrive any day now. But, there was something else: a different cold, worse than any other.

"High in these mountains stands the Crystal Blade," said

Matufinn, "the sword left for our people to claim, at the spot where Morthadus saw the rest of the Blessed Ones fall into darkness. This has been the tradition of our line since its start, signifying a young man's rise beside his fathers. And now, on this day, you will take your place among us."

Wondering aloud, Morlen asked, "Why here?"

His father smiled glumly. "To truly know the light, you must know the dark as well."

Coming to a stop at the mountain base, Matufinn bade him to unstrap the rations he carried and set them on the ground. "Food and water will do you no good in there," he said. "You must keep them here, for when you come out."

Morlen's heart sank at the idea of leaving behind the only sustenance for miles all around, and he tried to focus his thoughts elsewhere. "When did you first come to make the journey?" he asked.

Matufinn's expression was solemn. "After my first battle with the shriekers, before I came to Korindelf," he answered. "And after I failed the quest, your mother truly saw emptiness in me, upon our first meeting. And still, she saw fit to fill it."

Then he withdrew a leather scabbard from within his cloak and handed it to Morlen. "This will have to do," he said, "until Edrik can make one more suitable."

As Morlen's bones froze in the mountains' shade, he tied the vacant sheath to the belt around his waist, unsure that it would ever meet the weapon for which it was intended.

"Remember, Morlen—with each step you take, you draw closer to an abyss that consumes all. You must be stronger in mind and heart than in body. None who went before you, not even I, were able to endure long enough to reach the Crystal Blade. He will lie to you. His power will turn your mind against yourself if you let it. And when your inner voice fails, His voice will prevail."

"He?" Morlen asked, dreading the answer.

Matufinn cast reluctant eyes on the treacherous cliffs he and his forbears had walked, where even daylight was no guide. "The one who lurks in the shadows," he said.

Fixed to the unfurling path that was imprinted with the footsteps of stronger men than he, Morlen said, "No one ever came back the same from this, did they?"

Matufinn fought hard not to show his apprehension. Shakily, he answered, "No one."

Morlen took a step closer to the mountains, pulled by a force that would not easily let him leave. Slowly, he looked at Matufinn again. "I am ready, Father."

Matufinn nodded. "Good." And, able to say no more, he turned quickly, fingernails stabbing into the palms of his hands. Morlen watched him shrink amid the abandoned wasteland, and then faced the trail that called out to him now, its slope so wickedly inviting.

He held still for many long minutes, the sun's heat barely a tickle on the back of his neck. The Dark Mountains loomed over him, steeped in a silence that could drown out the shrillest screams. With a mere pace between himself and ground where even the foulest insects dared not tread, he reached out with his mind to grasp all light that shone brightly behind. The light held him, begging him not to leave, not to go forward where there was none.

He stepped across, touching one boot heel down upon rock, then the other, and the cold immediately impaled him as he gasped for air, though each breath stung worse than the last. Suddenly the sunlight was dimmed by an invisible field that seemed to hover above this place, shining only on the world that felt so far away now.

As his hands scraped against the jagged outcroppings, a familiar flash of gold danced behind his eyes—not like the bright auras he had come to sense in the Isle, but something artificial. He strained to remember its source, and thought perhaps it could be a trick played upon him by the malevolent energy that lingered here.

Knowing he must strengthen himself against such threats, as his father had warned, he tried to cling to the many nurturing entities he'd left behind, summoning their collective radiance to light his path. But they were too far away, mere flickers now behind a sludge in which his sight quickly became mired, unable to break through. And finally, he understood he was alone.

But, what brought the most despair was not the unfathomable distance between himself and the prize. Rather it was the question that if somehow his mind and heart stayed intact through the journey in, would he have the strength to make his way back out? Or, would he be too weak? Would he be too nestled in the dark to even remember the light, falling limp with the Crystal Blade in his cold hands?

No. No, he must go on. Though his spirit might soon be spent, it had fire yet. Wrapping the cloak against his body, though it provided little warmth, he forged ahead over rocks so cold that they burned.

As he climbed through the meandering terrain, he felt he was being slowly choked by hands that crept unseen. Remember... he must remember. He had risen up from the shame of his old life and become something, when all had thought him nothing. But, truly, had he attained any greater knowledge, or tapped into the dormant reservoir of potential his father had been compelling him to unearth? Perhaps none existed for him. No... it did... he had always known of its presence, and had begun to see it more clearly in recent months.

Air was scarce now, and each labored breath coated his lungs with another layer of chilled poison. Standing in the murk of his own undoing, all he could do was move knowing it brought him closer to the vacuum that might shatter and absorb him. He must go on… He could not return to his father empty-handed and set out to face their enemies weak, as he had been upon fleeing them. They had watched a mere boy escape into the Isle; would they see a stranger emerge from it now? Or, would they recognize him clearly as the same fearful child?

The cold scorched his skin as he pushed higher, making his bones feel hollower with each step. How far had the others gone before turning back? How much did they withstand before their drive to go on simply broke? He suspected that his might begin to fracture before long.

Overwhelming isolation became a cascade of tar that weighed him down. His mind was a capsized boat in a sea of shadow, bobbing helplessly, sinking. Only silence remained, in which all experiences of growth and joy he'd ever had were laid out one by one like leaves, insignificant and brittle as they scattered away, leaving him empty.

And then, he heard it.

"Hello."

It sounded so friendly, giving him the only comfort he'd felt after what seemed an endless age in this place. He waited, praying he hadn't simply imagined it, though hope had all but gone.

Then, suddenly, it spoke again. "You think that you are lost."

Yes, there was no question about it. He knew that he was.

"But," the voice continued, "how can you be lost, when I have found you?"

Excitement began to stir him as he pressed on sluggishly through the mountains. "Can you hear me?" he asked sheepishly. Quiet was all that followed, and he feared the voice had gone.

But then, out of nowhere, it returned. "We are together."

He swelled with relief, certain that if he were to be left alone again after sensing another presence in this desolate place, it would destroy him. Keeping calm now, he climbed, listening intently for it to speak. And, when it did, he welcomed it more than he would the sun.

"I am here." The voice sounded young, and it was aching with the same pain this place inflicted upon him. "You will always be with me," it reassured, like a companion traveling with him while he braved the steepening cliffs. "You have been here long... but not as long as I."

Long? How long had it been? Hours? Days? How much longer could his mind last as his body deteriorated?

"I can help you. I can make you strong, though you are weak... weak..."

The bolt of gold struck behind his eyes again, and he started to remember. Strong... something that could make him strong.

"You could be so powerful. Come with me. Not far now. Come closer, and you will see."

"Where are you?" he called hoarsely, scaling the rocks like a blind man whose other senses had perished as well. But, there was no answer, stranding him in a deathly panic as he trudged higher. "Please!" he begged. "Please don't leave me!"

Rocks gave way beneath his ill-placed feet when he clawed upward, forcing him to cling for dear life onto white-hot needles. Gasping uncontrollably, he pulled himself up with arms in spasm, finally writhing onto a ledge like a slug.

And then, so quietly, it returned. "I am coming."

As he lay face-down in a cloud of dust made by his own wild panting, elation from hearing the voice soon overrode exhaustion, causing his legs to slowly spring to life. He stood shakily and looked around in all directions, though visibility was scarce. Coming from where?

There was nothing. No refuge, no aid, no end to this ordeal except for the path behind him. But then, something strange caught his eye: the faintest gleam, almost a sparkle, up high in the distance, like a single star in a dead galaxy. Could it? No, it couldn't be. His father hadn't mentioned seeing it even from afar.

"I am here," the voice repeated, louder now, luring his mind away from the mysterious object that was quickly veiled as he marched on. The cold was so thick, like quicksand latching onto him. He wanted to rest so badly. But, were he to bed down anywhere on this unnatural ground, he feared he wouldn't wake.

"Others have come before you, and they knew me well. Soon, you will see the plan I have for you." The voice was like a rope to embrace as he thrust himself farther up. Plan? Perhaps it knew the way to the Crystal Blade. And perhaps it could lead him back out again! He climbed as the blood retreated from his fingers, turning them to sharp ice. "Please," he panted, "please… What is your name? Where are you?"

"I am here," the voice repeated. "You will come to know me well. Closer… you must come closer."

The cold was upon him worse than ever, and he soon realized it was no longer coming externally, but from within. "I…" he muttered, "I… want… to be with you." The slope forced him to flatten his body and crawl slowly upward. He ripped through a thousand hungry mouths and cried out, wishing for the agony to simply end him.

"I am the only way," the voice returned. "Follow me, and you will be spared."

He knew it was his one lifeline, and that he must cling to it, no matter what. But, how far away did it lead, and what would meet him on the other end? Hours seemed to pass with each eviscerating slither up the mountainside, its unseen heights mocking his feeble gains.

"Please," he called out to the voice's hidden source, "please help me." He was weak… so weak. He was lower now than in the years he'd spent crouching in weeds to escape boyish scuffles. He was nothing.

Moving inches at a time, he was sprawled out limply like a corpse, and suddenly he could no longer hold back the tears that encrusted his eyelids with ice. He had no conviction with which to make them cease... no enlightened outlook that could overcome them... nothing. He was still as hopeless as he'd ever been.

But then, he began to remember: buried... something buried... gold. Yes! That was it! He remembered now. It waited to be unearthed, to make him strong, because he was weak. He could use it to change himself. Why did he even bother to keep climbing? What prize existed that could possibly be greater than the one he'd left behind?

"You are so close, so very close," the voice encouraged. At that, Morlen wiped his tears and continued upward, gingerly. "I will not be here forever."

Was the voice's source as lost as he was? Perhaps in so deep that it had become a part of this place? It sounded different now. Almost hungry, luring him.

"But you will."

He stopped cold, clinging tightly to the cliff as though about to fall. What? No... he must have misheard. The wind pressed him into the rock wall as though to fossilize his misery. Still, his muscles pushed on despite being fed by a choked furnace as he stretched over ground that even the drifting moon had forsaken.

"I will show you." The voice returned even fuller.

Show him what, how much farther he had to go? The journey back out already seemed insurmountable.

"I will show you," it repeated, losing its gentleness, "what you must be."

His skin stuck to the cliff with each grasp as he rose higher, coming free with a sickening suction every time he sought a new hold. There was something different now—a new danger—nearer than he realized.

"The darkness," the voice whispered, though agonizingly loud in his head. "The darkness is so sweet."

And suddenly, utter anguish enveloped him. He had brought it into himself, let it pull him up until he was completely vulnerable. He screamed in pain, the intruder's influence pervading him. He drove himself to break through the bewilderment it cast upon him, and kept climbing though his extremities now felt only the slightest tingle.

"Your flesh has already begun to rot, and your soul swims in the darkness. And the darkness is so sweet."

He was nothing… no one. He deserved to suffer and perish.

"Let the lights that guide each man along his own path be lost, for I am the only true path."

Light… There was no light anymore. Not for him. The realization that he would never escape began to take hold, jelling around him like a putrid cocoon. Still, somehow, his arms dragged him farther, and the trickle of blood in his wake would likely be a clear road back down, though he knew he would never take it.

Then, his numb hands slid over a ridge, resting flat on level ground that spread just above. Far too exhausted to care, he merely sighed and wondered if his torturous climb up the cliff face had only amounted to a few yards. He decided this would be his tomb, certain that once he lifted his head to see the vast distance beyond, he would finally be unmade, and would then submit his broken body to the foul rock that now dissolved it.

"You belong to me." The voice burned now. "The others who came before were weak, but you are the weakest of all."

Growling away all the toxic vapor his lungs now held, he heaved with every last ounce of sorrow and pain, channeling any emotion that hadn't yet vanished to lift him. His shoulders and chest extended over, teetering pitifully on the ledge, lurching forward bit by bit to drag the rest of his dead weight. And finally, his quivering body made it up in a flat crawl that quickly collapsed, and he dryly kissed his doom.

He dared not even look forward; he already knew he was finished. But, the strangest glow beckoned his reluctant gaze. Scanning the ground, he realized with a shiver that this place already entombed the remains of countless others. Rows of decayed bones lay in mounds of dust, almost resembling the skeletons of men, but twisted, unnaturally stretched, with misshapen skulls bearing powerful jaws and fangs.

Finally, his sight braved the space past the scattered graveyard, and he wished immediately that he could retract it. But his wide eyes would not even close while they beheld the infinite chasm a few yards ahead.

The absence of light through which he'd trod now seemed a warm summer's day as he lay prostrate before the unyielding shadow, basking in its slow erosion of his entire being. Its waters surged, rocking, as a beast rears back to swallow its prey, bellowing an utter silence that submerged him.

There, between him and the dark ocean, stood the Crystal Blade, its razor tip piercing the rock floor and its winged hilt extended to be taken, casting the gentlest warmth on his face.

Getting up slowly, he felt like a feather. And with each step closer to the abyss, his feet seemed to flutter, like he would soon evaporate into the black mists that beckoned him with ghostly fingers.

"YOU WILL ALWAYS BE WITH ME."

Slouching at the resting spot of the sword for which he'd come, he looked on with awe to see many other swords stuck in the ground ahead of him. They stood together in a line along the darkness's edge, each one with its own small crystal centered in the guard. The swords of the Blessed Ones, he realized, dropped from the grips of their masters who fell into the black mists. But, since the story held that Morthadus had escaped this place and lived on in the Isle, why was there no link missing?

"ALL WILL FORGET THEMSELVES, AND KNOW ME." The voice stung.

And as he stared helplessly into the outreaching gulf, he wanted it to take him, crush him.

"THE LIGHT IS A MERE INTRUDER. IT CAN BE SWEPT AWAY, EXTINGUISHED. BUT NONE CAN EXTINGUISH THE DARK. GIVE YOURSELF TO ME NOW, OR SUFFER."

His toes stretched forward, arching up, preparing to step forth. He was fading, giving in to the darkness. But then, stopping just inches away, he wrenched his focus from the dreadful sea.

"I…" he stammered, legs wobbling, "would rather… suffer, than let myself be chained." Then, wrapping his trembling fingers around its fine white marble grip, he drew the Crystal Blade swiftly from the cold ground that had housed it for so many centuries, and savored its gleam as he turned his back on the mists.

"YOU CANNOT LEAVE! WE WILL NEVER BE APART!"

A thousand minuscule icicles punctured the back of his neck, driving him faster down the unforgiving cliff, whose deceptive footholds sent an avalanche of small rocks tumbling below. But the Crystal Blade shone like a torch onto trails that had been hidden before, and it held the cold somewhat at bay.

"THERE IS NO ESCAPE FOR YOU. WHATEVER ROAD YOU TAKE, I SHALL BE WAITING AT THE END."

The freezing blast enclosed slick fingers around his limbs, trying to pull him back. But, he pressed on, scraping urgently down the sheer slopes he'd taken ages to scale, giving a fair amount of skin and blood to one ledge after another. His sight was fading quickly, as were all other faculties, his lack of sustenance no longer going unnoticed. He had to get out; he could not bear the thought of perishing here, after coming so far.

"I AM YOUR ONLY STRENGTH... ALL ELSE HAS GONE FROM YOU... ONLY I REMAIN."

Walls were smashing him, shaping as they saw fit. He would never make it out of this place. His body would freeze to become a snugly-fitting boulder upon the mountainside. Each step was slower than the last, invisible ropes binding his feet to the presence that still felt so close behind.

"POWERFUL... YOU COULD BE SO POWERFUL."

He would soon be nothing, pulverized into the dirt. But, the treacherous incline began to slacken, gradually tapering off, until—there! He saw the end, waiting far below. Now, more than at any previous point in this trial, he wanted to scream, stepping toward the boundary that seemed more distant than on his climb up, the boundary that divided him from the light.

"THERE IS NO ESCAPE. YOU BELONG HERE NOW."

Dragging chains through a magnetic swamp, he drew closer to the base... closer... not much farther now.

"I AM COMING."

Closer... he was almost there... it was below him... only a few feet. If he could just tilt, fall forward...

"YOU WILL ALWAYS BE WITH ME! ALLLWAYS..."

The voice faded to a sinister echo as he threw his body past his feet, tumbling painfully down the sharp mountain base. He slammed chest-first onto the flat earth beyond, gasping for the soft night air as though having just escaped the clutches of an ocean grave.

His throat's utter dryness finally revealed itself along with all other bodily hunger in the wave of heat now flooding him. With marionette's arms, he clamped both hands around one of the awaiting ration skins and hastily undid the tie that sealed it. Pulling it to his mouth, he sputtered violently as each gulp of water washed down the sands of a timeless thirst.

Urgently undoing another pouch, he chewed handfuls at a time of the sweet boiled oats it contained, speeding them to his stomach with more generous swigs from the water skin that he soon emptied. Finally, his throbbing muscles could move no more. Letting his consciousness slip away, unconcerned by how many hours, or days, had passed, he sprawled out beneath the moon's offered blanket.

And behind him, the Dark Mountains sat indignant, no longer holding their potential captive—or the sword they'd guarded for nearly a thousand years, which sparkled so elegantly now, ready at his side.

CHAPTER EIGHT

THE INVITED ENEMY

MORLEN SPENT THE next two days trekking back across the Dead Plains, with his cloak drawn against the newly falling snow. But this winter chill was mild next to the cold still clinging to him from the Dark Mountains, and now that he basked in it, he found it less severe, less threatening.

All mystery was gone this time when he approached the Isle, recoiling slightly as its thick mists swirled to receive him. Warding off a shudder, he let his body sink through, and breathed a sigh of relief when he emerged free on the other side. The dangling apples shone in vain as he passed beneath the trees, but their lost appeal to his appetite was nothing mourned, instead making him more aware of a hunger for things untasted.

Soon he was met by a radiant outpouring of affection, one he had long taken for granted until feeling it now like soothing ointment over a wound. They were waiting for him—all of them. Hundreds of lions gathered near the Isle's southern edge, ready to greet and follow as in their first meeting.

But, he could not do with the permanence of such a welcome, knowing he must soon set out again for a world of decay. They seemed to sense this in him, parting like bright waters to either side while he strode through the woods, though still he felt their potent energies holding close.

The frost pressed a gentle embrace against the ever-temperate forest, and penetrating flakes decorative and soft like flower petals only made him long for the sleet and sunken steps of the outside. His father worked in the distance with his sword against a whetstone, grinding a razor sheen that reflected a dance of flames beneath it. And when he drew near, neither of them uttered any sound in acknowledgment. They merely stood, as aware of one another now as when many miles had stretched between them.

"I felt a great presence leave the world, when our backs turned, and you confronted your trial," said Matufinn. "And I grew afraid when the short number of hours it had once taken me to be turned away from that realm passed, and passed again, and again. But still, even before you returned, I knew"—he looked at him now— "if our paths diverged again, I would never have any reason to fear for you."

Matufinn's pride held him warmly, slightly cheapening the imminent display of his prize. His possession of it, too, seemed already a foregone conclusion. Still, he withdrew the Crystal Blade from its makeshift scabbard at his hip, raising it up with both hands for his father to see.

But, it was not the weapon itself that drew Matufinn's wonder, but rather the validation it brought. "It was there," he said, "just before the dark mists?"

Morlen nodded, pleased to be providing the answers for once.

"And," Matufinn continued, "you saw the other swords? *Their* swords?"

Morlen affirmed again with a grin, "All of them."

At this, Matufinn's eyes held him tighter. "All?" he whispered. "Then, that means Morthadus must have returned there at some point." This weighed heavily on him, though his expression of delight grew much wider. He felt as though he had stood beside Morlen and seen this for himself, knowing too that there was still so much more for them to see. And they would see it, together.

Morlen nudged the Crystal Blade higher in a discreet gesture to let him hold it, but Matufinn graciously declined.

"It is yours," said Matufinn humbly. "You are the most worthy." A final smile followed in the wake of this, no longer shining down at Morlen, but straight on. "Come," he said more seriously while Morlen sheathed the sword and retrieved his bow. "We must—"

But Matufinn stopped short, mouth tightening as though against some knifing pain, and Morlen felt it too, like a thousand locusts clouding his vision. Someone else was inside the Isle, a large number of them. An entire legion, an army, was passing through, moving quickly toward one destination.

"Felkoth," Morlen said, knowing Matufinn already understood. But how could he have possibly gained entry, unless… they had been betrayed. He needed not even declare it over the indignation building in his father from the same realization.

Matufinn boiled, pacing closer toward the invading force. "Veldere. He means to position his entire army there. They'll fill the city in a matter of seconds, and the Eaglemasters won't be ready. That is why he never tried to stop me… so I would let them in." His eyes peered far off, swimming with guilt for the danger he'd inadvertently brought to so many.

Morlen suddenly had a sneaking notion as to whom Felkoth might have planted within the prisoner group. The image of his disquieting stare unearthed a memory of peril he'd left far behind. Now, it was returning for him, and for what he'd taken, what waited, buried, tantalizing his mind brightly.

Looking at his father, whose reluctantly returned stare melted from one of triumph and adventure to one of goodbye, Morlen opened his mouth to stop him speaking, but he was too late.

"Get to the lake, Morlen." Matufinn's voice held no panic. "Get to the lake before they do, and do not stop, don't turn back, no matter what."

His own voice still scrambling clumsily as he struggled to stall his father, Morlen found no words as Matufinn darted off, summoning deadly speed toward the enemy horde. Not here... not now. They were going to set out together, begin their journey far off at a place of strategy, in secret.

The lake would soon be overrun, and to flee the Isle on foot would only invite Felkoth's servants to track them. But, his father had spurned the notion of retreat altogether. There would be no escape for them both, at least none of Matufinn's design.

He started to run along his father's trail, though it would soon mingle with the tracks of those who wished to torture and kill. He had to catch him, reason with him, before the chance was lost.

"Swords ready!" belted the leader of a battalion on the army's flank, marching behind Felkoth within the Isle. The torches they carried through the sunlight were unintended for illumination, and the pounding of their steel-toed boots rose like war drums. "If he shows himself, do not take his head right away. First cut seventy pieces of flesh from him, one for each of ours he's killed."

"It isn't man that troubles me here," answered one at his back, glancing nervously around their perimeter into the dense, silent forest. "You've heard the stories about them, when they came out long ago, so many..."

"Dry your skirt!" the leader looked back contemptuously, brandishing his torch. "You know what to do if we come upon them." He gestured to the round clay vessels slung in sacks over every man's shoulder, each full of oil with a small hole bored into the top, corked by cloth. "But pray they eat you if one more whimper leaves your mouth, or I'll light you myself."

Mocking jeers broke out on either side of the reprimanded soldier, only to be just as abruptly silenced. "And I'll cut the tongues from each of you if you don't quiet down."

Their expressions hardened behind him, offering no apologies as all continued forward silently. The overnight reversal of their roles as unchecked slave-drivers to expendable cattle was wholly unwelcome. Power-drunk off of a year's reign over all of Korindelf's people, they shivered now under the sobering call for structured obedience.

"The king says two dwell here," the captain continued. "The scum who thought himself worthy to take your wretched lives, a privilege reserved only for me, and a boy, the one who outran you limp fools even as you gave chase on horseback, with the shriekers under your whips. To think, that his blood is worth more to Felkoth than yours.

"He sends us into this alien realm, and leaves his pets to hold the city," the captain hissed. "As though there'll be a soul left to rule over in Korindelf when we've sacked Veldere, and roasted the Eaglemasters on spits with their birds. Better to enjoy what sport we can now before none remains, after we've made a corpse of the dog who calls this place his home. Better to begin with the young one, see how many flies he can draw strung up from tree to tree as I improve my archery."

He let out a loud cackle that those behind him halfheartedly echoed, thinking it their obligation, when suddenly a stout whistling arrow cut it short and hammered through his chest plate. He staggered back in shock as his shaken subordinates sounded the alarm, and the stealthy attacker flew at him from the woods, snatching his torch with a menacing flash. Then the man bolted with it raised like a beacon to draw their fire, all in such a fluid motion they could barely get a glimpse of his bearded face. Battle horns erupted from neighboring ranks as they unleashed copious volleys at the streak of flame near the army's edge. And they ignored the fallen captain now under their feet, unaware that the wicks of his projectiles had been lit.

"He's still in range! Fire!" the other members of the group bellowed at each other. "There! He's slowing! Fire! Fi—" A quaking blast abruptly muted them, decimating the battalion and spraying the nearby woods with flames. Thick smoke rolled over the legion, driving fear into the concealed soldiers as they sputtered through the toxic haze, unable to get their bearings.

Their allies waited for them to regroup, shouting into the billowing fumes so those trapped within might hear which direction to follow. At first, they seemed to give calls in response, beckoning more guidance as they neared safety. But then, all at once, they fell silent.

Willing to wait no longer, the scattered soldiers formed up again as Felkoth's army pressed onward, its missing forces merely notches carved from the sides. Still, every man scanned apprehensively for any sign of the one who pursued them.

"He means to divide our number," said one through gritted teeth, nursing a burn on his neck. "If we separate, we'll crumble one by one."

Then, many heads turned focus just beyond their perimeter. "What's this?" another grumbled, viewing a round object that appeared at first glance to be an apple hurled at them through the trees, soaring in from above. But as it somersaulted in a bright arc with a burning cloth protruding, they quickly understood what it was.

Those in its direct path scrambled to avoid the destructive impact, when an arrow flew out from the same location and shattered it yards above their heads. It erupted in a fiery fountain that rained down while they took cover beneath their shields, completely enveloped in the shroud that fluttered lower amid blazing foliage.

Soon, similar warning cries rang out farther up in the midsection of the force, followed by another explosion and more chaotic shouts, indicating that the entire army was being strategically split up. Coughing raggedly, eyes in searing pain, the disoriented invaders knew they now had no choice but to abandon rank and file, diverging from their intended path. With flickering torches as the only light to guide them out from under the smothering blanket, they forged into the uncharted Isle and whatever snares its troublesome inhabitant might spring.

Morlen stumbled as the legion's collective menace singed him like hot coals. Gradually he began to see rising flames through the canopy of trees, and the fire leapt from grove to grove around the smoldering epicenter where the first blows had been struck.

Felkoth's army was still dangerously strong—merely bleeding from its wounds, not crippled. There was no more space to observe now; every stride would bring him deeper into the fray, beside sightless dogs that walked with teeth bared.

And while the thickening plumes drifted closer, he could not help but see ghostly hands take shape, reaching to choke him again. How long would it be before he could look into the dark, and laugh heartily, unafraid? There was no better opportunity than now for him to find out.

He stepped as though tracking the keenest of deer, though the role of hunter no longer belonged to him here. Many beasts were distressed, fleeing the Isle's northern stretch that withered in fire. But, he could feel some near, watching him carefully, though the threatening flames kept them at a distance. He only hoped they would have the sense to stay back, or soon there would be no refuge for them.

Throngs of intruders were close, following the blaring horns in a wayward current he'd have to cross as quickly as the one whose surprise attack they still feared. The nearest wave ambled across, stragglers batting at curtains of ash that clouded their view when he seized his window, lunging out from the trees to whip by the last of their group. Panicked yells summoned a dozen reckless shots that hit the ground long after he'd already passed, and he had no chance to stop, as the next battalion was far more dispersed.

He slowed for nothing, skirting more bewildered ranks to press through the engulfed forest as apples blistered open with steam overhead. Then suddenly, he careened into someone, one of the soldiers, who slammed to the ground while three others wasted no time swarming in with arrows drawn, and he stumbled to a halt.

He stood motionless, staring back at his enemies, frozen to the core.

"Is it him?" one rasped, aiming for his throat.

Fear shut down his instincts. All training, every lesson counted for nothing in this moment, wiped clean from his existence as he absorbed the intent of those before him and finally had his answer. He was not strong enough.

They released their volley, and still he could not move, fixed to ground that would taste his death, when a great lion lunged from the trees and growled terribly as the three arrows pierced its ribs and shoulder. His heart wailed, though he had no breath to voice his grief as the sinking creature stubbornly straightened up, turning razor eyes upon all four soldiers who hastily tried to break away. It sprang forth and brought down the middle archer, and the rest fled while it gave chase out of sight.

A thunderous roar shook the air, unfading as it traveled deeper into the burning woods. And Morlen desperately tried to follow, no matter how far off course it drew him. The deafening rumble parted even the smoke, ringing louder in the truest declaration of courage, stretching into the fire where Morlen could no longer follow. Then finally, the roaring ceased its forward course, resounding in place but slowly falling quiet, until even its echo sank through the soil. And Morlen heard it no more.

Unable to blame the toxic fumes for his tears, he slowly turned away and focused once again toward his father, who had closed in on the army's front.

Matufinn swept aggressively between the scattered invaders, using the smoke to his advantage as scores of troops fired haphazardly into one another. Horns began to sound farther up in the clear, rallying the disjointed forces to one point. Eventually, he knew, they would draw their numbers together again, and the lake sat not three miles off.

But, he sensed that Felkoth was not intent on departing right away, instead seeking something here in the Isle, and *someone*: Morlen. Sword drawn, he busied himself no longer with the dizzied ranks that stumbled along his sides, and glided out of the billowing black cloud toward the army's head. Now, he would have an audience with their king.

Beyond the smoke, he observed the reduced horde that moved toward him alongside the river, while trailing forces blindly clung to lifelines thrown back by the sound of their horns. Soon they would pass into the lake meadow, where they would fortify their position. Felkoth was obstructed from view, as was the one who led their way, no doubt blanketed within the folds of those ordered to be shields if circumstances required. And indeed they would.

The time for concealed attack was over. He walked into the

open without apprehension, striding on a collision course for the lead ranks, and their eyes widened at his approach.

"Prepare to fire!" a captain yelled.

Matufinn pointed his blade at their center, so as to part them on command. "You dogs may leave now, unharmed. I seek only your master."

This did nothing to stall them, only hastened trembling fingers to their bows, and their pulses raced as he rapidly advanced.

"If you insist," he said, charging with speed that closed their gap so quickly that hardly a bowstring had been plucked when he crashed into them like an axe through wood. He splintered the frontlines into fragments that fell on either side as he struck again, and again, and those bold enough to raise swords against him instilled little confidence in their comrades to follow suit. Fifty spears at his sides dared not even thrust, since his could not be the flesh of man.

The embattled ranks diverged, soldiers having become mere cattle under his yoke pushed to the trees. He thought of Morlen, seeing the foe who sought his capture in every enemy, and cleared a path closer to the only presence that harbored no fear at his offensive.

Batting aside a forest of unremembered faces, he came at last to the one he recognized, with glistening scars stretched wide above sweat-drenched brows. And still the man seemed to swell with hope, as powerful as it had been beside him in the prisoner caravan, where, it was clear now, both of them had been quite in disguise.

Matufinn had no mind to spare him. "Those scars were well-earned," he seethed. "Though a weak punishment for your treachery." The scarred man slowly backed away, silent under his approach.

But, as he closed on the deceitful culprit, an unseen weapon tore him from his shoulder to the small of his back, its unparalleled sting tainting his blood, which circulated now in a cruel pulse. He lost hold of his sword, and his balance too, though he stood as long as his stiffening muscles would permit. Turning while he slowly fell upon the fast-decaying gash, he looked up to see Felkoth with the Dark Blade dripping red at the end of a broad stroke.

Matufinn felt heavier by the second as the poison spread deeper, numbing every sensation but pain, yet he fought to hide any sign of this, leering at the triumphant huddle with indifference.

"Give him air, for goodness' sake," Felkoth ordered, stepping beside him as they shuffled back a space, tilting his head with a satisfied grin. "He's been hard at work for some time now."

Matufinn had no choice but to look into the bleak depths of his stare, and Felkoth relished such captivation, prolonging it as he bent closer, as though expecting to see a helpless shudder at any moment, though none came.

Losing some of his mock sympathy, Felkoth paced around him. "You've made a great deal of trouble for me this last year. Why, first I thought perhaps the wizard had returned, sneaking people from their given place in my kingdom, leaving none the wiser. But, foul as Nottleforf was, it is a man, not a wizard, who leaves a stench." Felkoth stopped with both feet on either side of Matufinn's head. "And you are just a man, aren't you?" he gloated, holding him in an upside down smile that slowly began to spin.

"And"—he resumed his stride—"when my beasts brought to my attention how unmistakable this stench was, and where it led, I was quite curious, since not long before someone else of great interest to me had vanished into that very same place." His self-aware enthusiasm poured down like stinking waste, but Matufinn showed no weakness.

"I know we've had our quarrels, you and I, from afar and up

close." Felkoth's silky speech turned steadily colder. "But, I'm willing to let the past die." He stopped near Matufinn's shoulder, glaring down at him. "Where is the boy?"

Matufinn's saliva bubbled in the back of his throat while he tried to conceal the difficulty of his efforts to breathe. Knowing how sparse words were for the picking, he mustered what he could. "There are no boys here," he answered, half smiling. "Except for you, Prince."

The gathered soldiers gasped as one. Felkoth, too, let his nostrils flare out, though his expression remained otherwise unchanged. Straightening up, he regarded Matufinn for the last time. "When I find him," he whispered, "I'll have the shriekers keep him alive." Wiping blood from the blade on the corner of his cloak, he added, "For as long as they can, at least."

Slowly turning, Felkoth headed for the river once again as his servants quietly followed, making their way toward the lake meadow. "Come, Nefandyr," he called as the man whose face was scarred lagged behind.

Squatting to smirk at Matufinn with amusement while patting his shoulder, Nefandyr taunted, "Careful who you trust, old man." Then, heeding his master, he rose without a second glance and took his leave.

Matufinn lay still, mind and body deteriorating fast. The lake was now cut off, and the blast of horns from every direction indicated the other forces were drawing close as well. Morlen was coming. And though he silently implored against this, all he could do was watch.

*

Morlen sprinted through smoke, choking on discolored spit as he strained to detect his father. He staggered as an acute twinge shot from the base of his skull to his toes, and winced in pain as the energy guiding him abruptly began to fade. Matufinn was in trouble. Perhaps he fought the enemy now, at this very moment. And perhaps they'd gained the upper hand. He refused to entertain the grimmest possibility, going forward despite the assembling battalions that marched to the same goal. He would not stop. They could still get out, together.

Dense trees parted to reveal the river, making its way toward the lake. Felkoth's horns rang out up ahead, stabbing dread into his heart as he realized they'd prevailed over the last attempt to halt them. Perhaps, though, his father merely waited to spring one more assault.

Soon, bodies strewn across the ground forced him to navigate far more cautiously, and he refused to search for Matufinn among them. His knuckles turned white as he scanned the sprawling scene, ready to unquestionably reject whatever his eyes might catch.

The remains of battle spread in a wider pattern, allowing him more space to continue. Matufinn's presence flickered so close. Any farther and he might pass…

He stopped, defying every urge not to look, and saw that his search was over. His father lay on his back, unmoving, just ahead, chest barely rising with each short breath. He rushed to his side, kneeling to see the veins in his face had turned a sickly green. His eyes were sunken, though not glazed yet, and still they recognized him.

Morlen's heart boiled as he bitterly cursed Felkoth, certain this could only be the work of the Dark Blade. Matufinn grumbled while he lowered his face to listen, fighting to suppress despair.

"Nuh… no," Matufinn uttered softly.

Morlen wanted nothing but for them both to leave right now, to stop the tears that knifed their way out so painfully, falling upon his father's hair.

"No..." Matufinn repeated. The horns blared, and a rising beat within the soil announced the approach of Felkoth's remaining legions, but he would not be moved, paying all attention to his father's words.

Matufinn's left arm twitched just a few inches upward, fingers stretching out toward him as he grabbed them with his own and lifted them to rest upon his shoulder.

"Know... it... Morlen," Matufinn exhaled, smiling fully now as he took in his son. His face brimmed with a joy that defied grave injury and dire circumstance, a transcendent attainment that Morlen could only watch unfold. As his fingers began to go limp, he drew one more breath, slowly let it fill his lungs, and released it at last behind one happy word: "Morlen."

His bright smile faded while Morlen tried in vain to cling to his receding energy, begging it not to leave, to stay with him, to no avail. And Matufinn's breath did not return.

Morlen became a cold statue, wondering if the earth would swallow him up if he knelt long enough, still clasping his father's lifeless hand. Voices broke out from all sides as Felkoth's troops rejoined one another, coming across the first wave of their slain brothers in arms. Many emerged from the lake meadow as well, no doubt sent to track him down.

Though his will to act was diminished, he knew he could not linger. Nor could he abandon his father's body to the vengeful hands of the fast-returning soldiers who would fill the area in a matter of seconds. He had to flee, now, as far away as possible.

Looking sorrowfully at Matufinn's empty eyes, he closed them tenderly with an open hand. Then, as the quake of boots crashed nearer, he shed his cloak and draped it over the body, hoping it would be a sufficient shield from view.

They were here. He had to run, just as he'd done a year before. Only this time he knew not where to go. He bolted through the trees, forsaking the now cut-off lake, his only chance for quick departure, but too late. He was spotted, and uproarious calls for pursuit sent Felkoth's men tearing along his path.

This was no exhibition of sport with the beloved lions, all of whom stood blocked behind the partition of flame at the Isle's center; second place in this race would bring death. Doubt was all that remained in him, and the cold voice he'd left in the Dark Mountains reverberated more strongly than any other memory. He was weak, as much now in leaving the Isle as upon entering it for the first time. And, while arrows zipped through the adjacent brush, he suspected he would not get far. He was not strong enough; he knew that now.

"He's here!" snarled one man a dozen paces back as Morlen lunged around the base of a hill, throwing himself farther into the woods. "This way!"

Crushing pain began to pierce Morlen's sides, stealing from each breath, but still he ran. Then, something shone out to him, as it had many times before, so friendly, and warm. Buried... he'd buried it. And suddenly, he understood his course. He was not moving toward escape, but to the one thing that could erase all fear, and make him whole.

He had to reach it, or else Felkoth might come to have it. That is what Nottleforf had charged him with when entrusting it into his possession. Nottleforf had also told him not to turn to the power it offered. But, that choice would soon be his, and his alone.

"To me! I see him!" another shouted at his heels.

He pushed on desperately, glad to let his own panting drown out the sounds of those tracking him when, thinking them a reasonable space behind, he shuddered to see a tall cloaked figure a few yards away on his right. Throwing every remaining bit of strength into moving ahead, he dared not waste a moment to fire at the pursuer while the others rapidly followed, their opportunistic shots guaranteeing loss of limb if he tarried. But as he wove farther through the forest trails, the shot patterns grew wider, less accurate, though still a threat. The darkly clad figure near his position vanished, though undoubtedly watching him, unwilling to let him break away.

Eventually the soldiers ceased their fire altogether, falling out of range as he drove on. Danger, though, was far from evaded when again the corner of a dark cloak through the trees caught his eye, spurring him on more urgently. Could Felkoth have caught up to him already? Was he leading the enemy to the very spot where it rested, waiting to be claimed? What if he retrieved it only to be apprehended before he could use it?

Again, as he focused all fading determination into moving forward, the elusive tracker haunting his steps disappeared into the brush, leaving him more than uneasy as he approached his destination. He could feel where it lay hidden, where he'd entombed it to conceal its rich luster. There was no more time; he had to reach it now.

After what seemed an agonizing hour treading water above circling predators, he burst at last into the wide clearing where he and Matufinn had first sparred. Seeing the large stone draped in a year's worth of moss on the opposite side, his spirits soared.

With determined calls for his capture advancing like a net, and the more ominous foe at his heels sure to emerge at any moment, he sprang across the grass and threw himself upon the cool, damp stone. Digging frantic hands beneath its rounded edge, he struggled to wedge it out and was only reminded how much he truly needed what lay beneath, which drew him closer with memories of its dancing sheen.

Legs bent and back straining, he wrenched the stone free of its resting place and flipped it out of the way, pulling clear the worn-out cover to reveal the shallow hole that held the object he sought, just as he'd left it. He knew someone was nearby, even though he had tentatively scanned the perimeter and found that no others had entered the vicinity. Fearing they'd soon be upon him, he hastily reached in and unearthed the small relic, wrapped in the torn brown sleeve of his old garb from Korindelf.

As the tattered cloth brushed his skin, making him feel he'd donned his boyish dress all over again, he parted the coarse fabric and dropped it aside, holding the jagged Goldshard tenderly within his palm. A rustling in the woods abruptly jolted him to his feet, and, not wishing to greet its source, he ran again.

This was his chance, now as he sprinted along the crest of a valley that sloped down within the forest. They were still coming; he hadn't lost them completely. And... someone, the same from before, was closing in, perhaps watching him even now. Slowing to a halt, he lifted the Goldshard and stared hungrily into its smooth, bright center. "Make me strong," he begged it. "Make me strong enough to defeat Felkoth. Strong enough to defeat all his armies. Give me all that I need... please."

He waited for it to respond with some mystical infusion of power, squeezing so tightly his fingertips ached, when the cloaked man suddenly emerged from the nearby woods and came directly at him. Stepping back in startled surprise, Morlen lost his footing on the ravine's precarious ledge and tumbled down as one rock after another took a hefty toll. Each boulder forcefully slowed his fall until he came to rest on his back, bloodied and disheveled, still firmly clasping the Goldshard.

Head spinning as his body screamed out, all he could make out was the blurred outline of the hooded figure, observing him from above, and then slowly descending toward him against a faded backdrop.

And then, finally, all went dark.

CHAPTER NINE

THE GEM

MORTHADUS KNEW THEY were close. He'd dwelt below for so long, undisturbed, but the youngest would soon seek him out, and the other would no doubt show him the way. And though he had eluded that one for so many centuries, he could not elude them both, not for long.

He would never have peace, he lamented. They would find him, sooner rather than later. It was only a matter of time now, and he would have nowhere left to retreat.

Morlen quivered as they stood so menacingly around him, cold eyes stabbing deeper than their blades soon would. They barked with satisfaction, savoring each torturous moment while preparing to finish him. But then, the murderous huddle parted to reveal someone who stood in the surrounding brush: a boy, watching the scene fearfully. Lying in agony on his back, it took every ounce of dying strength to reach out to him, begging for help. But, the boy would not move. He was merely going to watch him die.

Screaming in sorrow, he rolled over the shadowy edge of a

cliff, falling to his death. He slammed chest-first to hard ground, and the impact brought his nightmare to an abrupt end. Turning over slowly with a resentful groan, he shuddered to realize that he was underground, deep in the belly of a torch-lit chamber with jagged rock walls that rose to meet a ceiling of stalactites. Had Felkoth brought him back to Korindelf and locked him away beneath the castle?

Straining to push his body upright, he ascertained by the presence of select items—a fleece-covered armchair, a table strewn with cups, even a raised pallet off of which it seemed he'd fallen to the floor—that someone lived within this place. And, as far as he could detect, they were absent for the time being.

Thoughts of Felkoth quickly shot another pang of dread into his mind: What had become of the Goldshard? Had his captor taken it for himself, and used it? Searching frantically, he left no corner unchecked, when a bright ray flagged him from beneath the makeshift bed. There it was; it must have fallen from him when he'd rolled onto the floor, meaning whoever had brought him here hadn't wanted it.

Its prickly edges were so welcome against his hand, and he placed it back within his inner chest pocket as his bruised memory gradually recalled bits and pieces of what had transpired before he'd awoken here. He'd used it, he suddenly remembered with a thrill. He'd used the Goldshard, during his final moments in the Isle! It was the last thing he could recollect; everything following the act remained blurred. That was why he ached so terribly; the shock from being imbued with the treasure's power must have overwhelmed him, and would not soon pass.

Examining his muscles under the torchlight, he swelled with confidence, and hungered to face down Felkoth and all his men, wherever they may be. He would not be weak, not anymore.

His bow and quiver lay beside the sheathed Crystal Blade,

close to where he'd been sleeping, and notions of capture partly faded. He appeared to be in the anteroom of a much larger complex that sprawled out into other chambers and passageways, and behind him a corridor held a small stairwell that led up to two trapdoors. Hearing voices above ground, he ascended the steps to push both wooden panels open in a cascade of displaced snow, and emerged in the middle of a clearing surrounded by tall firs and pines, drably colored by winter's arrival.

"Well, you always do seem to find your way into some sort of trouble, don't you?" spoke a voice he knew well, one he'd feared he would never hear again. Looking behind him, he saw the gray-bearded face he'd nearly forgotten, realizing the identity of the cloaked figure who had pursued him in the Isle.

"Nottleforf?" Morlen said with disbelief when the old man removed his hood.

"Yes, young Morlen," he replied as Morlen came to stand before him. "My," he marveled, now eye to eye with him. "Were I a lesser wizard, I might have taken you for Matufinn back in the Isle. He was close to your age when last we…"

Images from recent memory stabbed Morlen cruelly upon mention of his father, a pain that Nottleforf left alone before it bled worse.

"Let's move along," said the wizard. "Needless to say, we have a great deal to discuss."

But, Morlen could not avert his eyes from the black clouds in the distant sky, which billowed from the burning Isle. He worried for its many beasts and realized, from its location relative to his own, he must now be at the edge of the Eaglemasters' realm.

"The Isle's bloom will live on," said Nottleforf sullenly, following his line of sight. "For all who remain inside."

Morlen's fists tightened as he pictured Felkoth's army gathered in droves ten paces from his father's body, knowing the poor measures he'd hurriedly taken to conceal it must have failed shortly thereafter.

"Have they come yet?" Morlen asked hotly, eager for the second chance to engage his pursuers.

Nottleforf's voice carried warning. "No, Morlen."

"They reached the lake before I fled," said Morlen. "Felkoth's bound to lead them through at any moment."

"I mean, no, this battle is not yours," Nottleforf clarified when Morlen turned to face him.

"Not mine?" Morlen protested. "You saw what he and I were up against in there. You saw them come for me after they'd finished with him. I'm ready now. I won't run, not this time—"

"The Eaglemasters are well aware of what is coming," Nottleforf interjected, holding up a hand to halt his restlessness. "King Valdis has suspected for some time that people from Korindelf were being brought into his realm, finally discovering exactly how after tracing members of the last group your father sent over. I brought warning to them after collecting you, and evacuation was already under way. Now Valdis and three thousand men-at-arms fly ready above the capital, waiting for foe, not friend."

The wizard held him with a firm look, one he'd seen many times growing up that asked him to cease his advances into certain areas of discussion. And now, a year after learning what many of those questions would have uncovered, he stared back just as pointedly.

"You felt I was in danger?" he asked. "That's why you came?"

Nottleforf's eyes calmed. "It is quite rare when I do not feel you are in danger. And though you were no longer under my care, the instinct to care remained very much intact."

Thinking back to his years in Korindelf, Morlen could not imagine any specific experience being very different if the wizard had not been there. But then again, he might never have grown to have any at all without Nottleforf's involvement, however remote it was. "What was I to you, back then?" he asked dryly. "And what am I now?"

He detected a strong urge in the old man to look away, one he seemed to take great pains to fight. "Someone," Nottleforf answered, "whom I would gladly see realized." Then he motioned that they should make their way through the forest, and Morlen followed beside him.

He enjoyed the abrasive, musty shroud of falling pine needles, reveling in how distant he now felt from the Isle's pleasures. This was cold and wet, and here there were things that scratched and bit. He could not walk twenty paces without tearing through a sticky web, its uprooted occupants stinging him with their grievances.

"I've no doubt you were somewhat shocked upon waking this morning," said Nottleforf.

Morlen suspected the wizard must be aware that he'd turned to the Goldshard's power. Surely he'd been found unconscious in the Isle, still clutching it. Why did Nottleforf not rebuke him for using it, when he'd emphatically prohibited such an act?

Wary to delve into that topic, Morlen kept to the one at hand. "That place wasn't made by men."

Nottleforf smiled. "No. It is a ferotaur hive, or was, rather, out from which they'd slink in the night to Veldere in its developing years, taking captive any they could, until the Eaglemasters finally hunted them down and emptied it. Now, it sits vacant, dead, though the legend of hungry whispers from the forest where many were taken, never to leave, is alive and well."

"And this is where you've lived?" Morlen asked. "Since Korindelf?"

"For one who can travel to the ends of the earth and back, a residence is unbefitting," said Nottleforf. Then he grinned. "Though I've come to find, an empty tunnel beneath ground where no man dares to tread can once in a while provide a much-needed night's sleep. But when I journeyed to Veldere last night, seeing that its people were being shipped downriver to the four lower cities, I proposed Valdis send some here, as well, to ease their brimming capacity."

Trees swayed up ahead, pushed by heavy gusts beneath wings of departing eagles, and their delivered cargo gradually stepped into view. Walking among them, Morlen soon came to realize that every face evoked memories from the last several months.

Each person smiled kindly while he slowly passed: mothers with children in much better condition than he recalled; men gripping canes to steady themselves against pains of past abuse, with marks that would never vanish. Every one of them offered the same look of gratitude, of reclaimed life, that he remembered seeing when his father had first brought them into the Isle.

More recent faces caught him as well—those who'd elected not to depart for immediate safety, instead taking up arms to help free others. Members of the most recently rescued convoy beamed at him now. There were so many—hundreds, all standing together in tribute to the one who'd saved them, stretching far toward some sort of altar. And, finally drawing closer to it, Morlen slowed his breathing, seeing the dry logs upon which rested a shrouded body, broad and tall.

Turning to Nottleforf, his expression widened to ask what his choked voice couldn't.

Looking back sympathetically, the wizard gave a somber answer. "You were not all that I brought here." The two walked to the altar's edge, from beneath which Nottleforf withdrew a folded garment, letting it flow out as Morlen realized it was his cloak, which he had shed to cover his father's body. Holding it out for him, Nottleforf said reassuringly, "He would have wanted you to keep it."

Weighed heavily to the ground, Morlen took the cloak, glad to feel its sturdy softness around him as he donned it once again. Then, Nottleforf waited patiently, looking to him for permission, and, taking one last glance at the silent, still outline beneath the unwrinkled sheet, he gave it. Nodding in acknowledgment, the wizard pressed both hands flat to the air until kindling sparked into flame, and soon the pyre raged high, consuming all upon it. Morlen turned and walked away, needing to see no more as the mountain of light released its smoke high above the forest roof, then slowly crumbled to dust in his wake.

After an ensuing hunt, Morlen and the rescued prisoners congregated in the underlying complex for a festive banquet. The center tunnel opened into a modified great hall flanked by roaring hearths with chimneys that pierced the forest floor above, and they dined together at many tables. Each was laden with steaming bowls of rabbit stew, platters of roasted wild pig, and goblets that brimmed with dark ale brought in casks from Veldere.

Morlen savored the melted marbling throughout each tender cut while he sat beside members of the recently freed caravan, with Nottleforf at the head of their table. All of them appeared to have grown much closer over the past week.

"Terrible shame," the burly farmer among their group wheezed after a large gulp of ale. "I could tell there was something not quite right about that fellow. Scars like that... from what I saw the guards do to so many, if they ever were driven to burn, they were driven to kill. They made no exceptions... I should've known."

"None of us could have," assured the bearded man opposite him. "I was the closest to him of all of us; he even helped me, though, I didn't understand his true motives."

"Enough talk of him," spoke the woman close beside this one.

"He'll get what's his, as will all who ever carried a whip behind any of us. Probably at this very moment they've pooled into the capital, right under King Valdis's spear. The Crystal Spear, mind you, a powerful weapon against such foulness."

Grinning next to her, the man placed his hand over hers. "One of the many fine things I've learned of my new wife is how talented she is at regaling an audience with all sorts of legends and stories buried by their respective kingdoms."

She smiled in return. "Buried, but not forgotten." Then, facing the rest of them, she asked, "You know of the crystals, yes?" Their blank faces baffled her. Morlen casually focused on his meal, unready to divulge any knowledge on the topic. "They were formed almost a thousand years ago, in the time of Korine the Ancient. And just as Korine was said to be powerful and kind, there was another being who lurked in the shadows, who conjured tremendous destruction and despair, turning men to beasts, and beasts to things far worse.

"He lured thousands with promises of power and long life, twisting and deforming their flesh and bones so they would make war on all others, until the Blessed Ones rose up and halted their oppression, for a time. And Korine cast Him down from these very mountains above us. But, the Enemy dragged Korine down, too, and they both slammed to the ground with such force that parts of them were fused together, creating a crystallized pool.

"And Korine washed Him away with the river that mingled with both of their shed energies. The Speaking River, it came to be called, as some who later found themselves immersed in its depths claimed to have heard prophetic messages from it. Then Korine, gravely wounded, gathered up the crystals and entrusted them to the land's protectors."

Morlen's hip suddenly felt quite bare as he couldn't help but think of the sword lying a stone's throw from where they sat. But the Goldshard's comforting embrace reminded him he was well-equipped for any danger.

"Speaking of whom"—the woman smiled at Morlen now, her attention a pressure he struggled to bear—"you wouldn't happen to know anything about the first inhabitant of the Forbidden Isle, would you?" she asked hopefully. "The hero who helped the Eaglemasters drive out the shriekers in the Battle of Korindelf? Surely he's a celebrated figure among your people, isn't he?"

Morlen pretended to be intrigued by the table's surface, chewing far more than his current portion required. Know? What did he know of Morthadus besides an ancient origin story, besides a claim that they were of the same bloodline? That blood's potency had been greatly diluted before flowing through his veins, and he doubted Morthadus would even recognize him as an heir if their paths crossed.

But, maybe such an encounter could help him grasp the heritage his father had always wanted him to find, or finally verify that he had no connection to it. If he found the one for whom the legend was told, he could learn the truth and no longer need the legend.

"Morthad—" Nottleforf suddenly broke the silence while everyone turned to listen, abruptly drinking from his goblet before Morlen's gaze reached him. He held up a hand to beg their pardon as though he'd been choked up. "More than… a few times," he resumed with a scratched voice that slowly cleared, "I have heard of the Isle's first warrior."

Could Nottleforf really know Morthadus? Or, at least, could he have known him at some point long ago? Why hadn't he ever considered the possibility before? Nottleforf had kept so much else a secret from him. Maybe he knew where Morthadus resided this very day, where he'd been since departing the Isle.

"But"—Nottleforf coughed and took another sip of ale—"his

legend was limited to the Battle of Korindelf. And it endured long after the city's liberation, bolstered by the many courageous acts of his descendants, whom I came to befriend, to my true benefit." He looked across at Morlen this time, raising his cup in a humble salute, and Morlen lifted his as well, though comforted little by the gesture.

How could Nottleforf presume to recognize him as one of those he mentioned, after witnessing his failure in the Isle? Only now would he be able to demonstrate real courage, real greatness, when before he'd just been fooling himself. Now, relying on that which had brought him true strength, his potential would be endless.

Nottleforf cunningly changed the subject. "In my exploration of this hive, which, I will admit, still contains scores of passageways I've yet to travel, I discovered something extraordinary embedded within a crack along one of the rock walls. Something even my eyes would have likely missed had it not revealed itself through a chance flicker of torchlight.

"And, prying it out, I held it to the light: a fine gem, rare beyond measure, so beautiful that I kept it, and would like to show it to all of you now." Sounds of delight traveled around the table; Morlen, too, was not uninterested to see.

Pleased by their eagerness, Nottleforf pushed back his chair and drew from under the table a strange copper contraption that resembled a disproportionate spider. It had a central compartment the size of an acorn, from which projected a circle of many long, narrow scopes like stretched legs, each one fitted with a clear magnifying lens through which to look.

Levitating it over the platters of food, he brought it gently down at the table's center, its protruding scopes resting mere inches from each of their enthralled faces. "Due to its size, I've housed it within this device," Nottleforf said in response to the questioning looks from all sides. "This way it might be seen up close by many at a time. Peer now into the chamber where sits the gem, and describe it."

Smiling at one another as though about to partake in the night's entertainment, the guests lowered curious eyes to the scopes before them. Morlen strained at first to see anything at all through a brown web of lashes that brushed against the circular glass. He retracted his head and then set his eye to the scope repeatedly, when finally, a bright core within the blurred cylinder sharpened as the gem appeared, clear as could be.

It was rough, and irregularly shaped, neither square nor round, with grayish silver veins etched through sky blue stone. Strange, it was not quite as extraordinary as he'd imagined, and he withdrew to look around at all the others, none of whom had yet uttered the fairly simple description he was about to give.

"What a gorgeous red hue," blurted the man beside him without raising his head, "almost purple near its edges, and so smooth too." Morlen furrowed his brow at this, hovering over his own lens as the qualities his neighbor announced remained completely absent.

"I'd check that eye if I were you, friend," the gruff farmer snickered down the table. "Maybe you took one too many blows to the head while we were in captivity, or else you'd see the grassy green here the rest of us do."

"What?" the woman opposite him laughed. "You've the worst eyes of any of us to see cloudy orange as anything near green."

But, looking to her husband for support, she found none. "Cloudy I'll grant you," the bearded fellow said tentatively, "but, quite distinctly yellow... maybe orange near its top corners," he added.

"Corners? It's shaped as an oval, isn't it?" she asked,

turning to Morlen, who, in courtesy, looked once more, finding it quite unchanged.

Rumbles of dissent echoed from everyone present, none of them abandoning their emphatic appraisal.

"Lenses," shouted one. "It's a trick with the lenses. They must change color for every scope."

A man beside him waved this off as nonsense. "Mine is clear as a well's still water, and shows me the gem as you'd see it too if you hadn't already drunk three goblets."

Nottleforf's hearty laughter mingled with the table's stubborn unrest, growing stronger until all fell quiet, staring at him quite puzzled. With a wave of his hand, the central compartment out from which the scopes protruded opened at its top, and from inside rose an object the size of a blueberry, floating above for all to see. It was colorless, shapeless, composed of thousands upon thousands of different hues and forms, textures and shades, all connected together in one indefinable mass.

"What you each saw," said Nottleforf, "was but a minuscule part of the whole. Yet, you asserted that it *was* the whole, that there was nothing to be seen past the edges you perceived. There are those who will look at something so small, so incomplete, for so long, it becomes their everything, and they forget how much is outside of it. To them, I would say, do not mistake a facet for the gem."

Nottleforf's attention fell firmly on Morlen now, silently imploring in a way that so closely resembled the unwelcome look Matufinn had often given, searching for awareness that was nowhere to be found, until the only response could be to look away.

The farmer broke the silence. "Well, I'll say this, lord wizard. Caring little for your trickery myself, I'll gladly listen to any advisor whose lessons are accompanied by meat and ale." Others at the table laughed with him, but Morlen remained quiet as Nottleforf placed the gem back inside his multi-scoped device.

Soon the clatter of empty plates brought the large gathering to its feet, signaling time for rest as many retreated to their respective quarters. Offering nods of respect to both Nottleforf and Morlen, the rest of the group took their leave, and, though Nottleforf stayed seated, Morlen rose with them. After one last studious, prolonged glance at the wizard, he strode swiftly back through his own chamber and exited up to the surface.

Veldere was just visible beyond the treetops, and Morlen found its stillness far more unnerving than the clashes of steel against steel that were soon to fill it. Felkoth's army would flood the city any minute now, expecting their sudden appearance on its streets to spell doom for the king and his people; instead they would find themselves tangled in the Eaglemasters' awaiting snare. But, would they break through it nonetheless, spreading their flames through every home, to every bird and rider?

Coated in snow, he shuffled at the sound of doors creaking as Nottleforf came to stand beside him. His presence was slowly becoming more distinguishable through the bustling energies of so many others nearby.

The wizard stared far off through the trees and said forebodingly, "Felkoth will not be beaten so easily. He may not realize what sits prepared for him, but neither do the Eaglemasters know the true extent of his drive to conquer. Whatever the outcome of this night, I fear it may be just the beginning."

Morlen stood unmoving for a long while. "You knew him," he said, still looking ahead while the wizard turned to him.

"Knew?" Nottleforf asked, pausing for clarification, though Morlen was sure he anticipated his aim already.

"Morthadus," he answered with certainty, the wizard's mealtime slip having left no room for doubt on the matter.

At mention of the name, Nottleforf faced sharply forward, giving no answer. Morlen's eyes followed him this time, and would not soon leave.

"Do you know him still?" he persisted, though this remembrance was the closest to anger he'd ever seen in Nottleforf, whose jaw tightened disdainfully at the question. "I don't know what conflict existed, or still exists, between the two of you," Morlen pressed on cautiously. "But, I think it might do some good, for me... maybe help me better understand where I come from, if I could find him."

Nottleforf's face relaxed a little, his many wrinkles gradually unfurling again while he peered far away. "It's been centuries, Morlen," he replied at last, in a voice far more somber than usual. "I no longer know where he is, or how I could possibly find him."

Even this dim admission made Morlen's heart beat stronger, leading him to a trail that was faded yet not completely lost. "But, you did know him, and you know, or at least suspect, where he might be now."

Nottleforf fell silent once more, raising a stiff shoulder between himself and Morlen.

Desperate to keep this chance from vanishing, Morlen maintained pursuit. "You may have believed you were protecting me by keeping me from the truth when I was younger. But, I'm asking you now, don't keep this from me. Please."

Nottleforf stayed rigid, refusing at first to acknowledge him, as though the two of them would stand forever to see who could outlast the other, until finally, he lowered his gray head, breathing out heavily before lifting it again.

"I will help you find Morthadus," Nottleforf said reluctantly, turning as Morlen's spirits rose. "But, not tonight," the wizard added stubbornly, leaving him in the clearing as he reopened the door at his feet.

Descending the stairwell, Nottleforf said with finality, "You should get some sleep. There's no telling what the next few days will bring." The two doors shut behind him, and Morlen stood alone, looking to the sky above Veldere, where the Eaglemasters flew ready for Felkoth's imminent arrival.

CHAPTER TEN

ROFTOME THE UNTAMABLE

ROFTOME BORE NO weight but his own. Never would he surrender his wings to the command of men, who sought only his submission, his servitude. And many had come, more than the feathers that covered his body and tail.

For he was greatest of the mountain eagles, strongest, fastest, behind whom all other wild birds followed, and no prize shone brighter in the prideful minds of kings, princes, and heroes. All had sought him out, braving bitter cold and razor cliffs to gain his allegiance, and all were harshly cast away. And now war, the device of men, was coming to pollute the lands on which he gazed day after day. He could see them bracing for invasion, swelling like a red cloud above their high walls, those who called themselves masters.

He splintered a boulder to dust at the very sight of them, and his unscratched beak billowed sedimentary powder that scattered in frosty winds. Most of the self-proclaimed masters had come to him before all others of his kind, swiftly recanting their title the very second they dared seat themselves upon him. And all were lucky to draw enough breath afterward to communicate with those who would be ridden. He pitied his brothers and sisters who'd bowed to such a station, whisking their keepers into battle while watching over the king's domain, perching themselves within structures of wood to be groomed till they became as soft as those they carried.

Peace had forever eluded those dwelling in the five cities below, and tonight might see it vanish altogether. As much as he despised their meddlesome efforts to gain his loyalty, far more troubling were the forces that sought their overthrow. Fouler men and creatures were coming, and they would feast on every flock if given the chance.

Never before had he flown to war for any king. But, tonight, if his vantage point proved too distant to ascertain the stock of this conqueror who invaded his lands, he would have to fly in for a closer look.

King Valdis sat atop his eagle as it treaded air above the empty capital, with the Crystal Spear clasped firmly in hand, imagining Felkoth's ribcage to be a fitting sheath. Three thousand Eaglemasters swarmed around him in the night sky, ready to rain down a final greeting upon the treacherous masses they'd once served as allies.

For a full year he'd wished to meet Felkoth in the field—longer than that, really, though duty had bound him to maintain a guise of civility. But no longer would he watch, powerless, while a once-bright haven for the free crumbled to a pen of torture and death. There would be no stalemate, not after this meeting.

The glittering surface of the Speaking River drew his gaze, bringing hope to the forefront of his mind. He'd been just a prince, hungry for glory, when the eagle Roftome tossed him into its depths. But, even now, he remembered its message quite vividly, a message he'd never repeated, though it had emboldened him every time he flew to war:

When the Crystal Blade meets the Crystal Spear

And fire soars to rule the sky

Your victory shall then be near

And the eastern war shall finally die.

His youth had slipped away, and countless battles had come and gone while he waited for the hero with the Crystal Blade to join him, dreaming that together they could cripple the hordes that oppressed so many. But, after decades without ever laying eyes on the elusive weapon or the warrior who wielded it, he suspected now he only waited in vain.

"Did all three of you pursue Roftome, after you'd completed the Wildland Test?" he asked his sons, who were near his sides. "There seems to be hardly an Eaglemaster who didn't."

"After what he did to this one?" joked Ivrild, gesturing at his older brother. "After hearing that the honorable heir boldly ventured into the mountains in search of the greatest pair of wings, only to wind up with two broken legs? No, I chose the most docile eagle I could find, just in case the responsibility to rule abruptly fell to me."

Verald was glad he could now laugh at his near-death experience, though the memory still jarred him. "Broken legs were a mercy. He spun me so fast I was a foot away from splattering my skull against the cliff before I finally let go. And when I lay there sprawled out in the snow, he perched over me just to show that he could peck out my liver if he had a mind to. I almost froze before the others I'd traveled with flew me to the infirmary."

Keen for chances to compete with his more seasoned brothers, Ondrel boasted, "I almost got him to let me mount. The first three paces of your approach are all that decide whether you hear any words in return, and if you mount without hearing, you're as good as dead. When I came upon him, I looked him in the eyes before moving one inch closer, and I must've stood there for an hour waiting for his expression to change. But his eyes alone told me that nothing I did would convince him I was there for anything but my own gain, and all I'd gain from him was an extra orifice or two.

"I tried to show that being able to protect him, care for him, would make me as happy as flaunting him to my brothers in arms. But I think he knew that was a lie before I did." He restlessly surveyed the city's vacant streets, disheartened to see a normally booming hub of activity lying so dormant now. "I wish Felkoth would come already. I've got women to visit downriver. All this fuss shipping them to the lower cities is a great inconvenience for me."

"Valeine will be just fine without her closest brother there to play swordfight for a day or two," Ivrild replied, egged on by their older brother's laughter. "I'd wager Veleseor's the safest city in the realm, for once, under her watch."

"Though it couldn't have been easy to keep her there," added Verald. "I'm sure Father's relieved the worst is over after incurring her wrath at being denied a place here tonight. She's liable to skewer any ferotaur within five miles of her city, knowing one of us may let loose the arrow that nails Felkoth to the dirt."

Valdis turned to look south toward his farthest city. "I don't want her here, not for this. She's been raising a fine crop these past few months; her place is there, with them."

"Besides, should Felkoth surprise us all and show up there instead of here, she may give him a brutal fight," Ivrild declared, making light of the grimmest prospect.

Valdis shook his head, resenting the urge to laugh at the remark as he envisioned his daughter with only a handful of veterans and trainees. "Felkoth will not go there," he said plainly.

"With no way to hold the ferotaurs under his yoke as he does the shriekers, he'd only be fighting them too if Veleseor fell. He will come here.

"And, with my head on a pike and the capital burnt, he'll press the four lower cities into submission." Valdis chuckled loudly now, concealing his worry as his sons joined in, each of them eager to see the look on Felkoth's face, and on the faces of those with him, when he arrived.

"How does a boy elude you, not once, but twice?" Felkoth's voice carried strongly to every soldier as he stood looking out over the Isle's lake.

Each man quietly begged him not to turn, to forget his disappointment at their failure and simply lead them on to where others would suffer instead. "A little boy," he said more softly, though even those at the very back could not escape his words. Then, every heart became synchronized in a growing collective pulse as he slowly pivoted around to approach them.

"You were a boy, once," he uttered sharply to one in front, whose breathing pattern quickened. "But now you are a man," he added, drawing the Dark Blade into sight, and the ground seemed to move as all troops shifted slightly, preparing to hastily step back.

"What separates man from boy?" Felkoth asked, still studying the same soldier. "What is it that ought to have given all of you the advantage over this pest? I ask only because, since you failed, you obviously are not using it."

The soldier's throat tensed through a frightened gulp as he blinked rapidly, face still forward, avoiding Felkoth's examining stare at all costs as the Dark Blade came nearer.

"How am I to trust any of you to deliver my rule upon the

people of Veldere, upon countless children, women, and men, when you cannot even do this to one child when I ask it?"

Another man in the frontlines fervently declared, "We will serve you faithfully always, my k—" He gagged, his last words choked by blood, body collapsing upon reddened snow after Felkoth's swiftly delivered sword pulled away. All others fought to hide their notice, while the unlucky one who'd been scrutinized before this began to tremble visibly.

"I cannot abide those who speak out of turn," Felkoth continued, stepping closer to the clearly shaken soldier. "But, neither can I abide those insubordinate enough to keep silent when I ask very plain questions. What separates man from boy?" he hissed through a chill whisper, until the one he addressed barely opened a quivering mouth.

"I..." he muttered, while Felkoth craned his head with intrigue. "I... don't know, my lord."

Felkoth smiled crookedly. His tone bordered on the paternal as he patted the man's shoulder. "No. Of course you don't. What are we, anyway, besides what we want, and what we take? You wanted things, took things, when you were a boy, just as you do now.

"But, the only distinction I can make is, when you were a boy, if you wanted something that another had, and you couldn't take it from him, well, you would just storm away in a huff, I suppose. But now, if you want something, and someone prevents you from having it, why, you would just cut off his head, wouldn't you?"

The soldier's knees bent weakly at this as he stammered again, believing Felkoth would act according to his answer. "N-no, my lord," he whispered.

Felkoth focused on him more sharply. "No?" he asked. "Then you will be of no use to me against the Eaglemasters, whose heads I expect to see piled higher than their towering walls, and the same for any of their people who refuse to kneel. Is that understood by the rest of you?"

"Yes, my lord!" his army chanted in unison.

Felkoth grinned again through the dancing shadows. "Good. Start with this one whose lack of stomach offends me." He pointed at the distraught soldier, and the man cowered until his comrades' swords stifled his wails, the small thud of his severed head against the ground preceding his body's fall.

Felkoth waded into the open lake, raising his sword for all to see. "We go now to taste the blood of Valdis and his men!" he yelled, and the loyal host cheered close behind, following their master down into the rippling water. The boy could not elude him forever. Once he seized Veldere, his vision would be doubled in scope, and he would cut down any who tried to block it from falling upon what was his.

He'd bested the Eaglemasters when they first crossed him at Korindelf, forcing them to abandon their predictable maneuver of dropping indiscriminate volleys. He would employ that very same strategy now, as none would see them coming—pillage and trample the masses through the streets, in their very homes, bringing Valdis to fall upon his sword.

He submerged with his scarred lieutenant Nefandyr while the others swam together toward the same luminous rift up ahead. Bogged down by armor and shields, they fought to move forward, concentrating diligently on their destination as the pocket inflated tenfold. It drew them in like a starving mouth until all had finally entered, finding themselves swallowed within the sealing doorway that swirled them about like beans in a cup, slamming each soldier down feet first to stand dry upon the paved roads of Veldere.

Felkoth straightened tall while breathing deep, marveling that he could stand so easily in the very heart of Valdis's realm. But, with swords already pointed to flay the unsuspecting townspeople, his men glanced at one another, crestfallen at finding no targets. There was not one soul in plain sight, nor any sound to be detected, not even the grind of wagon wheels against stone or distant calls of merchants from scattered shops.

It couldn't be—had Valdis truly anticipated this occupation? Charging through vacant snow-covered streets, they broke down door after door to no avail. Felkoth's ire churned, and he confronted his lieutenant as the army overran a village square. "Nefandyr, you said the others would not divulge the secret of their transport here, that they thought it might lead Valdis to prevent any more from being sent over."

The scarred man's brows lifted high around wide eyes as he stared back in shock. "My lord..." he mumbled, "they wouldn't have told anyone openly... the king himself must have suspected them—"

"The king?" Felkoth growled, raising his sword as Nefandyr backed away in fright.

"No, my lord," he begged. "I didn't mean... please... pl—"
An arrow suddenly struck Nefandyr like a lightning bolt, vertically through the chest, slamming his body hard to the ground.

With his blade still reared back, Felkoth slowly tilted his head upward, and the others followed suit, seeing Prince Ivrild reset his bow as Valdis and the Eaglemasters swarmed above, far out of reach. Like beasts circling before a grisly fight, both armies watched one another quietly for a few slow-passing moments, the confounded invaders sizing up an amply prepared counter-offensive.

"Come for blood, young prince?" Valdis's unmistakable voice boomed from the dense red cluster, followed by a crashing silence like thunderclaps foreboding rain. "You came to the right place." Then, he raised the Crystal Spear high in a blinding flash and swung it down to point directly at the army's center, bringing a volley that poured down in torrents upon Felkoth and his men.

"Take cover!" Felkoth shouted, scrambling to swing his round shield up for protection, his men doing the same though many were not quick enough. Their screams filled the air as the shower of arrows enveloped them.

"Sons of Veldere!" Valdis's words pounded the sky again. "The Tyrant Prince has traveled far to taste our fabled hospitality. Give him and his servants the rich welcome they deserve!" The Eaglemasters let out a collective guttural bellow that rattled the eaves of houses around Felkoth's pinned army, soaring closer in a sweeping formation while dropping wave after wave of projectiles with each pass.

Taking advantage of a brief gap between assaults, Felkoth rallied his archers frantically to load their bows, waiting for the next approach. "Fire!" he yelled with rage, the command sending up a thousand arrows that merely drooped in a pitiful arc as their intended targets responded with devastating precision.

He was trapped, and his wary head darted around to see dozens of corpses strewn within a slowly crumbling legion, those who still lived crouching beneath heavily dimpled shields. He could inflict no damage like this, not while Valdis and his buzzing flies held such a superior position. But, suddenly aware of the tactical potential posed by the rows of structures along his perimeter, he grabbed hold of the nearest battalion leader. "Burn the houses!" he commanded. "Burn everything now!"

Ducking low to avoid another volley, the soldier shook his head in confusion. "My lord, we dropped our torches before coming through, we've nothing to light—" but Felkoth snarled as he retrieved a bow from its fallen owner as well as his sling of oil pots. After hurling them through the doorway of a nearby house to smash all over its stone floor, he shot a steel-tipped arrow to scrape a trail of sparks through the combustible liquid until it burst into flame, tongues of hungry fire crawling up the wooden beams.

"There's your torch!" Felkoth fumed, shoving the battalion leader violently toward the engulfed hut. "I don't care if your arms and legs get charred to stubs—I'll light you myself if every house in this village isn't a hill of smoke by my next breath!"

Nodding to conceal his shaking, the captain collected his troops and ushered them to the growing blaze, though many fell prematurely as the Eaglemasters gleaned Felkoth's strategy and took immediate action. All who dodged the relentless downpour ignited their own fire pots and cast them upon neighboring structures, until soon the occupied town square swam with smoke that jutted a swirling needle into Valdis's ranks.

"All of them! Burn all of them!" Felkoth shouted as adjacent buildings went up in flames, standing more at ease under the canopy that brought each hammering burst from the airborne fleet to a halt. Now they would have to fly through the blinding haze, well within range of his bows, to continue their onslaught. "Arrows ready!" he called out wrathfully, eager to confront those bold enough to breach the makeshift ceiling.

His soldiers stared upward at the gray dome's center with bowstrings drawn tight, waiting with bated breath to pierce any flesh that entered. Without warning, a turbulent wind swept through from behind them, driven by the wings of at least five hundred, and the accompanying riders promptly felled entire lines at a time with blankets of suppressing shots. But dozens of them were unseated by well-aimed arrows from below, plummeting dead as their departing comrades eviscerated the smoky curtain. It remained open just long enough to provide another opportunity for clear fire, which the Eaglemasters used to full advantage before the heavy plumes resealed.

Felkoth seethed, his shield now riddled with arrow tips, hundreds of his swordsmen lying dead beside a meager handful taken from above. They thought he would be defeated? They thought he'd collapse soon enough under their heel? They knew nothing.

"Valdis!" he howled toward the dark barrier. "Coward, dismount your spectator's seat and come face me, and let it be decided who the true king is!"

High above the rising partition, Valdis pressed the Crystal Spear firmly to his side like a knight at joust, no hesitation in him as he prepared to lead the charge.

"Father, let *me* go," implored Verald with a steady hand upon his sword. "I'll finish him quick and clean. Well... quick."

"No," Valdis answered, leaving no room for debate. "You follow me, and circle closely with the others to ensure I'm not disturbed, until every one of his men lies broken. I'll take him in five hits, and rejoin you. Understood?"

All three sons stared back in silent protest, disdainful of his resolve to deny them the task they'd each gladly spare him, though none doubted he could accomplish it. Nodding once in a plain show of his station and nothing more, Verald acknowledged the orders.

"Good," said Valdis curtly, ready to fly as his mighty carrier cupped the wind. "Besides," he said with a reassuring smile, "an Eaglemaster is deadlier on the ground than in the sky."

He reared back to spur Clodion forth with the Crystal Spear thrust up as a beacon for all to follow into the fray, when a rising commotion suddenly stalled him. "Look!" he heard several shout in disbelief, summoning his attention toward a distant swarm whose size surpassed theirs: the mountain eagles, unmanned, at the head of which flew one unmistakable to any warrior.

"Roftome the Untamable flies to war!" they hailed as the greatest of all birds shot past their flank. Thousands of wild eagles flocked along his path, and they broke through the cap of smoke shielding the enemy horde that shrank from them in fear, hearing unavoidable doom in a ringing chorus.

Roftome wove seamlessly through haphazard waves of arrows while all who fired dispersed at the sight of his outstretched talons. But no man got far as his brothers and sisters crashed upon those beyond his immediate reach, every section of the invading army falling beneath the same terrible shroud.

Felkoth sprinted as close to the flames as possible to avoid the eagles' main concentration, his potently deadly Dark Blade swiping down any that drew near. He stopped to withdraw the last clay oil pot from the sling at his side, holding its cloth wick to the inferno's edge. Then, waiting while the lit fuse crept toward the round vessel's opening, he lunged out and hurled his projectile into the winged masses, on whose stout backs it shattered, spilling liquid fire that engulfed six birds and his own screaming soldiers beneath them. Still, this was a weak vengeance for the unforeseen delay of his conquest. He had to get out, now, before the eagles had less prey to chase.

Screeching mournfully at the morbid conflagration, Roftome latched his gaze onto the malicious fire-thrower whose blade dripped with the blood of eagle-kind, and bolted out toward him. With honed reflexes, Felkoth sheathed his sword and withdrew a sharp dagger, planting himself with legs apart to wrangle the charging beast.

His spread wings dwarfing his target, Roftome pounced with a forward thrust of his heavy skull to deliver shattering death. But Felkoth narrowly dodged the blow sideways while filling his hands with thick neck feathers, and pulled himself up to a mounted position, jabbing his knife's point into the eagle's back.

Enraged far beyond caring about the open gash his would-be master had inflicted, Roftome flipped hard off the ground, soaring in a great spiral with as much speed as he could muster. Felkoth clung tightly atop him, sticking his flesh repeatedly with the knife to spur him away as his dying men wailed for help.

Roftome wanted blood, entrails, anything he could tear from this foe who still rode him despite his most violent efforts to shake free, careening higher with each tormenting prod until they were beyond the smoke-draped city walls. He unleashed every maneuver in his arsenal—rolling, plummeting, speeding upside down. But each time he attempted such tricks or deviated from a steady course, he received another dizzying cut, forcing him along a consistent path while they left the city farther behind.

Hearing cries of two wild eagles in pursuit, Felkoth knew he hadn't escaped completely unseen, though it was doubtful the Eaglemasters would realize his absence until long after the battle's end.

Roftome maintained a smooth trajectory under a painstaking guise of obedience, hoping this would lead his foul rider to become more relaxed, till he suddenly broke course and spun hard sideways, brimming with outrage as unwelcome arms continued to constrict him. Deeper stabs goaded him forward as he released an earsplitting whistle, which, though no man had ever won words from him, still conveyed the shrillest contempt.

Soon the forest where the long-horned savages had once dwelt spread low in the distance, and his parasite pushed him toward it as the two following birds drew closer. The blade slowly dug into his neck, threatening death if he did anything but land safely, quickly, within the dense shelter. In his descent, he saw only one opportunity, one chance to disobey and break apart, which he would gladly die taking.

The knife stabbed deeper, spurring him forward. Drained from each cruel cut, till the dawn revealed emerald fields peppered by a trail of blood that trickled from his feathers, Roftome descended toward the forest roof. He hoped only that he would have strength enough to rip out his deeply rooted flea, and limp away as long and far as he could, free, with dignity reclaimed.

He dashed ahead, despite harshly disapproving knife prods, through snapping foliage and into a thick branch that ripped his flesh and dislodged the reviled passenger, who managed one last long slice as he tumbled off. Collapsing wing-first against the snowy floor with a sickening crack that yanked from him a high-pitched cry, Roftome rolled sluggishly onto his butchered back. His white downy head turned left, then right, trying to glimpse a sky that had all but vanished, leaving only speckled patches that now felt too far out of reach.

But, basking in a shower of irate growls from the enemy he'd finally unseated, he waited with a defiant glare that burned the failed conqueror who stood over him, a bloody gash across his cheek.

"Filthy mountain vermin," Felkoth hissed, replacing his dagger to draw the Dark Blade once again. He aimed its point directly at the eagle's heart, clasped the grip tightly with both hands and raised it high, savoring the moment.

And Roftome the Untamable lifted a firm beak, lying quiet, without fear, under the imminent final blow.

CHAPTER ELEVEN
FRIEND

MORLEN AWOKE WITH a jolt in the blankets of his makeshift bed, and silence from the adjacent tunnels indicated the hour was quite early. Fumbling groggily through his coverings, he searched for any sign of a stowaway insect, feeling a faint sting that gradually began to throb along his neck. But, regaining his faculties, he realized this accompanied his growing sense that something familiar approached above the surface, or rather, someone.

"Felkoth..." he whispered, baffled as to how the Tyrant Prince could have ventured so far beyond the ambush prepared by the Eaglemasters. At last he had what he needed to prevail. Now was the time. Now he would stand up and be strong, unafraid, and defeat him as he should have done within the Isle.

He donned his boots and cloak hurriedly, not even thinking to bring his sword as he rushed through the entrance passage, bolstered by the Goldshard against his chest. He swung both panels open above, revealing dawn's silver sheen into which he exuberantly emerged, and charged through an ice-laden forest toward the intruding presence.

A piercing call rang out unlike any sound he'd ever known, echoing with such distress, such pain. Stamping urgently through snow, he knew it was one of the eagles, and the ensuing silence stabbed deeper with the same sting that had awoken him.

Finally he stormed through a cluster of trees, seeing Felkoth, bruised and torn, poised menacingly with the Dark Blade over a sprawled-out eagle whose crooked wings spanned at least twenty feet. Its reddened chest puffed determinedly despite many wounds along its side.

As though interrupted by a hiccup, Felkoth brought the sword to his side while casting all interest now upon Morlen. "You…" he said, arm outstretched, fingers clenched as though around his adversary's throat. "The boy who escaped Korindelf… not so scrawny now as when I last saw you." His voice cut with a chill as he smiled at Morlen's lack of any weapon. "You must have turned to the Goldshard by now. And to transform yourself into such a formidable specimen. How wise a choice," he mocked. "What a fuss you brought, taking my prize. So many in Korindelf who could have lived, who would've obeyed instead of dying, had it not been for your thievery. And if this is truly the extent to which you've used it," he said, pointing the Dark Blade rigidly at Morlen's gut, "I'll have you spilt across the snow alongside this one in two seconds' time." He gestured at the flattened eagle, whose head blurred into the white carpet, leaving visible only its beak and blazing eyes that now locked on Morlen.

"Lay down your sword," replied Morlen, feeling clad in impenetrable armor as his full heart tapped at ease against the weapon in his possession, "and I'll persuade the Eaglemasters to give you a quick death."

Felkoth scoffed at Morlen's very existence, lunging out to flay him limb from limb as he stood still, trusting that he'd been empowered to win this contest. But as he watched Felkoth approach for the kill, throes of panic began to set in, when suddenly a thunderous crash froze them both in their tracks. Two wild eagles burst down through the trees and viciously hurled Felkoth out of view with taxing swipes, and Morlen could hear him scurrying back to his feet, fleeing northward through the woods while they pursued closely from above.

As if bolted to the ground, he waited for all sounds of the chase to gradually fade, and the eagle lay low while he strode closer. All power he'd observed in the Isle's fearsome beasts was momentarily swept from memory by its penetrating gaze.

He'd never seen such an embodiment of lethality, nor such strength in fear's place, and knew any physical approach was foolhardy as he beheld the godlike creature. Considering his already dangerous proximity, he merely stood, careful not to blink as he offered a sympathetic mien to one that would offer nothing so easily.

"You are wounded," said Morlen, thinking of few worse fates than for such commanding wings to lie broken on dirt and ice.

Looking up at the one who knowingly stood where talons and beak could still manage a final thrash, Roftome's instinctual defenses slowly withdrew in the face of such open surrender. His deep voice transcended the predatory calls of his kind to man's plane of communication for the very first time. "I know that."

"Do you wish to be helped?" asked Morlen, encouraged that the eagle was not immediately inclined to repel him.

"Do you wish to help me?" The words held an innate cynicism Morlen dared not underestimate.

He nodded, oblivious to any alternative. "Yes."

Roftome strained to lift his head a few inches, studying him keenly. "Why?"

Morlen knelt at eye level to ease the creature's appraisal of him, aligning his neck with its unstoppable claws. "Because," he answered, "since that man was prevented from killing you, it would be a shame to let your wounds finish the job, or the snow if it works faster." He held the eagle's stubborn face in his sights, refusing to stray.

Roftome stared back, waiting for a subtle tremble, any telltale sign of concealed intent that could be unearthed by his threatening scrutiny, but none came. Begrudgingly he acknowledged the offer of aid. "What would you do?"

Pleased by this progress, Morlen answered, "I know someone who lives in these woods. Someone powerful, of many arts and skills. I will take you to him, if you permit me, and I've no doubt he will be able to repair your wing and sew your wounds with the greatest care."

Roftome snapped a ridiculing beak at his proposal. "You will take me?" he mocked. "How?"

Unfazed by the eagle's disbelief, Morlen replied matter-of-factly, "I will carry you."

Roftome did not jeer this time, looking at Morlen now without trying to gauge his ability or ascertain any foul play, only trying to understand. "What do you want?" he asked plainly, far more curious than accusing.

"What do you mean?" said Morlen, knowing time was running short as a blanket of red spread over the eagle's bed of snow.

"I mean what do you want, with me?"

"I want to help you fly again, instead of leaving you here to die." Morlen set his jaw firm.

For many long breaths, Roftome lay quiet, focusing on Morlen with greater suspicion, though relinquishing his acerbic tone. "You would carry me?"

Morlen rose tall, nodding again. "Yes," he declared. "And I'll see no predator finds you without finding me first, and no ice freezes you without freezing me."

Roftome gave no indication he intended the least bit to be moved. Yet the man lingered still, silently inquiring for an answer, until finally, he cast aside all misgivings, nodding in acceptance.

Elated they'd reached terms, Morlen wished to give in to optimism that the most difficult task was done. But, beginning to truly take in the eagle's immensity, his enthusiasm quickly melted to desperate hope that he could keep from choking on his words. Fearful that any jostling might stir the pained creature into a frenzy that left them both in need of rescue, he crouched and set reluctant sights on its black, gleaming talons, despite his best efforts to find a better anchor point.

"Can you move at all?" he asked with calm patience, trying to instill the same in his potentially volatile cargo.

Barely able to lift his head, Roftome needed not reply. Morlen breathed out slowly, realizing he'd have to lever the great beast up in a flipping motion, though his own body was the size of its abdomen alone. He removed his long hooded cloak, shivering through chill winds while he tied the top and bottom of it securely to either hand, bringing the center portion of its slack to the eagle. "Bite down on this as hard as you can," he said through chattering teeth, bunching up a thick wad before the deadly beak.

Looking up at him questioningly, but with guarded trust, Roftome kept silent for a few moments, wondering what pains his carrier planned to inflict that his beak would have to be stuffed. But, seeing the way his hairs stood so defensively upon arm and leg in absence of protection, Roftome took what was given, clamping a spine-crushing hold on the thick garment.

Morlen tugged hard in response, ensuring the grip was tight. "Good," he said, easing as seamlessly as he could into harsher proceedings. "Now," he began, trying not to sound grave, "the ice will have numbed you somewhat, but there will be more pain for this next part. I'm going to lift you up as gently as I can, and you must latch onto my shoulders when I say so. Understood?"

Almost relieved to be gagged under such alien measures of consideration, Roftome bit visibly harder on the makeshift strap, indicating his preparedness.

Morlen then turned his back to the giant raptor and walked slowly forward with legs apart on either side, both arms wide as the slumping cloak grew taut. Each labored pace pulled the eagle's body upward to fold in on its lower half, which remained dug-in, almost resembling a crude catapult that would snap under strain. Then, he clenched his muscles to hold steady while squatting low, and locked himself in place against both wide, golden-brown feet, knowing the eight jutting talons could bleed him dry with the slightest shift. "All right," he said with steaming breath and no small sense of apprehension. "Hold on."

Bracing for both shoulder blades to be promptly fractured, Morlen remained intact as bladelike claws fastened beside his neck, while two more jutted into his ribs. With his elbows point-ing down, he hoisted the eagle's body as far forward as he could manage while his thighs propelled them out, heaving the eagle's tremendous weight off its snowy deathbed to drape over his upper back.

Feet crunching through the precarious frost surface with each step, Morlen swayed forward dangerously and struggled to stabi-lize himself as the eagle's wings hung like curtains on either side. Eventually he slowed to a sustainable pace, fighting to disregard the fiery twinges he sensed in the eagle, who still pressed no disap-proving scratch upon him.

Unable to pivot, Morlen lifted one leg at a time gingerly around a wide radius to face the way he'd come, pulling tightly down on his cloak that centered the teetering bird over his bent back. "Well," he groaned, hoping conversation might lure their minds elsewhere, "I can understand why Felkoth must have chosen you. I'll wager you're not of common stock among your kind."

The eagle remained slumped without uttering a sound, its head a guiding mast out in front. Its chest sagged heavily onto him, undoubtedly limiting air intake, but even so, a full voice rumbled down to Morlen's core. "He is not the only one who chose me," it replied, keeping the cloak hooked against its lower beak while the upper flapped softly.

"No, that would not surprise me," said Morlen, laboring to hold his mind off each bone-shaking step. "And you're not the only one he's tried to rule, though perhaps one of the few he couldn't."

He felt his own blood begin to trickle down through a freezing sheen of sweat. Cursing the light running distance for one man that now may as well have been an acidic marsh, he devoted all concern to the heart that beat like a hammer to his skull, and let hope for its uninterrupted pulse be his only fuel forward.

"You fought in that battle, then?" he asked, short of breath. "You flew against him, for King Valdis?" The pounding grew stronger now, like a sharp rebuke as the eagle stirred, and he swiftly shifted his hands to steady the tipping weight before it toppled them.

"I serve no king," Roftome declared with muffled indignation. "I flew out because, though the city men offend me, they take only those who trust and go willingly. But, he who came to the city last night... he takes all."

Morlen grimaced, knowing how easily he'd let Felkoth escape, deferring to two birds of prey the task that had been laid so opportunely before him. Why did he hesitate, as though stalled by some familiar haze? He was strong enough to defeat Felkoth now, and always would be, under the Goldshard's influence. Perhaps his mind simply hadn't yet adjusted to the new power that had been seared so abruptly into him.

"What are you called, by the other city men?" Roftome inquired bluntly.

The smallest chuckle escaped Morlen's lips under building pressure that threatened to pop his lungs. "The other city men… called me… many things," he wheezed. "None of which… I would now repeat. But, you can call me Morlen, friend."

Roftome tilted his head downward, thinking a closer look might help him better hear what was said. "What did you call me?" he asked.

Stamping the weight of four men through each narrow, snowy path, Morlen grunted, "What… friend? You understand it, don't you?"

Roftome's sight lifted up again as he gave no answer, looking out on the bouncing white landscape beneath which he would have now been smothered and forgotten if not for this human. And Morlen held their course, snarling through each caustic exhalation that only made him want to stop and rest, after which, he knew, both of them together would not continue.

Desperate not to lose his dwindling momentum, he drove on with a surge that would flatten him in a matter of minutes, realizing he did not need to endure longer than that as they'd surpassed the halfway mark. They were now merely a hundred feet or so from the hive of refugees and the opening of his quarters, where Nottleforf dwelt close by. "Hold steady now," he panted, doubling his efforts in a final march that would see him either reach his destination or crumple short of it with ruptured organs.

As his faculties began to recede, Roftome shivered as the pressing cold overwhelmed his draining life's blood, which still trickled out through a dozen stab wounds. He bit down on his carrier's cloak with a laughable force that any captive fish would surely escape unharmed.

Morlen felt the eagle's rapid faltering, too, and moved forward while clutching the dangling garment tight in his fists, steering through camouflaged contours that threatened to bring them down. His lower spine shot one blinding flash after another behind wind-burnt eyes, and he kept them open only because the tall oak above his chamber finally came into view. He could not stop... not yet; the eagle had but minutes left.

His feet scuffed the ground with each pitiful stride, leaving not foot prints but long tracks, and he could not even lift his head. His thighs and calves lost their ability to anchor and navigate simultaneously, throwing him ahead on feet that would no longer hold him, till his only remaining option would be to dive as close to safety as he could.

Breaking through one last row of trees into the open clearing, his flesh seemed to lose its structural form altogether, careening immediately at the sight of the trail's end toward a violent fall that could inflict irreparable damage to both of them. He gathered one last breath, kneeling with legs half-submerged in snow before the hidden stairwell while pressing wobbly arms upward to brace the eagle's body, which sank chest-first against the ground. Then he wrapped his hands around each set of talons to pluck them delicately away as the remaining weight slid off his shoulders with a soft thud.

Collapsing atop the icy soil, too numb and drained to reach for his cloak that was still clasped in the near-unconscious eagle's beak, he was relieved to find it unnecessary to yell out to Nottleforf, who ascended quickly through the opening door.

"Don't," Morlen urged at sight of the wizard. "Don't take him underground... not underground..."

"Easy, now," Nottleforf soothed in reply as a warm gust suddenly pried Morlen away from the frost. It landed him upright while supporting his swaying body with centrifugal force that kept weight off of both buckling legs, and heated his blood.

"He's stabbed, dying... Felkoth..." Morlen muttered, arms and legs gradually tingling back to life under less strain.

"Shhhh. Rest a moment," said Nottleforf, delicately hoisting the eagle up on another bed of air that rose higher until both dangling wings touched no ground. Then, he set four tall pieces of timber as corner-posts, over which he threw a flowing blanket that draped down as a makeshift tent to ward off the snow.

Revolving ancient, wrinkled hands around one another as though winding yarn into an invisible ball, Nottleforf rotated the eagle over slowly to study each slash through the crimson-dyed feathers. And Morlen watched over his shoulder, still cradled by crutches of air.

"Can you stand?" Nottleforf called out, his attention fixed on the eagle as Morlen tested his recuperating legs and lower back, which were sorely responsive.

"Yes," he answered, half-sure, and the wizard waved a hand to disperse the encircling breeze, leaving him to limp until he gradually straightened.

"Bring me rabbits," ordered Nottleforf, certain that he needed not repeat himself. Morlen scuttled down the open stairwell into his awaiting quarters, emerging with his bow and quiver, and bent stiffly to don his cloak where it had fallen from the eagle's grasp. He strode as quickly as he could into the nearby woods, scanning for any movement in the pure white landscape.

The eagle's energy swam in his periphery, pulsing weakly. To carry was not enough; he would have to feed, nurture, or all else would be in vain, no matter how extensive Nottleforf's skills. He had to work fast, and return even faster. And he would, before it was too late.

Morthadus watched him from below—the youngest, brimming

with hunger and enthusiasm. Soon he would begin to search; there was no doubt. He would first search high, search every slope and peak. Then, inevitably, he would search low.

No man could tread as far down as he dwelt, but still, he knew, with the other's help, the youngest would find him... they would both find him.

He withdrew his gaze quickly, collecting it back within himself, as the youngest was always keeping alert for his presence now, and would know its source if he was not careful.

Know... He cringed at the notion. The youngest would not want to know, or even see, what was left of him.

Pleased with the heft of two fresh kills that swung from his hip, Morlen meticulously followed the trail of faint indentations that forged out from some adjacent brush. Slowly he pulled his arrow back, gritting his teeth through each creak of the drawn bowstring that warned his prey, which he spotted now. Its short teeth whittled away at a stalk until the thick arrow struck it squarely and plunged it through inches of snow.

He hurriedly grabbed just below the fletching that stuck out like a flag, and wrenched up his spoils, tying the carcass to the others at his side. Confident his provisions would prove sufficient for the immediate care Nottleforf needed to administer, he rushed back along his own tracks to deliver them, knees and back throbbing with each impact.

A fire now crackled in a shallow pit beside the occupied tent, and over the flames sat a kettle, steam rising from its unknown contents. Nottleforf worked busily along the eagle's torn back and neck. Every gash was coated in a gleaming aloe salve, some of the worst ones already sewn shut while the wizard continued to maneuver needle and thread.

Without a glance, Nottleforf beckoned him, taking the three rabbits. Gently spinning his winged patient to face upward, he made a small incision in one of the carcasses and hung it from the tent above to allow a few droplets of blood to drip every few seconds into the half-open beak, and both eyes on either side abruptly gleamed with a whetted appetite.

"You possess strong shoulders indeed, young Morlen," he lauded, skinning and gutting the other two.

Morlen followed with great intrigue as Nottleforf carried both pink, fleshy kills to the fire, dropping them through the greenish-brown surface of the kettle's glowing liquid, which immediately billowed a pungent metallic aroma. It made him nauseatingly certain it would be well received by any creature whose diet contained a great deal of blood.

"To bear the greatest of all eagles through such unstable turf, let alone hoist him up from his flattened, broken state," Nottleforf continued, stirring the thick concoction while Morlen turned to study the unmoving bird, who lay silent though increasingly awake beneath the steady trickle of sustenance.

"Greatest?" he asked, rubbing sore muscles around each tender disk in his back. "I was sure he had to be one of a select few, but… how do you know, exactly?"

"Morlen," said Nottleforf, looking at him now, "do you think one who has traveled as far and wide as I could mistake such a creature, the object of lore and quest for so many? That is Roftome, the mountain eagle whose unmatched size and speed have made him a coveted acquisition for the men of Veldere over the last two centuries, at least."

Morlen's brows arched high, though he had little difficulty believing this. "Roftome," he said warmly, glancing over at the eagle with pride. "He seemed opposed to all men when I first made my intentions known, though I can understand why, given his condition."

"All eagles are opposed to men, initially," replied Nottleforf. "Until their aversion is overridden by trust and affection, cultivated by those who seek to ride them and become masters. But Roftome is called 'Untamable' for a reason; he is not just slightly more difficult to win over than his brothers and sisters. I've not heard of any hopefuls he's ever put to death, but he's sunk the fear of it into many the moment their armored backsides presumed to rest between his wings."

Morlen flinched while brushing the eight shallow puncture marks unintentionally inflicted on his back, pitying any who'd fall under those talons when driven by even modest strength. "Will you be able to heal him?" he asked.

Nottleforf nodded in cautious affirmation. "The next day will tell," he said tentatively, testing the viscosity of the boiling medicinal mixture before him and grunting in approval. "The eagles outlive generations of men, a quality that may pair quite well with what skill I possess, but Roftome here appears to have encountered a predator whose thirst he underestimated. This remedy will work to replenish his depleted blood; that is the gravest concern. Then, after we set his bones, he must rest."

Nottleforf lifted the searing-hot kettle off its seat in the fire and twisted it down into the snow to yield a palatable temperature. After constantly stirring it to hasten the cooling process, he then brought it still steaming to the eagle's side with a large wooden spoon. He prodded the murky contents wherein the meat of both rabbits seemed to have dissolved, leaving only polished, bobbing bones.

Without fear of a violent recoil, Nottleforf lifted a brimming spoonful toward the awaiting beak. Yet Roftome looked only at Morlen, either for approval of the feeding hand or to further assess the aim in bringing him here. Regardless, he took the muddy green helping in one subdued snap which Nottleforf quickly followed with another, repeating through many servings.

"Good," said Nottleforf, pulling away to return the kettle, now half empty, to its fire. Then, gesturing for Morlen to stand behind Roftome's head, he said, "Now, carefully lift his wing."

Morlen was reluctant to handle Roftome's broken limb, as he was certain the eagle had already experienced enough discomfort with which to associate him. But, gently hooking both arms under the dangling left wing, he elevated it slowly to be parallel with the ground, squinting through each disorienting ache that struck him like an electric current through Roftome.

Nottleforf did not need to look closely; the wing bone was snapped, with one half's jagged end pinned beneath the other, and dislocated too from its joint below the eagle's neck. "Hold him firmly now," he charged, old hands clamping both dexterous and strong on either side of the fracture, and Morlen pressed up with equal resistance. He willed Roftome to keep calm, to trust that this procedure was only meant for good despite the agony that threatened to expel every ounce of his ingested medicine.

Suddenly a hot wave pulsed from Nottleforf's fingertips throughout every feather and tendon of the crooked wing. His grip tightened around both split sections of bone that slowly repelled one another as though by some building energy field, until, when enough separation had been gained, he drew both together with an unnerving crunch. The radiating warmth concentrated more intensely on the spot of their merger, seemingly melding the pieces as one bone, which Nottleforf forcefully pulled back into its socket with another sickening pop.

Morlen exhaled with relief, sensing a swell of ease in Roftome, as though the worst had passed. He waited while Nottleforf expanded the eagle's dense bed of air to support his now-mended wing, and released it with great care.

Nottleforf smiled under a glistening brow. "You both did well," he praised, exposing the lacerated back once more. "After he's stitched, we'll be in smoother waters. Bring the kettle, and let the remainder cool a bit while I finish with these." He drew his needle and thread out again, weaving nimbly through each open wound while Morlen took the pot from its fire.

Nottleforf parted one reddened downy tuft after another, and finally broached the subject that Morlen wouldn't open. "Felkoth escaped, then," he said flatly.

Morlen silently resented the bitter reminder. No matter how hard he looked, Felkoth's sinister presence now eluded him. Whether this indicated that the eagles had overpowered him, he could not be certain. "I don't know," he answered, discouraged. "He may not have gotten far, hunted the way he was. But, King Valdis and his men will find him, won't they? I doubt they'll rest until he's captured, dead or alive." He waited expectantly for a heartening response, deflating a little as the wizard seemed not so sure.

"Soon, the Eaglemasters will have to decide whether to move on Korindelf, once their capital has been secured," said Nottleforf. "They'll know it will be prudent to free the remaining prisoners, before the shriekers get the notion that he will not return."

"It matters little whether he does or not," Morlen replied, envisioning Felkoth ruling his obedient horde even from afar. "He commands them at this very moment, and if the Eaglemasters drive them out of Korindelf, they'll still be a weapon in his grip, no matter where he goes."

Nottleforf continued working busily, his thread passing higher through Roftome's mended flesh. "Yes," he said, "and I fear, as I did before the battle, that this will certainly not be the last we see of him."

He delayed his efforts with the eagle momentarily, facing Morlen now. "But today is a day of victory, and you must savor it while you can, for seldom will such days repeat. The greater of Felkoth's two armies has been crushed, leaving him cut off from his seat of power, stranded in the very realm he failed to conquer. His deepest concern now will be to survive, to find cover and plan his next move somewhere remote. Yours must be to gather your strength, and take joy, too," he urged, turning to regard Roftome. "If not for yourself, then for this creature, who will ride many winds to come, because of you."

Morlen's tense expression relaxed at the sight of the eagle's stout chest inflating with full breaths. The few wounds left to tell of his ordeal would soon be closed, and his feathers were kept warm above the piling flakes. Looking again at Nottleforf, he was glad to have made good on his promise to deliver Roftome to one who could provide such skillful healing.

Recognizing this, Nottleforf resumed his sewing, bringing it near completion. "You'd do well to eat something yourself," the wizard urged. "Performing such a feat as you have is troublesome enough, but on an empty stomach…"

Nottleforf needed to say no more. Morlen understood that he could do nothing else to help for the time being, feeling far more in need of rest than a meal. With another long glance at Roftome, he made for the trapdoor.

"I've prepared some food already in your quarters," Nottleforf called over his shoulder. "I'll finish here in no time, and set a small perimeter so he's not disturbed, but you can still see him whenever you like."

Morlen bobbed his head in acknowledgment through a wide yawn, limping down to the warm chamber where a heated pot emitting aromatic waves of cinnamon did not tempt in the slightest. He surrendered himself to the well-blanketed pallet, and quickly faded to sleep.

Felkoth ground his teeth with each throb, tightening a torn section of cloth above a deep gash in his arm. He spat on the feathery corpse whose blood drained from a poisoned slash, smelling already of putrid rot, and the bird's overzealous companion lay close behind, with its beak and face nearly hewn off.

He'd reached the base of the Eagle Mountains, and would have to scale the cliffs while keeping out of sight. As soon as he found a secluded cave or fissure, he could lie low for a few days, since the Eaglemasters would quickly be out in droves, searching until he was found.

He would let the Eaglemasters sniff every tree until his trail went cold. And when they departed to claim his city, he would re-enter the forest, take the Goldshard along with the boy's head, and lay waste to every bird and knight.

Wiping it clean of the sticky mass of blood and feathers, he drew the Dark Blade close, speaking to address the awaiting shriekers. "My faithful beasts," he whispered reassuringly, "I shall return to you soon, with the flesh of thousands for you to feast upon, I promise. Hold my city, at all costs. May not the presence of any Eaglemaster in my realm go unanswered. Gather all the people close around you; let them shield you from every arrow, and swiftly unleash your own, until the bird-riders' ranks fall from the sky to your jaws. Hold my city. Hold it for your king, and I will reward your loyalty for ages to come." The Dark Blade absorbed each word, transmitting them to the endless packs around Korindelf, who heard their master clearly.

Sheathing the sword, he dabbed at a trail of blood that still ran down his face from an open wound, carved in his violent dismount from the eagle he'd left for dead in the forest. He gripped a nearby outcropping and slowly climbed the sheer brown mountain that was marbled with so many white veins. His enemies might rest a little easier, thinking him gone for good, but soon they'd see he could not be beaten. And he would never be forgotten.

When Morlen awoke, he pushed himself upright with both arms to spare his back. But he was glad to find such precautions unnecessary when his muscles stretched more easily after a few hours' sleep, though truly he couldn't tell how long he'd been out. With hunger now refusing to be neglected, he strode eagerly to the kettle stationed in his quarters' fiery hearth, and found its enticing provisions had changed from porridge to rabbit stew, leaving little doubt he'd indulged in more than a mere afternoon nap.

Filling a smooth clay bowl with generous helpings of thick broth, tender meat, and carrots, which smelled so pleasingly different from the blood-building slop they'd fed Roftome, he sat and devoured one gulp after another. Nottleforf's soft approach through the connecting passage diverted little of his attention at first, despite nagging curiosity as to the time of day. But more earnest concern for the eagle's condition pulled his steam-soaked brow in the wizard's direction.

"Finally up?" Nottleforf greeted, visibly wearied by his exertion of energy in the healing effort. "Roftome improved so well over the day's course, when night fell and still you slept I hoped he would stay until you had a chance to see him in decent strength."

Morlen could not help but sink, though thrilled by news of Roftome's rejuvenation. Still, he would have wished to see him off, watch him take to the air and leave his small forest tent behind.

"He's gone then?" he asked glumly, though the answer already seemed apparent.

Nottleforf smiled, leading Morlen to only guess what was so amusing in his sleeping for almost a full day, and missing the eagle's return to health. "No, Morlen," Nottleforf replied. "He hasn't gone, not yet."

Unsure what exactly Nottleforf meant to convey, Morlen set his bowl aside and stood up. "I don't understand," he began, trying to bring himself up to speed. "He's still here, but no longer in need of care?"

Nottleforf appeared to enjoy his suspense, making him feel he grasped at something in plain sight. "I told him he was healed enough to fly hours ago, but he will not leave," said the wizard. "He has been standing perched above the entrance for some time, and remains there still."

"Why won't he go?" asked Morlen.

"I believe that he is waiting for you."

"For me?"

"Yes," Nottleforf repeated. And then, studying him more inquisitively, he said, "Morlen, do you understand what you've done?"

"I helped him," he said dismissively. "But anyone—"

"No," Nottleforf cut him off. "Not anyone, Morlen. No one. No one before has ever done what you did."

"Done what?" Morlen asked, furrowing his brow.

The wizard grinned more widely, intentionally letting Morlen's curiosity build while withholding the answer. Raising shaggy gray eyebrows, he nodded encouragingly toward the stairway to the surface.

Well-versed by now in Nottleforf's nonverbal directives, Morlen did not need to be nudged twice. If the eagle was truly waiting for him, he would soon know why. Taking one last look at the wizard, who clearly found more delight in this than Morlen himself knew possible, he donned his cloak and made for the entrance passage. And when he emerged into the wintry daylight, even brighter were those two bronze eyes, cutting a path to his through the air.

Morlen took a few short steps. Keeping a reasonable distance, he cleared his throat and tentatively asked, "You are healing well?"

Like a sculpted cloud with earthy tones spread throughout, Roftome stood silently for a few moments, looking into him. The recognition in his voice was soothing as he answered, "Yes, Morlen. The wizard's remedies worked quickly. But, it is because of you that I am alive, that I may fly and have not left."

"You don't need to thank me," Morlen quickly replied, anticipating the reason for his reluctance to depart. "There's nothing you owe. But let me see you go free, now, while you still can."

Roftome beheld him again in a way that nearly made his deadliness easy to forget. "Many men have crossed my path. And my freedom is something they've never sought."

Then, releasing the earth from the grip of his talons, he stepped forward, closing the gap between them in one stride. "I do not linger here now because I wish to merely give you thanks, and I do not feel as though there is a debt I must repay to release myself from some sort of obligation, for none exists in my mind. As you say, I am free, and freely I choose to carry you, as you carried me, wherever you wish to go."

Morlen was held motionless by this declaration, oblivious to what could have inspired such devotion from the mightiest of eagles, known so well for his scorn of men. "Why is this your choice?" he asked.

"Because," said Roftome, "while all other men would force their weight onto my back and call me servant, you took mine onto yours, and called me friend. Unasked, and asking nothing in return, you lowered yourself for me in a way that I never would for another, until now. Now, and from this day forth, I am your friend, and you are mine. Your weight shall be my weight, and my speed shall be your speed."

Swaying just a bit, unsure how to show he accepted such an offer—though his heart filled to welcome it—Morlen found his stuttering response stifled altogether when Roftome swept an open wing and flipped him away from the ground. He grabbed on tightly for balance, dropping in a seated position on the eagle's well-repaired back as though to ride a horse.

But there would be no constricting reins to impose any course, nor any kick of heel against flank; there was only the mutual trust that now existed between them, and an understanding that the word "master" would never apply.

Pushing away from the icy mire with one powerful flap of healthy, broad wings, Roftome blasted up out of the sheltered clearing and drove them higher like a great arching arrow to pierce wide skies. They soared far above the small green patch in which they'd seconds before been housed, no longer limited by the border of any realm, as all in sight was now theirs.

Drunk on the lapping wind, Morlen marveled to see every territory he'd ever known, whether city or wood or sprawling frontier, surrounded by many more, which beckoned them now with no obstructions in between.

He cared not in the least which direction they took, as long as they didn't touch down, not for a long while, at least. There would soon be days for battle and blood and grief, but not today, as danger lay far on the horizon that stretched before them. Now there was speed and height and invincible pursuit, where nothing would be unreachable.

So Morlen and Roftome embraced the greeting clouds, letting each gust bear them forward, together, and left all else far below.

Chapter Twelve
The King's Fear

VALDIS PEERED DOWN from the city walls with a pitiless expression, watching as his flock removed Felkoth's slain troops to a mass pyre outside the capital. The bulk of them had fallen under the smothering assault of the mountain eagles, who had withdrawn at battle's end after Roftome's disappearance from the fray.

Many underlying villages sat scorched and collapsing around the epicenter, while other homes farther across the city remained unscathed. Closer to the citadel on raised wooden altars burned the corpses of many young Eaglemasters, clad in the armor and red capes they'd only recently earned. All had their spears and swords crossed over still chests while their unmanned eagles called out mournfully above the rising smoke, departing with heads hung low for their ancestral home in the mountains.

"Still no sign of him, Father," Verald announced, swiftly ascending from the bloody streets atop his carrier. "He's not among the rest, and we searched too for his sword near those who fell under the flames—nothing."

Ondrel replied, "The doorway that brought them here must've

sealed behind them. Otherwise they all would've gone back as soon as they laid eyes on Roftome and the others coming down through the smoke."

"Agreed," said Ivrild. "Even my stomach did a few turns when the entire flock shot past us. Imagine being under them all at once—no wonder there's such a stench down there now."

The king turned at the sound of nearing wings, seeing his daughter approach unexpectedly to join their huddle.

"Did you really think I'd let you all bask in victory without me?" Valeine greeted with a smile. "As soon as the messengers flew saying Felkoth's army had been crushed, I had to see it for myself." She looked patiently at her brothers, and then her father, waiting for one of them to take credit for Felkoth's death. But, when all remained uncharacteristically quiet, she realized the dread that pooled in their hearts.

"How?" she demanded, trying to keep calm.

Valdis stared out past the city limits, as though to trace a scurrying rodent before it returned to destroy his crops. "I know the birds well," he began, with his children all watching him diligently. "If indeed he managed to harness one, it would not have gone willingly, meaning however far he managed to stray, his landing was likely violent, and low."

Ivrild held up his bow with an eager hand. "Let me lead a hunting party, Father," he urged. "I'll draw him out and have his head on the wall by night's end."

"No." Valdis waved this off. "What does a rat do, but burrow deeper at any sign of danger?" They glared back with tongues held tightly while he concealed his worry for their shared ambition. "We will watch every path near the Speaking River, as his only remaining haven lies on the other side. Let him sniff apprehensively for our approach, and when he feels safe in assuming we've halted the search, he'll crawl out from whatever shelter he's dug and make himself known."

He needed not look twice to determine whether they accepted this answer; each of them knew their station well. He only hoped he'd been convincing enough in his tactical reasoning, when his plan was only to keep all of them close.

"Do we move on Korindelf?" Valeine asked, leaning forward as though to forgo deliberation and simply lead the charge herself at his signal.

Valdis admired her resolve, though he knew he could not yet act as she sought. "When Felkoth senses the shriekers have all been destroyed, that Korindelf has been stripped from his grasp, what incentive has he to emerge?"

"You mean to wait for him to gather strength and make a run back to his kingdom, instead of taking it now while he lies beaten? To let those people linger in captivity as bait?" she seethed.

"That is the only hope to keep him from stowing away so long that he cuts our throats in our sleep!" Valdis replied, leaving all four taken aback by the first distress he'd ever shown openly.

He cast his gaze downward and slumped ever so slightly. "I suffer with those people, knowing what they face each moment we delay," he said. "But I will give him no reason to hide so long that we forget the danger he still poses. If I must sleep with one eye open, I'll wake with both inside our borders, and let neither wander until they fall upon him."

At this, all four avoided trading second glances or signs of defiance, and Ivrild hovered closer to him. "I'll always follow you, Father," he assured. "Though you're not the fairest sight from behind. He'll make his move soon enough, and when he does, rest assured that I and the hundreds flying behind me will be the last he sees."

Valeine shook her head in ridicule, making as though to depart, but Valdis lifted off as well, gesturing for them to follow. "Come," he beckoned, and she reluctantly flew alongside her brothers.

Flying wingtip to wingtip, they left behind smoke and ruin for brief serenity, together, as their wide open country stretched out below, and came to perch on one of the many hills that often provided them a quiet retreat.

"I can't stay long," said Valeine. "I need to return to my city before sundown."

"*Her* city, Father!" shouted Ivrild. "Doesn't she know you sent her there so her squawking voice would scare off every ferotaur within a hundred miles?"

"You forget he first tried to sacrifice her for a few decades of peace," Ondrel countered. "Only for them to give her back the next day."

Verald could not help but smile too. Being eldest, he'd always felt compelled to set a chivalrous example and refrain from all jokes at their sister's expense, though he was hard-pressed to see if this instilled affection in her, or resentment. "I'd wager Father brought each of you as close to the ferotaurs as he could after you were born," he laughed. "Their twisted faces no doubt made yours tolerable to look at, after he'd grown used to my perfection. It's a wonder you've both attracted so many girls over the years."

Despite her brothers' incessant jests, Valeine never felt short of loved or looked after in their presence, and she fought the urge now to laugh at the way they emulated their father's regal composure. "No girl would go willingly to any of you in the first place, were it not for your tendencies to promise each of them a seat beside you at the throne."

"And I keep my promises, little sister; make no mistake," Ivrild replied. "Which is why I'll need you along with your loyal host to come and expand the great hall to a capacity that will accommodate those seats."

Unable to stay quiet between them any longer, Valdis declared, "There's ample room even if you three were king jointly; fitting, as I'm wary to entrust the crown to any one of you."

Ivrild reared his head back at this notion. "The three of us might just make one competent king. Cross legs with one another to squeeze into the throne, just like old times."

"We'll have to grovel at her feet every time she threatens to let the ferotaurs rush in to take our heads," Ondrel scoffed.

Valdis failed to hide a grimace that quickly withdrew beneath his hardening expression. His troubled heart settled down somewhat, as it always did whenever he could get lost with them. Gladly would he relinquish his high station, no longer to be king, only father. But, he knew such solace would crumble as soon as it was indulged.

Even as one invading horde lay shattered in their wake, others marshaled, resilient and vengeful, at their quivering borders. Yet no rabble in plain sight threatened with such gravity as the single gnawing tick at the back of his mind, whose eager face he would seek among his own people if he had to, until it was extracted and crushed.

Suddenly, blaring horns tremored through the wind, repeating a distress call from their farthest city. Turning to his daughter, he felt no surprise to find her attention already upon him, with no hint of trepidation.

"I have to go," said Valeine in a curt farewell, preparing to turn her carrier homeward.

"I'm going with you," Verald's voice was lost beneath those of his two brothers, who emphatically declared the same.

Finally allowing a broad smile at each of them, she said, "Sweet brothers, an overconfident fleet of ferotaurs prodding our defenses does not require the attention of busy princes such as yourselves. Quite a common occurrence really, at my city." She made to veer off, when Valdis halted her, willing to take no chances despite her display of daring.

"Verald, you go too," the king said sternly, though it was more directed at her, while she made no secret of her scorn for the command. Nodding his goodbye, Verald hastened forward to catch up as she'd already bolted far ahead, leaving them in her trail.

"What about us, Father?" protested Ondrel. "You think them better warriors?"

Ivrild teased, "Well, better than you, most likely. He probably wishes to keep me close for his own sake, with Felkoth hiding under our feet and all."

Valdis rolled his eyes at them. "You're both staying with me," he grumbled. "If I can't enjoy more than a few minutes' peace with all four, I'll at least settle for you two."

Grinning, Ivrild responded, "I didn't know you held us in such high esteem. I always reckoned myself tolerable at best in your regard, with occasion to stretch toward potentially respectable."

"Rare occasion," Valdis replied, driving them around. "Keep up," he bade, and they continued on together, sweeping back toward the heart of their kingdom, in which, somewhere, the enemy lay quietly.

Morlen looked down on the highest peaks as Roftome defied repellant winds, carving their own undisputed domain above winter's shroud, where all was blue and warm. Every tree or hill he'd ever climbed was a mere speck at such open altitude, where he could drink in each ray purely from its source, unfiltered by any cloud or flake. Filling his hands with the rising breath of all mortals inhabiting the earth below, he for one fleeting second counted himself apart from them, invulnerable to dust or decay.

"Your wings swim the air well, Roftome," he praised. "I'm soon to believe they were never broken at all."

"Nothing is broken that may heal, in time." Roftome's deep voice resounded over the underlying clouds. "My kind have endured far worse through the ages, whether biting snows or crushing tumbles of rock, or the arrows and nets of many intruders, and still we thrive."

Morlen felt disturbed by this, never before having heard of such atrocities perpetrated by men against eagles. "But I thought the Eaglemas—" He caught himself. "The city men never harmed your kind."

Roftome turned his white head sideways, with one eye aimed up like a spearhead in Morlen's direction. "I spoke not of the city men," he answered, holding course in silence for a moment, and realized he waited in vain for Morlen to acknowledge those he meant. "There are others who have come for us," he said. "And they have taken many."

Blaming the cold of a turbulent breeze for his sudden inner chill, Morlen drew his cloak tighter while they skimmed the thinning outer reaches and asked, "What others?"

Roftome had no fear of delving into memory of those who had come, and would again. "The pale men from the Mountains of the Lost," he said. "Who fly atop those they took before, the Pyrnaq, no longer bright-feathered or singing our songs. They throw their nets over my brothers and sisters and bring them underground, and they are never heard or seen again… not as they once were."

Looking far to the northeast, where unwelcoming bergs jutted through a dense white carpet, their lower reaches anchored in the menacing range where no man dared tread, Morlen asked, "How many have they taken?"

Roftome bowed his head solemnly, looking ahead to the

mountains of his birth. "As many as are left of us, if not more," he answered.

Morlen's heart slowed its beat. Having yesterday seen what he imagined was the worst possible end for a creature so free, he realized now that far worse fates crept nearby. "Then even the eagles can be corrupted by force."

Roftome gave no immediate response, flying in another foreboding quiet. After a few moments, he spoke. "There is one of my kind who has gone willingly," he said. "In the days of Korine the Ancient, He who brought many shadows came to our mountains, calling the eagles to be corrupted into serving His design. But all refused. All… but one, whose wings were stretched wide to shroud all lands, his feathers and beak melded with rock, and chest filled with fire, erupting behind dreadful notes that brought crippling sorrow before death."

As they dove beneath the damp caress of fog, Morlen shuddered as he knew well of what Roftome spoke. He was no stranger to the tales of Korindelf that rumored its first people to have cowered beneath a monstrous silhouette, whose debilitating call brought downpours of destruction. "Bloodsong," he whispered, the beast's name carved deep in his mind. "He was born an eagle, like you?"

"Not like me," Roftome assured. "There is no brother of mine who desires the weight of stone, or spout of flame."

Morlen took comfort in Roftome's pride, sitting well at ease even while they swayed in a surveying pass over the heights where thousands more flocked. There were no rulers here, no subjugated masses—only those made kings by their own strength, sharing snow-capped thrones with one another. And none would be led who did not wish to follow.

He envisioned this place serving as one of many homes he

made for himself in later days, which would not keep him settled long, since he would not be confined to one edge of the world.

"Let's make a pact," he said. "To leave no cloud untouched, and no peak unexplored, when less-troubled times call to us."

Etching an elegant path flanked on many sides by foreign realms, Roftome raised his sturdy head in acceptance. "No peak unexplored," he repeated boldly. "And no cloud untouched."

Morlen's face brightened despite thickening overhead wisps of gray when they descended in a stealthy sweep, aiming for a closer look down each cliff and into every sheltering hollow.

"You truly think he'd be fool enough to venture here?" said Roftome. "Perched on any ridge, I could spot and crush a rabbit sitting motionless at the mountain base, as could any of my brothers or sisters."

"He is no rabbit. You underestimated him before." Morlen choked slightly on his words of warning, realizing he still carried neither bow nor sword. "Felkoth is unlikely to remain in the forest, knowing the king's men will soon be searching. He'll seek refuge someplace out of sight and far less accessible."

"I owe him no higher estimation than previously given," Roftome retorted stubbornly. "I merely let my eagerness to end him get the better of me, but never again."

Suddenly, the glint of light upon metal drew Morlen's passing gaze back as he urged Roftome to slow, and, hovering, they both focused on the same vertical grid, waiting for the sign to hail them again. Minutes passed with no result, leading him to wonder if maybe he'd simply caught a frozen stream at a deceptive angle, when once more the elusive glare repeated unmistakably. This time they pinpointed its location high on an icy slope.

Leaning into each breeze that hit harder the closer to the mountain they forged, Morlen saw the outline of a form that became gradually defined. Soon, he realized, it was a man, but not

Felkoth. "One of the city men?" he asked tentatively. "I see no others around him."

"No," Roftome answered assuredly while he prepared to land, the curious figure standing unthreatened by their approach. "Not one of them."

Setting down against the white-blanketed rock, Morlen dismounted, looking on as the silent stranger stepped nearer, a full head taller than he, and, by his appearance, not much older. He was suited in armor, silver and bright, his helm crafted as an eagle's head (though its design seemed quite antiquated), and he was caped in red, with a dark scar through his cloven left pauldron.

Walking closer to them, he halted an arm's length away, and the snow did not even buckle under his weight. A more formidable warrior than Morlen had ever seen, the man's face shone in warm recognition, as though to greet a close ally.

"You are seeking someone," he said with barely the force of a whisper, though it resounded powerfully through the quiet, chill air.

Morlen gave no response at first, wondering if the hallucinations that often visited miners and smiths in sweltering heat could be brought on by fierce cold as well. But, studying his stately addresser, whose stance was broad and solid, he cast aside such notions. Instead he wondered how far this man's watch extended through the mountains, and if he alluded to Felkoth's whereabouts.

"Yes," he finally replied. "I am trying to find—"

"Morthadus," said the man, and Morlen was immediately taken aback.

How could he know this, of all names? Its relevance to himself could not possibly be suspected by any stranger. Still, as this rare opportunity reared its head, offering answers for which he'd lately found himself at a loss, he nodded.

Brimming with knowledge scarcely seen in one so young, his

smooth visage masking an ancient memory, the man smiled at him now. "The father of your fathers."

Again, Morlen tried in vain to understand, though he felt encouraged by the man's acute perception. "How…?" he cautiously began, but found no need to finish.

"You will find him," the man interjected, "where the halves meet."

Looking kindly at Morlen for a moment longer, he seemed to know his message was received. And yet, Morlen gleaned no meaning from it, no interpretation that could shed any light whatsoever, resolving only to remember it.

Then, the man strode smoothly to Roftome, who gave no warning at his advance, merely standing calm with beak relaxed as he stroked his neck feathers. "You have a good friend here," he praised. "I too had such a friend. But, I lost him, long ago."

Proud to have borne Roftome's stout frame on his own shoulders, and taking solace in their mutual loyalty, Morlen was aggrieved by the man's words. "Your eagle?" he asked, unable to expel many dark images stirred by the thought.

"No." The man continued to pat Roftome with loving regard. "A man. Like my brother." Withdrawing from Roftome, he stood farther apart this time and faced Morlen. "Farewell," he bade encouragingly. "I believe we shall see one another again."

Morlen drew a quick breath, seeing now that no flakes touched the man but fluttered unhindered through his wide, translucent form, which showed the hazy terrain behind as he gracefully took his leave. He walked far into the open white background, fading with each steady pace until they saw him no more.

Shielding himself from razor-edged winds that swept more forcefully now, he felt these unexpected words of counsel slowly uproot his determination to scour the frost for Felkoth. Instead his aim was diverted toward someone who, with Nottleforf's promised help, might yet be found.

"Come," Morlen said, reclaiming his place atop Roftome. "Felkoth will not move far under the city men's watch."

Preparing to take off at his companion's behest, Roftome asked, "You mean to give up the chase?"

Morlen looked below where a thousand places of cover were now frozen closed. "There may soon be nothing left to chase, whether he lies low or rears his head. But, right now, there is someone else I need to find."

They kicked off from the white peaks, passing over hundreds of icy trenches that could be housing the Tyrant Prince. Steering back toward familiar stretches of forest, Morlen hoped Nottleforf would uphold his reluctant promise, and finally send him in the direction he sought.

"You allow yourself to become far too troubled, Father," said Ivrild at the king's shoulder, as the three landed again in fields of emerald green centered in their realm. "If I were king, I would not bear so many burdens alone, as you do."

Ondrel cut him off. "No, you would assemble a council to bear them for you, and then fly away in the night with an ale in hand and a farm girl on your lap."

Ivrild's rejoinder was swift, punctuated with a smirk. "No, actually, I thought I might appoint you as my top advisor, in matters of feather grooming, crop distribution, and the like."

Knowing the attempt was futile under their scrutiny, Valdis nevertheless took pains to avert his half-smile.

"You see?" Ivrild laughed harder now. "He's redder than your backside was that night we gave you your first lashing."

Ondrel's tone grew indignant. "Don't think I've forgotten that. Letting me think it was Father's doing for all those years."

"It will be, this time; that goes for the both of you," said Valdis, "if you cannot take your fill of this rare quiet, perhaps the last we find in a long while."

Trading jovial glances, the brothers ceased their banter, finding it in their hearts to indulge his request, though Ivrild would not be completely silenced. "As I was saying before, Father," he jabbed affectionately, "as king, your crown should weigh heavier than your troubles. What is the point of having a host of subjects under your rule if you're unwilling to let your pain spill over a little onto them?"

Valdis's face relaxed under the watch of his second-eldest son, who brought more laughter than his other children by far, and he felt no need for concealment this time. "To be king is to be alone," he answered tersely. "You exist merely to give the people an illusion that they sleep each night behind someone keeping vigil with spear and sword in hand, ready to repel ten thousand snapping jaws from their doors at a moment's notice.

"And if, perchance, they learn that this is well beyond your power, that you are in fact just as vulnerable as they, and that even you at times feel terror, how soundly will they sleep each night? How confidently will each soldier carry out the orders given him when the relentless hordes finally come? And rest assured, they are coming.

"But, to be father," he went on, his lighter voice summoning their more optimistic attention. "To be father is to see your shortcomings erased, to feel your fear unravel when the faces that reflect the very best in you absolve every weakness, every doubt. You will be better kings than I, and fathers too. Your subjects will sleep far more peacefully than mine, and your men will fight far more fiercely. Your children will torment you with their keener intellect,

sharper wit. Their strength and speed will make you consider yourselves relics in the dust. And you will thank them silently for it
each day."

He grinned at both of them now, letting go of any bravado
he'd ever donned in their presence to make less of the perils toward
which they'd flown. He knew more were on the horizon, as near as
the cluster of men speeding at them from the capital.

"Suppose they've come to enjoy this enchanting quiet as well?"
nudged Ondrel, his brother snorting in response as they hastened to keep up with the king, who took off to meet the fren-
zied messengers.

"My lord!" the first of them bellowed out in front. "He's been
seen... our scouts in the mountains just sent word!"

"Where?" Valdis demanded.

Wiping frost from his glistening brow, the man panted,
"Climbing near the falls. They say he jumped as soon as he was
spotted, and they couldn't find his body in the river. He may very
well have drowned."

"No," answered Valdis with certainty. "Not him." Feeling his
sons' eager stares fixing upon him, he would not deny them the
task they sought. "Gather every warrior at the capital to arms," he
charged both princes, knowing the confident enthusiasm they frequently inspired there could mean the difference between finding
their target and coming up short. "I'll round up all who are able
to fly from the two middle cities. Track him wherever he goes, and
wait for me," he ordered, seeing their reluctance to obey. "Wait for
me—do you understand?"

Giving barely discernible nods in answer, the two brothers
turned their eagles to lead the group back. Knowing how quickly
impatience would seize them if they came upon Felkoth, Valdis
descended to summon a force great enough to finally eliminate his

enemy, though a part of him suspected that three thousand spears and bows might still be too few.

Spat upon a slick bank by roaring waters, Felkoth slowly slithered through muddy gravel, one elbow dragging after the other until he rested flat upon dry land. And, scanning out over the former Freelands stretching ahead, his spirits soon soared as he realized he'd reached his own territory once again.

Even so, he was days away from any haven. And, though unsure how long he'd been on display beside the river, he sensed the Eaglemasters with their abundant spies would soon be on his trail. Lying still, he merely listened for any sound of the massing fleet that would quickly swarm above, ready to hunt him to the ends of the earth. He hoped against hope to see Valdis at the head of their ranks, and kept the Dark Blade ready to bleed him slowly for all to see.

Then, quite abruptly, the smoothest splash caught his ear. Slowly turning over with his body low against the ground, his spirits swelled once more as he laid eyes on a very familiar mode of deliverance. The mountain eagle stood a dozen paces away, talons submerged in glittering shallows as the lower half of a blue-tinted fish wriggled limply within its beak, and its head feathers showered the glassy surface with falling droplets.

He had to strike fast if he meant to evade the Eaglemasters. And he would not be unseated this time, judging the bird's size to be significantly smaller than the previous brute he'd harnessed. Dagger drawn, he slit through the upper left side of his robes, tearing out a long strip of fabric. Wrapping each end around his palms like a garrote, he pushed himself upright, eyeing the unsuspecting creature's spacious back.

Careful not to disturb even a pebble from the loose terrain, he paused to look over the river and adjacent forest, and saw thousands of identical red figures in an airborne formation that pointed like an arrowhead straight for him. Pulling the lengthy cloth around white knuckles, he bolted forward, letting each stomp announce inevitable capture to his prey, and lunged out with arms extended as the raptor leapt from the bank in an attempt to escape.

He crashed hard between its wings, hooking the makeshift rein under its throat with ruthless force, and the ensnared creature thrashed violently with no choice but to fly in the direction steered. Forcing its thick head to the right against screams of protest, he drove his carrier away from the coming assault, squeezing out every ounce of speed it would relinquish.

Its windpipe bent under the unrelenting strain while he struggled to maintain altitude, cursing the only harbor offered him in the Quiet Waste. Still, he would not allow Valdis the satisfaction of bringing him down, even if it meant descending into the depths of the earth, where the Eaglemasters dared not fly.

They were close now, and his shrinking lead would hold their fire at bay only a short while longer. Passing into caustic air pumped from their destination, the bird fell dizzily in a sharp decline that required all his strength to counteract. He nearly snapped its neck until they leveled out again.

He had no time to contemplate what might be found within the crater's boiling depths, having heard nothing more than old men's fireside tales about it. His closing pursuers had begun testing their range, and hundreds of arrows fell close behind him. It would not be long before he became a viable target, and the beckoning mountain sat miles away.

He unsheathed the Dark Blade and bashed it flat against the eagle's lower back, bringing a distressed burst of speed, taking care not to make any cut that would bring the flight to a premature end. Again he struck even harder, and this time they teetered upward as the eagle's backside bobbed low in response.

Then, rearing back for a third stroke, he found it unnecessary as a wayward arrow tore down through the bird's tail flesh, summoning another high-pitched shriek muffled by the rein he still held securely. It careened downward again, but was lifted by his urgent efforts to keep them above the hollow peak that was barely below eye level.

Hearing the Eaglemasters' emboldened shouts, he tensed his body in anticipation of the downpour to follow, beating his transporter once more across its broken tail. The shock traveled through every stiff feather, inducing a turbulent jolt that bucked his head just inches out of a zipping arrow's path, while others began to shroud them on each side.

"Faster!" he growled, pushing for the dark plume that spewed from the mountain before them, in the hope it might shield him from his attackers' aim. Above the toxic clouds, they continued to rain projectiles down on his position as he veered haphazardly through each volley, knowing the lethal walls would soon crush him.

As it succumbed to the fumes and smoke, the bird no longer paid heed to even the harshest lash. It merely resorted to a feeble repetition of wing flaps that sank them toward the pitch black opening, which gaped like an expectant mouth. The Eaglemasters' onslaught persisted nonetheless, blasting like a windswept storm.

"There!" He heard the cry high overhead when the black fumes parted, followed by a zealous assault that cut his thigh and back like lashes, riddling the eagle whose cries were finally silenced. They ceased gliding, and plummeted instead through the suffocating volcano spout while he clung to the aerodynamic carcass. Soon the creature's feathers ignited beneath him as he skidded down the scorched walls, scalding him through a steamy plunge that abruptly ended when he crashed upon a jagged rim that encircled the pool of magma below.

Hovering in a bright red cluster over the hot steam that concealed their fallen target, the Eaglemasters belted a united chorus of triumph that vibrated down the open rock to its orange depths, which bubbled a morbid greeting when Felkoth rose on trembling legs. There was nowhere to go now. Nothing to do but wait while each breath seared his lungs and brought them closer to rupturing, depriving the Eaglemasters of any true victory, after every one of their aimless volleys left his flesh only shallowly flayed.

Imagining himself the first ever to set foot within this fiery crypt, he examined its glowing innards with great curiosity, his attention particularly drawn to a light aura encasing the molten surface. Not thick like smoke, it merely lay, as still as an ancient shroud.

Suddenly the aura began to stir ever so delicately, swimming in his direction while he paced around the elevated platform. Moments later he felt an inexplicable pull on his sword, which lifted to meet the approaching vapors, stopping him in his tracks while the connection grew stronger. He had to plant his boots firmly to avoid being dragged over, until, like a scabby crust, the bluish haze peeled away from the dense, burning liquid, stretching toward him and wrapping deftly around the Dark Blade like silk from a spider. Then, it rattled his outstretched arm with an explosive blast and shot up out of the mountain in a burnt, smoky jet, dissipating beneath the huddled Eaglemasters.

Holding the sword as it pointed upward, unchanged, he looked more closely at the molten lake, which rumbled with an unprecedented shudder, causing the rock beneath his feet to crack open while he scrambled to find better footing. He kept both eyes fixed on the churning lava. Its bubbles popped much more turbulently, almost as if something breathed from below and was slowly rising. A groan quaked deep in the earth's core, growing louder, closer, like a gargantuan yawn that even liquefied stone could not silence. Standing rigid, he remained transfixed by the pulsing reservoir. Its inner disturbance grew as the surface rippled, hissed, no longer flat, but concave, sucked down to flood a newly vacated recess far below, while the remainder slowly lifted off, pushed out atop a solid berg that dwarfed him.

An immense beak of sharp black diamond protruded through the flaming sludge, followed by a boulder-sized head that shook clusters of white-hot slime all around the crater walls, its lava-encrusted lids peeling open to reveal dark red eyes. Folded wings emerged next, opening barely half their full span within these crushing confines, covered, along with every inch of its neck and body, in long granite feathers that overlapped like impenetrable armor.

Its lower half still submerged, the fiery leviathan sucked all breathable air out of the crater in one voracious breath, leaving Felkoth gasping for what slowly trickled back down through the clogged ash roof. Then the creature belted out globs of bright orange phlegm into the surrounding stone.

Blinking all around like a hatchling for its mother, its dreadful countenance soon found him, its massive neck bending down for a closer look while he held his ground, a mere sapling beneath a great shadowy hill.

"Bloodsong," Felkoth whispered, feeling his heels suddenly jolt upward as the beast's head-sized nostrils drew in a gust that pulled him to his tiptoes, pushing him back to stand flat again with a satisfied release. Retracting its head, it trained adjusting eyes on him.

"The blood of the One Hundred is on your blade," it rasped, every word sizzling, crackling, as though each took a charring toll when spoken. "You have slain one of the Blessed Ones, my captors."

Felkoth stared back expressionless, certain that he had encountered no such man. Their time was long past, and he would know beyond any doubt if he had ever come across one of them. But, perhaps his first ancestor to wield the Dark Blade had taken his share of blood from them, when the shriekers brought their fall.

"Long have I slumbered beneath those who once filled my shadow." The sonorous voice rattled the precarious magmatic structures around them. "I listen to their children laugh and stomp the earth, as though they have forgotten how pale the sun looked behind my silhouette, and dried the tears that soiled their faces when they heard my call, for in hearing, they knew my name."

Wrenching its lower body out of the sweltering soup, it revealed two monstrous arrays of talons, each curving longer than the height of any man into a scythe of polished volcanic glass. An enormous barbed tail followed with a jagged, clubbed tip that could devastate scores of foes in a single sweep. Hibernating muscles stretched against one another in thousands of grinding plates, and it broadened its chest as widely as the stifling walls would permit.

"I want them to know it again, Master," it declared hungrily, waiting patiently before him, as if the simplest command would hurtle them both skyward.

Felkoth was shocked to hear such a word uttered by this flame-dripping terror. "Master," he repeated.

Meeting him with a loyal nod, as though he now held the chains that would release it upon the world, the creature answered, "You have broken the seal which bound me to the depths, and, in breaking it have become my master. Only you may take me to the skies, where the feathered herds shall reign no more."

Rearing his soot-covered head back to peer up toward the lightless roof, anticipation penetrating what his gaze could not, he saw the amassed Eaglemasters gloating as though he were a charred ruin. He smiled, imagining their shock as he emerged, brief though it would be. Lavishing pride upon his newest and greatest servant, he was ready to bask in blood spilt from those above, and watch it mingle with their flesh into the dust.

"Yes," his voice resounded with a deep appetite. "They will know. They will all know it, soon enough."

Ivrild looked back to see that the king's haste to catch up with them had grown, despite their static position above Felkoth's billowing tomb.

"Whether he comes to congratulate or scold, I cannot tell," he said to his brother. "And with the army's entire remainder at his sides, you would think we waited here for aid."

Ondrel nodded, treading air triumphantly above all that was left to see of the Tyrant Prince. "In Father's mind there is always a worry. And more than one, I suspect, to accompany any beckoning peace."

"All that beckons now are the biggest flagons crafted by men," Ivrild replied. The mighty host laughed heartily, enjoying an overdue sense of elation. "After we reclaim Korindelf and the last of those skeletal abominations lies cold with our arrows between its ribs, I should like to take a short leave. Maybe there will be some advantage to be found in my standing as a liberator of the people."

Ondrel laughed. "Father would summon you back in a heartbeat, what with all the unknown dangers left to repel."

Lifting a carefree chin, Ivrild said, "All dangers now are those we know quite well. We've treaded within the shadows where they creep, dug them out of the holes they thought well-hidden, and they slink away at our approach. Whatever remains unknown is too afraid to reveal itself, and always shall be. I say there is nothing else to fear ahead."

Suddenly, the most silent calm swept all around them, and the underlying ash dome swirled downward, churning in a great spout of black to the very belly of the mountain. It drew their devoted attention through smoke, through flame, until they could not look anymore, could not see at all, for hearing alone became in that moment more than they could bear. The rising sound of wailing, inescapable death drew tears as profuse as the sweat that trickled from each pore, and they could do nothing but sit, helpless, while it furiously grew.

Valdis heard it too, though still a mile off from the ominous peak. His eagle trembled like all others in the fleet with the same staggering shock that would otherwise deter their advance, were it not for the two thousand souls, his sons included, hovering at the very source.

"Steady!" he commanded as every wing stroke drove them deeper into a stinging mire flooded by the unending sound. He had to reach them now. Something was wrong, terribly...

The cluster of men remained huddled above the summit, all of their faces angled down toward the volcano mouth, the eagles beneath them struggling to merely tread air, as though slipping through mud toward something climbing from below. And then—

A great mass, shrouded in smoke, erupted directly through their center as it sprayed liquid flame that obliterated dozens. Droves that were spared the initial impact scattered with renewed urgency, only to be swatted down like flies by an airborne mace that swung wildly left and right, which, Valdis shuddered to realize, was a tail. He traced its thickening stony length to the base of a creature grotesque and enraged, which spread razor wings of black rock to drape all beneath it in shadow.

Heartbeat smothered by every figure that fell burnt and bashed, pounding for those who still fled each malicious swipe, he led a desperate charge to the chaotic scene. The dead seemed to double with each enormous jet hurled from the beast's lungs, and all others broke off in every direction, forming new lines to launch rapid volleys that bounced pathetically off of every sought weakness.

"Ready arrows!" Valdis yelled hoarsely, and the ranks behind him drew their bowstrings uncertainly, releasing upon his command only to find—as had their beleaguered comrades—every shot was ineffective. Hundreds ahead had already fallen, the rest abandoning any further attempts to counter or regroup, dispersing like a ring of debris around the invulnerable predator that clearly had only begun its pattern of destruction.

Then, blinding him to everything else, two figures caught his eye, narrowly ducking a ferocious thrash that crushed many others behind them as they sped out directly toward him. The creature saw them, too, slithering around to follow. They were but a quarter mile away as he leapt forward to meet them, the gap in between refusing to shrink like in some torturous nightmare, while the stalking creature drew closer at their heels. And then he saw Felkoth, standing securely within its left talons that enclosed him all around like a fortified box, oozing laughter while peering out at the two princes, and then at him, as though to savor what was to come.

He reached for their distant outstretched hands, and saw only infants' hands, waving as he'd lift them to sit on his shoulders. He would lift them now, as he'd done then. One on each shoulder.

The dragon sucked in a heaping gulp of air, stealing every ounce within his own deflating lungs while his throat and mouth opened to give no sound, vocal cords rattling bloody and raw as he watched the fiery blast shoot forth in a polarized stream. It exceeded his sons' speed, licking their backs while they began to cry out with eyes seeking help that would not come. It crawled up their helmets and around their arms, melting silver into skin that soon cracked and lost all color, finally bursting within the orange and black cloud that enveloped, vaporized. The force blew him back, limp and grudgingly alive into the fold of his men, who whisked him away in retreat, though still he gazed into the fading smoke, seeing that where they had been, there was now nothing.

He heard only Felkoth's satisfied cackling, pounding each battered eardrum to a withered pulp no matter how far they flew toward safety that would undoubtedly expire. Then his trembling limbs convulsed with the rest of him into deep unconsciousness, from which, he would not willingly wake.

CHAPTER THIRTEEN

FATHER OF FATHERS

FOR MORTHADUS, SLEEP was no blissful withdrawal, but a tormenting excavation of all he wished to keep sealed away. Fatigue merely drove him deeper to a cruel realm where body was immobilized while mind was peeled like a poisonous fruit, its spines piercing all corners of him with an electric current.

His dreams carried him to the Dark Mountains, to stand nearly one thousand years in the past with the other ninety-nine of his order, whom he'd lost. Their eyes peered like beacons into rising desolation, swords glinting silver in the moonlight, each with a round crystal centered in the hilt.

"We were told never to set foot on His ground," he warned. In this memory he was tall and lean, with muscular arms and legs. His face was young, like smooth stone, and brown hair jutted down his forehead. "None of us fully understands the power that sleeps here, if it sleeps at all."

"He is defeated, Morthadus," one beside him replied. "Not for one thousand years can He return. And even so, you forget the power *we* have. Now is the time to cut each one of them down to the last."

"But Korine's wound has weakened him," he implored. "He can no longer safeguard the city. If we fall, it will be left defenseless." But they would not listen, instead marching high into the cliffs, and he reluctantly kept up alongside.

They searched all around, listening warily for familiar morbid cries as it grew difficult to see, though the bright moon bore down on their heads like an executioner. Each step only sapped their strength, making them recall the aches and pains of mortal men. And the voice... It slowly froze their blood, until finally, as they reached the summit, the enemy horde emerged behind them, pinning them against the swirling abyss.

They brandished their swords as one, countering high and low, though merely a sunken reef in ravaging currents. Their faces nearly touching those of their disfigured foes, whose ghastly breath burned their nostrils, they could feel the darkness clasp their shoulders with ghostly fingers.

"Weak... You are weak," it whispered. "Come to me, and you will be weak no more."

He broke rank and pushed forward alone, away from its malevolent caress, and his noble brothers wailed, backing away from the murderous beasts that replaced him and into the cold vacuum at their heels.

"Don't leave us, Morthadus!" they pleaded. But he could only look through the tangle of claws at their desperate faces, which vanished one by one as all agonized screams were smothered, and the black mists wrapped around their helpless bodies, swallowing them whole. Clattering to the ground, unable to go into the mists with them, their swords reverberated in a chorus of unanswered calls, finally fading to utter quiet.

He wept in grief, his body twitching against the ground

while every groan pulled him back from the replayed vision, and he shook violently awake. His tears imprinted damp pockmarks into the dusty rock floor, as many as all the lifetimes that had progressed, and ended, under his watch. Now, he wished only to cease watching altogether.

Yet lately, in allowing himself a closer glimpse from below at the youngest, had he renewed that bond he swore to forever keep severed? Could he truly embrace that part of himself which lived on in others, knowing that one day they would be lost while still he lingered?

Morlen abandoned any further efforts toward sleep, sitting up stiffly on his blanketed pallet as the dark tunnels echoed with a fearful din. He had returned the previous day and found Nottleforf distressed as though some growing threat approached, which finally compelled him to depart just before nightfall. Staying put at the wizard's request, he had soon been drawn out by a sound of insatiable ruin, and as he looked upward to the stars a great shadow streaked far across the sky.

Wondering restlessly what Nottleforf had ascertained, unsure of when or if he had come back, he donned his cloak and boots, heading up through the stairwell. He was splashed with snow as the trapdoors opened, and tentatively peered west looking for columns of smoke, feeling relieved to see none so far. But he still feared that the Eaglemasters would soon face devastation even they were ill-equipped to combat.

Hearing a most welcome rustling through the foliage, he turned to see Roftome, who'd kept to the forest since their day's flight, descending now with his beak stained from a fruitful hunt.

"Trouble for the city men," said Morlen, eyes furtively scanning above for any movement.

"Trouble for all," replied Roftome alertly, his voice intrepid as he worked his beak to dislodge tufts of fur. "Only the darkest heart among my kind could inhabit such lifeless flesh. And only one darker still would it call master."

Pacing numbly through the heavy frost as every extremity tingled awake, Morlen searched for the next prudent move. Only yesterday had he thought Felkoth wounded and buried. What inhuman resolve could have driven him to elude so many, to harness the unquenchable plague whose service could only be purchased with the blood of the Blessed Ones?

Their blood had run through his father's veins, there was no doubt, spilt with cowardice, used toward such a foul end. Yet each day he doubted its presence within his own. He had only one reliable solace: feeling the Goldshard's jagged, flat embrace against flesh made stronger, faster, by its power. He would use that gift to fight Felkoth and his winged bearer. But, he needed to walk a path yet to be revealed, at the end of which, somewhere, sat the one who could give him real answers. One who, he had been led to believe, was a part of him.

Thinking back to the strange specter's message high on the snowy peaks, he still had no understanding of what direction it pointed. Suddenly his attention was diverted when another concealed set of doors opened farther out in the clearing, above the wizard's quarters. And, groggy and disheveled, as though the night's reports had brought far grimmer news than expected, Nottleforf emerged and ambled over to them.

He feared to know how dire the Eaglemasters' position truly was, because if they stood no chance against Felkoth now, he felt he could make little difference. "Does King Valdis live?" he asked, thinking the monarch's death would surely leave the realm vulnerable to defeat.

Looking grave, almost as though the answer no longer

mattered, Nottleforf gave an unconvincing nod. "Barely," he said, studying the sky like a field of battle. "His two youngest sons were among those killed, four hundred in a matter of minutes when they met Felkoth, who flies now with the creature Bloodsong."

Fears confirmed, Morlen glanced over at Roftome, who knew the imminent danger. Were they really ready to fly out against such a storm?

"There is more," Nottleforf continued, yet to have reached the worst. "Valdis has issued a stay of flight for the Eaglemasters. They are to remain at the capital, on foot, since he has fallen to the fear that any airborne force is now futile."

His stomach sank, as any show of submission from the Eaglemasters was unprecedented. "And what about the four lower cities? What defense will they have?"

Nottleforf shook his head, visibly weary. "The king thinks they are beyond saving, and that is not altogether mere pessimism, not with the overwhelming weapon now at Felkoth's disposal. He has already prepared his last stand, thinking Felkoth will surely strike the capital as he did before. But... I am not so convinced."

"You think Felkoth would rather divide the Eaglemasters than take them all on at once?" asked Morlen.

"I think he would savor their suffering for as long as possible. I think he would first have them watch as every blood-lusting wretch kept for centuries at the fringe was finally given safe passage to take its satisfaction. He will use his ascended position to make servants of all those who creep in the shadows, and only when Valdis has seen every brick toppled, and every soul devoured, will Felkoth finish him."

Staring off in silence, Morlen knew the king must be swayed quickly if any challenge was to be mounted against such an offensive. But, to be heard, he would have to first prove himself a worthy ally, to instill in them enough confidence to meet the coming tide before it spread too far. He would need every advantage possible, all strength and guidance to be found, if he were to draw them out of hopelessness and add their momentum to his.

Nottleforf seemed to know where his mind was going, like the trail he had promised to help uncover now lay inescapably before them both, when Morlen finally said, "I need to find him now, Nottleforf. I need to find Morthadus."

Unable to abide his scrutiny, Nottleforf looked away through the forest, perhaps toward the very place he felt so reluctant to explore. "He may not help you," the wizard warned. "You may wish you'd never sought him out... as will he."

Morlen refused to withdraw his attention. "I must," he pressed adamantly, saying nothing more as Nottleforf pivoted, doubling the space between them.

They stood silently, until Nottleforf uneasily gave a deep sigh, ready to yield. "There is a cave," he said with reservation, "at the northernmost point of this system. If you fly to the corner of the forest just overlooking the river, you will find its entrance in a small crevice at the mountain base. The tunnel leads deeper than any man would dare crawl. It is there, I believe, that you may find him."

Back still turned, Nottleforf gave no other movement or sound, waiting only for his departure, and perhaps the peace in solitude that it would bring.

"Thank you," said Morlen, briskly climbing onto Roftome's waiting back and launching up while Nottleforf returned to his quarters.

Gliding along the bristly forest roof blurred by Roftome's speed, Morlen looked unwaveringly ahead. He felt great promise to be found in the small patch hugging the distant mountain base, and in the one who dwelt far below, no longer to be obscured from his sight.

*

The city of Veldere rang with mournful silence for both dead and living, as every Eaglemaster stood shoulder to shoulder on its walls, staring for the first time with dread up at the skies. Deep within the citadel's great hall, gilded with silver that now appeared dull and tarnished in the absence of laughter, King Valdis sat colorless and rigid on a cold throne.

"You cannot lie down before him like this," Valeine implored with stained cheeks, though she held firmly against more tears. Her older brother leaned against the wall of a nearby corridor with his head pressed against the inner bend of his arm, muffling each sob that was ripped forth by memory of the two faces he'd never see again. They still shone as clearly as when he'd left them the previous day, an act for which he would never forgive himself.

"The four lower cities swell beyond capacity with all our people," she persisted. "If you leave them vulnerable you erase all we've ever bled for, all reason to have ever called ourselves a kingdom of free men, women, children. You erase all hope... Father."

Valdis slouched forward, lost in every nebulous swirl rippling through the marble floor, as though to dive out might submerge him in a dense cloud that would crush all memory away.

Giving only a feeble rasp, he muttered, "He is coming. He will come... I know."

Frustration drew her aggressively toward him, though he paid no heed to her advance. It took every ounce of restraint in her possession not to reach out and grab him by each shoulder, knowing that even with such a physical act she stood powerless to restore any purpose in him.

"How can you be so sure he will strike here?" she demanded, louder now. "How can you yield the sky to him so openly, when he could just as easily roast you where you sit half-dead? What if he moves on my city first with the allegiance of the ferotaurs, who would gladly serve any with the means to provide them a full breach of our borders? Will you let my people fall first to them?"

His head bobbling as though barely attached, Valdis could not bring himself to look up. He merely studied the long spear laid down at his feet, its upper half of bright crystal beckoning to be wielded by arms he no longer desired to lift.

"He will come," he repeated. "He will."

Her stinging eyes remained locked on him, threatening to soon give way, until she was unable to look even a moment longer at what he had become. Seeing the Crystal Spear relinquished between them, she stepped closer and drew it up, striking its base forcefully to the floor, and the sound of it bounced across the hall.

Bending down toward him, she said without sympathy, "If you won't bear this any longer, I will." Then, unwilling to waste another moment, she turned and strode hastily out into the courtyard where her eagle sat ready to fly.

"Where are you going?" asked Verald hotly, following her out of the castle as he wiped his face of any smudge.

"Where I must," she replied, mounting her carrier with the Crystal Spear at her side.

"If he strikes Veleseor you'll stand no chance!"

"It is *my* city; they are *my* people," she answered, pinning him with a scathing glare. "They will stand a chance with me, and with you too if you have the stomach." Saying no more, she sharply faced forward as the bird launched away, flying far above all others who were committed now only to ground, and disappeared off toward the realm's southern edge.

Sitting alone in the rusting hall, Valdis clung to the only remaining comfort he had, envisioning what would cleanse him of all fear, all doubt, and bring him fully revived to his feet. Only at the coming of the hero with the Crystal Blade, whom he'd imagined so vividly for years, would he rise again.

And the hero would come, very soon. He had to come.

Morning had grown late when Morlen and Roftome neared the northeast corner of the forest, touching down on a carpet of needles just below the mountains.

"You really mean to crawl like the tiniest of mice through some unstable fissure?" Roftome protested as Morlen dismounted and approached the snow-packed base. "Such low places were not meant for men, not even the worst ones I've met in my long days."

Disconcerted to see no visible opening as Nottleforf had described, Morlen knew he would have to dig out a substantial area before pinpointing the entrance. "I mean to, yes," he answered, scraping away one small dent at a time. "I mean to face the first of my father's line, and see what value there is in my being the last."

Displeased at the sight of him toiling alone, Roftome reluctantly stepped beside him and used both feet with outstretched talons to sweep a flurry past his tail feathers. "It may not be wise to seek one who dwells so far below," he warned. "He may not be so welcoming toward any who would uncover him."

Morlen said nothing at this, though it slowed his efforts slightly to picture the hostile response his presence might incite, especially from one fabled to be so powerful, so long removed from any contact, light, or sound.

"If there is at least a part of him that wants to emerge," he replied as freshly exposed stone glistened between them, "then, finding that, finding *him*, might help me as well."

Mounds piled higher behind them while they spread across the frost-coated mountain base until, prying away another dense clump, Morlen found a narrow mouth in the rock that seemed to splinter farther out. "Here," he said, moving to what he imagined would be its center while Roftome sidled over, clearing more away.

The jagged fracture tapered only inches wider as Morlen began gutting the ice within the middle, and he realized he would have to flatten himself completely in order to even break through.

"I hope your back is as tough-skinned as it is strong," said Roftome, bending his neck to peer inside. "This will not expand for many long crawls."

Brushing away the last handfuls of snow from tight jaws that grinned before him, he listened to every cold drip inside their awaiting throat, echoing to the same recess much farther down, where he knew he must go. He removed his cloak and draped it over Roftome's folded wings, kneeling beside the inhospitable entrance. His left arm was the first to brave its scathing bite, until both were wedged in far enough that he could pull his upper body in next, and he slithered deeper, straining to keep his face elevated while his scalp scraped sorely above.

Pulling with chilled fingers while bent, cramping legs fully extended, he suddenly felt empathy for the slimiest insects as he repeated his slinking crawl many times. Each frigid droplet that fell on the back of his neck made him feel that the crushing roof was steadily lifting. He could see from what little daylight trickled in that the cave opened some twenty yards ahead to a capacity through which he could move more comfortably, though still on hand and knee. Beyond that point, though, all was concealed and quiet, divulging no sign of his uncharted destination, or of anyone within.

Morthadus could sense the youngest drawing closer while he lay still upon the cave floor. He hoped in vain for just a moment's peace in sleep; apprehension of the encounter only plunged him deeper into dreaded memory, bringing him back again to that night when his brothers had fallen.

Standing alone, he swung his sword wildly into the shriekers, sending many heads flying through the ranks that gave way to his path, and he pushed forward until he was away from the cruel vapors. Those who tried to strike him lost their arms, while any who bit felt his blade on their throats, falling dead by the dozens until soon those who remained began to back away, watching him with terror.

"This one is powerful," a fearful whisper seethed. "Who is he?"

The voice spoke again in his mind with softness concealing urgency. "Ninety-nine are here… only one more…"

But, standing before the savage host that trembled now under his burning focus, he could bear to listen no longer. Gathering every last reserve of energy left within, he pushed the shiver out of his spirit and shouted, "I am Morthadus of the Blessed Ones!"

Suddenly his foes stood suspended, unmoving all around, and the mountainside was flooded with brilliant blue light into which he stared, knowing it would give no sting. In the center of the light was a figure, like a man, who floated beside him amid the carnage.

"Korine," he said in awe while taking in the mystic form, which was encircled by the wind itself like a robe of infinite color, and across his broad chest was a long dark gash from which bright mists flowed.

"Morthadus, my time will soon be at an end," said Korine as his life force pooled on the rocks around them. "The greatest hope left to challenge Him when He returns, rests upon you."

Staring into the dense shadow that would one day return to engulf all of Cryntor, he wondered what possible feat he could accomplish. "What do you ask of me?" he whispered.

With a smile that drove out all fear, Korine answered, "I ask you to live, Morthadus. Live, so that the Blessed Ones may never be extinguished."

He writhed, half-awake, against each prodding rock, his

restless mind begging every faculty he had surrendered to sleep and dreams to return before the scene went any further.

"Your children will have your strength, your speed. But, either by the sword, or when they stand frail and soft while you remain of good flesh, they will die."

Then, turning to the ninety-nine swords that had fallen at the edge of the black mists, Korine raised his arms to draw them into the air together, and then drove their blades into the ground to line the great abyss. At the center of the line remained a space, wide enough for one more.

"There may come a time when you will no longer want to be Morthadus of the Blessed Ones," Korine warned. "When it does, return to this place, and lay your sword to rest beside the others."

Morlen stifled each groan while he dragged himself farther across the sharp, rocky floor, unsure how any sudden noise might affect the spiked ceiling only inches above. Finally, his head and shoulders jutted into a wider cavity past the elongated mouth. Emerging intact within far more generously spaced walls, he allowed himself a breath of ease, though visibility was now all but gone.

A small amount of light still reflected off the rocks, but its source was not the entrance left behind, he realized. This seemed to pour in from farther ahead, dimmed by every bend and slope. Still prohibited from standing, he tripled his initial pace and kept himself centered as the tunnel narrowed to a declining chute.

He disregarded each pinching bump to his ribs while space grew considerably scarcer, and soon was on his stomach once more, looking at the chute's end a short distance away, lit from below by whatever glow had led him this far. Clawing now just to gain a few inches at a time, he held the bright opening firmly with unblinking eyes, letting go all expectations of what, or whom, he would find on the other side.

Morthadus sank deeper as he knew the youngest would find him at any moment, and his dream carried him through time and space.

Korine was sending him away, and the ancient one's image slowly faded as radiant mists continued to bleed from the grim wound, bringing death closer with each passing second. The Crystal Blade shone between them now, left to be claimed by one who could make the journey. Feeling like scattered feathers in the wind, he held as long as he could to the shrinking picture—endless lines of ghouls soon to find him gone, the blanket of light that sat motionless over the ground, and the one standing within, who finally expired as the last of his power blasted a great distance between them.

He soared far until eventually coming to rest someplace warm, green. Lying face-down upon grass more fragrant than any he'd ever known, he rolled onto his back and looked up to find himself in a bright meadow painted with colors that defied earthly existence. Having barely the time to wonder if he was the only one within its sprawling wonders, he felt a smooth hand touch his shoulder, and turned without fear to see a young woman.

She was tall and sleek, with golden hair surpassed by the brightness of her smile, and her eyes met with the subdued blue of his own. Crouching at his feet, she held out a round, pink object that glistened in the early morning light, saying in a way that drove all memory of the dark voice from his mind, "Eat."

She seemed to delight as much in his presence as he did in hers, and he gladly took her offering, sinking his teeth into the beautiful fruit as it stained his lips and soothed his vacant stomach, filling him with a rich warmth. His senses broadened to encompass things far beyond himself, and he swayed with the caress of each breeze, watching creatures great and lethal pass by as though his entrance into their realm was no threat.

She heated his sluggish blood with a look he wished never to pass, gently pulling his hand closer while it still held the half-eaten apple to take a deep bite herself.

"Can you feel it?" she asked.

His eyes burned with their inner light once more. "Yes," he answered hungrily. "I can feel it."

Morlen released every ounce of air that his compressed lungs could afford to lose while both shoulders forced their way out of the shrinking passage, and his pinned arms finally wrenched themselves free. He grabbed hold of an outcropping from the low ceiling ahead, lifting himself out to land a few feet down upon a slope that descended into a deep opening. And the strange glow continued to flicker up, its source only a few footsteps away now, though he remained unsure whether it was indifferent to his approach, or unwelcoming.

The rough floor stretched beneath steadily sinking walls until he had to crouch down again, sliding through a cylindrical, bright opening less than three feet in diameter. Midway through the connecting space, he stopped short, dazed as the most bewildering flashes passed behind his eyes, carrying with them a multitude of images too rapid to take in.

He dragged onward, colors and figures blurring through his mind while he wriggled out into a round chamber, and rose slowly to see that he was quite alone. He stood immersed in pale vapors that poured in from a small crack in the rock above, and their potency was so increased in the confines of this room it was almost palpable.

Recalling the banquet story from a few nights earlier, he realized he must be directly beneath the basin in which the crystals had been forged long ago. A powerful haze collected there at the head of the Speaking River, rumored to bring strange visions to all who breathed it. But, here it was highly concentrated, and its effects coursed through him before he could decide whether he wanted to see what it might bring.

Inhaling slowly to only half his lungs' capacity, he shed more reservation with each calming release, feeling no ill effect. He gave in as a bright, blurry canvas solidified before him, until he could no longer be sure if his eyes were open or closed. All he could do was watch as the light bent to reveal things for no other, but him.

He saw his father—he was sure of it—looking strong, with fine color, not as Felkoth had left him. But, wait… It could not be Matufinn, though the resemblance was staggering. No… this man was younger, clean-shaven, his hair just as long but not so dark. His eyes were different, too. They were sharper, fiercer. No… this was someone yet to be born. He stood wielding a sword of bright blue flame, holding fast against a towering curtain that pressed down on him, enveloping, swallowing…

The canvas shifted, swirling the tumultuous scene away and condensing into another, closer now to the present. He saw a tremendous lion in a cage, enclosed behind golden bars it had secured around itself for protection. But, the bars were shrinking inward, constricting it, preventing any proper swipe or lunge. The lion was going to die, and by its own folly, no less—its own fear. Could it not break free, somehow? Could it never escape?

Then, the lion and cage vanished as present bridged with past, giving way to another image that gradually became more defined than the others. He saw a single tree, standing tall and broad—old, undying, and bearing many branches. Then, suddenly, it split vertically into two halves, one of which withdrew its roots and pushed far away from the other, planting itself again where it could be set apart. And the discarded half slowly withered and cracked without nourishment.

But, as many ages passed, the half that tried to flourish in separation from its counterpart soon found itself similarly afflicted, unable to endure such a broken state. Extending its roots back toward those of the other, it grew stronger the closer they drew, though fearful of the poison that would sting more powerfully if they rejoined. But, only together could they overcome it and have peace.

The abandoned half feebly reached out toward that which returned while both felt life rekindle within. Their roots became entwined, pulling each to the other until the two halves finally met again as one, mending over time.

Morlen gasped sharply, pulling away to fall hard on his back, and grabbed aimlessly for the opening through which he'd entered the chamber. He flipped himself around and urgently dug back through the connecting passage until he could breathe more freely, his mind violently spinning to rest, no longer exposed to the intoxicating vapors.

Forcing into the adjacent segment, he sat up, leaning against the cold rock with both arms wrapped around his knees, exhilarated at all he'd seen. He almost laughed, envisioning what he'd expected to find here when first entering. Crawling up again toward the narrow chute, he summoned the same effort that had driven him down to this place, feeling, as he had then, he must meet the one on the other side.

And, this time, he understood. It was clear now.

He knew where to find Morthadus.

Memory swelled and rocked like hostile waters, drowning

Morthadus in the recurring dream whose end he could only hope would finally bring his own. To wake, and face what was swiftly coming, would be more than he could bear.

He drifted back to the night he'd left the Isle, when he stood looking out on those who slept soundly over soil that buried others whose faces still branded him. He could not watch another grow, see them leave and come back to him with proven strength and new love, as though the extension of his progeny could somehow blur them all into one line. He could never forget the sight of each who shone so much brighter than he, each who crumbled like everything within his falsely youthful shell, into ruin.

The scene rose away from those who lay blanketed in color and warmth, crashing like foam over familiar cliffs. The Dark Mountains' poisonous touch was a minor sting as he climbed toward the only light amid an endless sea, and the streak of radiant blue mists still fluttered calmly over the very spot where he and Korine had once stood.

Stepping past the Crystal Blade, which sat untouched waiting for someone to claim it, he went to the ninety-nine swords dropped long before by men far greater. The gap in their line only shamed him at the shadow's edge while he stood, so unworthy, outside it. He shuddered coldly, hearing a voice that would never fully leave him.

"Weak… weak… weak."

His old eyes were faint embers of the light they'd once held, tears staining cheeks that had been kept smooth and fresh for too long as he bowed a mournful head. "I know."

Its gossamer touch could inflict no more dread than what already filled him, to have fled his brothers' fate for one just as dark. "You were right, Korine," he said. "I am Morthadus of the Blessed Ones no more." He drew his sword from its sheath at his hip, raised it high with both hands, and firmly drove it into the ground between the others, making their line complete.

Then suddenly, in his periphery, he saw the cloud of Korine's lost vapors begin to stir, and turned with alarm as they rushed to encircle him in a cyclone that tightened all around. They imbued him with energy that did not escape, but flowed from his very center out through his arms, collecting at his fiery fingertips while the glowing vortex shrank lower, until all of it was finally absorbed.

He stood boiling with power—tremendous power. And, seeing that his hands were now old and wrinkled, he put them to his face, realizing that it had finally caught up with his age, his chin covered by a thick gray beard.

Walking out to the sharp cliff edge, he looked out on all lands below, unsure of where he would go, or who he would be. He would never go back to the Isle; of that he was certain. They must live apart from him, and he from them.

As his body became lost in the wind like a pile of leaves, he was reminded of how Korine had sent him away, how he had sent him to her, so many years before. But, he could no longer think about that. When those things had happened, he had been Morthadus of the Blessed Ones. But now, and forevermore, he was not.

Day had grown short when Morlen finally emerged from beneath the mountain to rejoin Roftome, and the sky darkened to purple as they passed again over the silent stretch of woods. Returning to the familiar grove, he dismounted and strode toward Nottleforf's quarters.

He pulled the two trapdoors open over the wizard's stairwell, which, he discerned through the dim light, led only to bare, jagged rock. Never having given a second thought to where Nottleforf slept, he entered now to find it had no bed or blanket, no shelter of any kind except rough stone walls and an unkind floor.

He passed into the hallway, following it back toward his own compartment. There, he came upon Nottleforf sitting wearily beside the stoked hearth in a wooden armchair, giving no shuffle or nod to acknowledge his presence.

Standing before the wizard, who'd kept him always at such a distance though watching over him closely, Morlen looked at him now as if it were the very first time. "*You* are Morthadus."

Nottleforf's eyes, sunken above dark, wrinkled bags, slowly turned to blue ice as though all of his inner workings came grinding to a halt. His persistent silence sent the slightest tremor through the floor and up its earthen walls while Morlen held firm.

Still unable to return any attention, Nottleforf stared forward, clearing his throat of grief that could no longer be kept down. "Morlen." His voice was deep, unshaking though it seemed to be under the weight of heavy waters. "That part of me has been dead for a very long time."

Morlen would not withdraw his focus. "Yet you kept eyes and ears open for me always, even when it pained you to look after me, though I never knew why you did, until now." He thought back to the image of the severed tree, reaching so fearfully toward its forsaken half with hope that their rejoining might heal more than it stung. "And before me, you came to my father, in the place where you left those who followed in your bloodline. Where you undoubtedly vowed never to return. Look at me, and tell me it was chance that drove you to that. Tell me it was not your wish to restore that part of you that has always lived, to know us, and let us come to know you, Morthadus."

Nottleforf's gray head darted toward him at the repeated name, and his ancient brow stretched tight above a searing gaze meant for foe, not friend. "Do not call me that, Morlen," he rumbled so unfamiliarly, like a cornered beast. "I warned you what might happen, if you searched too closely."

Morlen held his ground, though as unaccustomed to threats from the wizard as he was to any outward display of emotion by him, and pressed stubbornly. "And still you helped me. Still you sent me where I would be shown what you were too afraid to bring yourself to say, just as when you sent me to the Isle, to learn what you'd kept from me for so long. Morthadus wanted me to know those things, and now that I do, I see him clearly. And he is good."

He stood at ease knowing he could be toppled at any moment by Nottleforf's visibly unstable reaction, and spoke again, boldly. "You don't need to be buried anymore. You don't need to be a faceless legend to those you left. If they all knew you now, they would still hold you in high regard."

"There is nothing," the wizard seethed in reply. "None to know, or see, but what sits before you now. I am Nottleforf, nothing more."

"You are Morthadus of the Blessed—" A dizzying flash knocked the wind out of his chest as Nottleforf bolted upward, sending him flying back to obliterate the wooden table in the chamber's center. Its splintered pieces poked into him while he lay flat upon the ground, disoriented and bruised.

Tentatively sitting up with no thought of any counterattack, Morlen saw that defense too would be needless, as Nottleforf now stood shamefully covering both eyes with the hand that had struck, and many tears seeped out to follow the lines of old wrinkles. Extending the other weakly as though to beg his trust of no further action, the wizard looked down at him, face smeared by his fingers.

"I'm sorry," he choked through a gripping sob. "I am sorry... Morlen."

Then, leaning against a nearby wall, he shook his head as

labored words poured forth. "Morthadus of the Blessed Ones," he said despairingly, while Morlen watched from the floor. "I was not blessed, but cursed. To have been made so deceptively invulnerable, all of us… so that together, as brothers, we prospered without a blemish, without fatigue, until we became numb to all that had once made us men.

"How awful it was to be stripped of that protection so quickly, to remember what it was to sweat and bleed. Each of them was stronger than I, brave while I was afraid. And they looked to me for help while I acted only to save myself. I stood watching as they lost their hope and stepped back into a realm worse than death. After that night, how could I go on as one of them while I rotted from the inside?" He slowly revealed his face again with this, and Morlen rose under his beseeching gaze.

"Do you understand, Morlen?" he pleaded. "I had to die. Morthadus… had to die. And all that remained of me had to live separate, far removed, from all that remained of him."

Morlen looked at him, seeing no disguise now. "I understand why you came back," he answered. "To us, and to him."

Unresistant this time, Nottleforf simply held his part of a rare quiet between them now, the first one he hadn't brought to keep Morlen from growing too close. This was the result of that long-dreaded encounter, and yet, in it, he for once found nothing to fear.

Suddenly though, it was broken by distant notes that penetrated even snow and rock, reverberating from the lower cities. Glancing toward the surface, Morlen hastily grasped the Crystal Blade and strapped it at his hip, securing bow and quiver to his back as well while running up into the open air, which was blotted with smoke.

Craning his thick white head to look down from a perch in the trees, Roftome alerted him. "The city men call for help at the southernmost fort. Their defenses are broken around the ferotaurs, who march below the enemy's fire-breather."

"Veleseor," Morlen uttered, turning as Nottleforf quickly strode out beside him. "He's struck Veleseor, as you feared."

"And they will stand little chance," the wizard replied gravely, scanning far across the southern horizon. "Even if they evacuate, they will not get far with the skies handed to Felkoth."

Morlen peered farther north toward the capital, its airspace unoccupied despite each desperate alarm. And, convinced that this would not soon change, he walked forth and summoned Roftome down to the clearing, climbing up quickly to sit between his ready wings.

"We will go," he said, and Nottleforf stepped nearer beside them, distress in his old face outshone by hope.

Looking up at him, no longer as a mere guardian to his ward, Nottleforf said, "Morlen, you go against more danger than I think you yet know. Hold to your strength. Hold to yourself, and to the one who flies with you, for you may find no aid in the air. Valdis will not send out his Eaglemasters tonight."

Preparing to lift off, Morlen's expression was kinder as he regarded Nottleforf now than at any other time in their shared experience, feeling the unseen arm that had always held him at bay finally slacken.

"Goodbye," he said, knees tightening against Roftome's sides. "Father of my fathers."

Saying nothing for a long moment, Nottleforf drew a slow breath behind only one word, though it was enough. "Goodbye," he replied quietly, and with that, Roftome's springing legs lunged away from the earth while powerful wings thrust them high above the forest, leaving him standing far below as he watched them shrink to a speck in starless skies. "Son of my sons."

Soaring upward through fierce wind, Morlen looked out

with no apprehension as Roftome carried his weight like it were his own. Knowing what an unexpected pair they would make in the eyes of the Eaglemasters' besieged people, the two companions sped on together, toward yearning jaws and fiery battle that undoubtedly sat ready for them, at the city of Veleseor.

Chapter Fourteen
BLADE MEETS SPEAR

"GIVE THEM NOT one inch!" Lady Valeine yelled with the Crystal Spear pressed firmly against her chest plate, with four hundred aspiring soldiers in tight ranks on either side. "You've been preparing for some time to venture into their territory and prove your worth; now, they've simply saved you the trouble!"

Their circular stone wall was broken and burnt, their archers charred beneath its rubble as hordes of ferotaurs spilled in, swarming up the central road toward the city's only line of defense.

"An Eaglemaster is deadlier on the ground than in the sky!" called Valeine. "And you are all the closest to Eaglemasters this kingdom has, since those previously honored with that title now stand hopeless behind the capital walls. Tonight, you will give them a reason to hope! And they will fly behind you, their betters, into many battles to come!"

The rallying youths silently planted themselves with weapons aimed forward, united by her courageous heart, while the first enemy wave lowered thick horns to crush their skulls.

"Front rank ready!" she ordered, pleased by the stumbling

advance of those that now saw the Crystal Spear positioned toward them. Their malicious eyes widened while speed drove them nearer, and thick pale arms raised rusted scythes as the space between both forces dwindled.

"Thrust!" she bellowed to her troops, skewering a gnarled rib-cage when a storm of metal and slimy flesh crashed into them. Every fighter beside her followed suit, impaling the foes before them while comrades in the second rank struck over their shoulders with synchronized precision.

Brandishing the Crystal Spear, she slashed its razor edge through the face of one assailant nearest her left, twirling it high to change grip while swinging its horned base down through another's skull.

"You've not forgotten this spear!" She scorned all that poured in, and rammed its shaft forward to shatter every tooth in an oncoming mouth. Then she ducked a swishing slice for her neck while severing the enemy's leg, and pounded its collapsed body into snow and dirt with a forceful strike. "It will taste a great many of you before the night's through!" She plucked the weapon free, standing ready while all challengers diverted to the men at her sides, who were doubly fierce now under her watch.

But soon, skill could not hold against sheer pressure as thousands now flowed against their makeshift dam, flooding every inch of space between them and the breached city wall. She glanced toward the north gate, relieved to see the last clusters of people filing out, and hoped only to buy them enough time. Blood began to splash within her own ranks as outnumbering swords defied every defensive measure, until they had no choice but to pull back.

"Hold formation!" she commanded, suppressing all grief for their dead who now lay flattened beneath the vicious onslaught. The battalion scuttled backward with quick steps while batting away every beast that jumped forth, trying to maintain a spear's length of separation from the endless tide. But it became clear the tireless assault would overtake them unless they ran.

"To the gate! Now!" She turned, driving the rest to do the same, and retreated behind them toward the open exit just a mile ahead, through which her people had finally escaped. "Seal it from the inside, and guard it to the very end!" she charged, hoping at least, when they no longer stood, the ferotaurs would be too inept to open it and become trapped.

The lumbering invaders lagged farther behind with every minute, giving them ample time to prepare a final stand when they reached the wide gateway. Each half of the battalion massed along its two thick doors of stone, pushing them closed as sturdy iron hinges squealed. Then, having climbed rungs centered in the right-hand door, one man went to a large winch and wound it while great metal claws slowly protracted into curved channels within the left, sealing both together.

"Make ready!" she called, assembling them once more against the gate. The advancing force was more scattered now, and an eager herd led out in front with viscous strings of slobber bobbing against fleshy chins and throats. She thought fondly of her eagle, whom she'd sent away not only to guard those fleeing the city, but also to deprive herself of any chance to become separated from her men and escape while they fell.

She held the Crystal Spear high for what she knew would be the last time, and those around her beat their weapons upon their chest plates, standing ready to meet their rushing doom. The incensed pack spread wider apart, breaking formation as every member came running for its own chosen kill, not stalled in the slightest by the dense arrays of outstretched spears.

"The pretty one is mine!" rasped the quickest among them, veering deliberately toward Valeine, who only dug her heels deeper, relishing its fatal choice.

"Which do you mean?" cackled another close behind, daggers aimed menacingly out.

"This one's head would look prettier on those shoulders," one pointed at two troops in its sights, only a dozen yards off.

Valeine watched steadily while each careless wretch stormed nearer with arms extended, until she could taste the rotting breath of the creature closing in on her. She reared the Crystal Spear back to swing, when an arrow bolted in from an unseen source high on their left, hammering her target off course so quickly that the two behind it had little time to react, before they too were shot in rapid succession.

Searching the smoky sky in vain, she allowed only a minuscule spark of hope to ignite. Had the other Eaglemasters finally come to their aid? If not all, at least enough to hold the ferotaurs at bay a little longer, and guide her people to shelter? Those shots were too quick and precise to have come from just one.

Four more beasts came stomping next, giving hardly a second glance to those that lay dead before them, when suddenly a single eagle swept down along their course. Its rider slashed with a strangely glittering sword in two strokes that took as many heads, while the other oblivious pair was snatched from the ground by talons that pierced and crushed with ease. Their monstrous wails were abruptly silenced, and both dropped lifelessly from above, where the two companions disappeared.

Bewildered like all others with her, Valeine stared upward, no longer looking for her fellow Eaglemasters. Six ferotaurs pressed in this time with another ten close in tow, aiming for the defenders' center like a jagged blade tipped with the largest and most fearsome brute of all. Its broad strides lengthened while thick foam stretched down its bloodstained lips, as it groped with oversized hands that needed no weapon.

Unsure how many spears she and her men would have to

deliver in order to bring it down, she felt her hair and robes suddenly flutter against a heavy gust that billowed over them when the stealthy airborne pair dove upon the threatening leader. The cloaked man seated above severed its long horns with one fluid slice, leaving pitiful nubs atop a slimy, sleek skull that soon shattered as the eagle struck with a crippling thrust of its beak.

Growls erupted while the two allies continued to cut their way forward, sword and talons flashing. Each strike's momentum carried the next in a perpetual cyclone that crumpled four enemies at a time, repelling the rest in a haphazard perimeter. Seeing a chance to move in against their stunned and divided numbers, Valeine darted ahead, and the city's last protectors finally went on the offensive.

"Follow their path!" she ordered, dizzying herself in an attempt to glimpse the man's face as her troops meandered like a tail behind him and his carrier. His sword stood out to her most of all, evoking a fear in every gruesome face beneath it just as her own ancient weapon did.

The horde's vast remainder halted its march into the fray, visibly daunted by the two who sat unchallenged, and Valeine rallied the battalion to split along each side. They extended like solid walls from the eagle's wide wings, advancing to pave a road of smashed foes before the sealed gate, until no more stood around them.

Shouting cries of opposition toward the onlooking legions, her men clattered a triumphant chorus across the sea of broken armor beneath their feet, each kneeling to cut a long horn from the head of one enemy he'd killed. And despite her fear that their jubilation would be short-lived, she was proud to see them take their rightful places as defenders of the realm.

She drew closer to the stranger mounted on his eagle that towered above all others she'd ever seen, and came to stand beside him while he peered out silently at the hostile tide. "Who—?" Her question was abruptly muffled as he looked down at her, lacking the cold fury she expected from one who had rushed in against such overwhelming odds. "Your name, sir?" she asked.

Morlen had not seen a woman his own age since his days in Korindelf, when most would hardly glance at him, and never one who appeared so passionate. Suddenly aware of how this winter night's chill had become utterly lost on him, he looked forward again, returning the Crystal Blade to its sheath at his side where she stood. "Morlen," he said quietly, and with a firm pat continued fondly, "and Roftome."

Slowing her breath, she momentarily diverted attention from him to take in the eagle once more. "Roftome," she whispered. "The Untamable." Following every arch and line of his grand stature, she knew it must be true, and returned her eyes to Morlen. "But, how did you—?"

He met her pressing focus again, and found it comforting. "He's still untamed, I assure you."

Never knowing that an outsider could hope to forge a bond with the eagles, as only her people had done for centuries, she found herself now pleasantly without surprise. And, having seen the mysterious sword he carried, she brought herself to inquire a bit further. "I was unaware that such a blade existed," she said, holding her father's spear up straight to reveal its similarity.

Looking for the first time upon the legendary Crystal Spear, passed down as an heirloom through the Eaglemasters' line of kings, Morlen realized her possession of it must mean that she was the daughter of King Valdis, and that he truly had lost hope. "Your king has never shied away from an enemy until now," he said. "If he'd seen you tonight, he may have thought you didn't need any aid."

She gave no response to the compliment, though it came

without the arrogance she often faced from others, and was relieved by one soldier's interruption. "Lady Valeine, do we charge?"

Both she and Morlen turned forward again, seeing that the ranks facing them were reluctant to cross the neutral area as scores of their boastful brothers lay in ruin. But, they seemed to stir with violent tremors that began with those far at the force's rear, as though some other disturbance rose from behind.

"He sits no more," said Roftome, digging talons sharply down in preparation to launch. "Bloodsong is coming."

Morlen unslung his bow, readying to take off while Valeine looked harder at him. "What is it?" she asked, as none but he had heard Roftome's words.

Before he could reply, the clearest and most unwelcome of answers drowned every inch of the besieged city in debilitating wrath. Then, with a brush of his hand to encourage Roftome, they flew while a dark mass grew more defined in the distance, tearing toward the protected gate.

"I doubt his eyes are anywhere as good as mine," Roftome assured, though his voice lost more strength the closer they pressed. "Caked in smoke with every blink, he'll see only what comes directly at him."

Morlen's mind was seared beneath hot needles while the emanating call solidified around them. But it made him remember a pain he'd endured in another realm, one that had seen him come and go farther, and longer, than he ever imagined he could. Clouds of smoke swam before them, puffing rounder with each breath from the creature within, glowing as it carved its way out.

"Hold tight!" Roftome bellowed, rolling low and to the right as a river of fire announced the emerging beast, which passed above in a shroud of flickering heat that illuminated its well-guarded master, who stood inside a closed fist of enormous talons.

A warming flash of gold suddenly wrapped Morlen's thoughts

like a blanket when the loathsome sound faded. And, hovering in its wake, he was reminded by the sharp, thin touch of metal concealed securely against his chest that Felkoth was not the only one with a weapon that had made him powerful.

"Follow beneath him," he urged Roftome, fitting an arrow to his bow as they soared to catch up with the dragon that threatened Valeine and her troops. Felkoth's white hands bounced in and out of view while they chased steadily nearer to acquire a clear shot.

"Destroy them!" He heard Felkoth order to the flying abomination, which obediently descended toward the steadfast battalion, drinking in gusts of breath while flames prepared to burst from its swollen chest.

Only seconds remained now. Exhaling slowly, Morlen released his arrow, which lifted upon the persistent breeze in an arc toward the creature's stony legs. It grazed through the colossal talons in a river of sparks to slice hard against Felkoth's left forearm, drawing a mad growl in response that promptly lured the dragon about-face.

Peering from between the talons with a fierce gaze, longing to incinerate whichever daring Eaglemasters thought themselves matches for him, Felkoth saw them straight ahead, hovering alone in a blatant challenge: the unruly bird he'd left to die, now healed, beneath the one who held his prize.

"Down!" Morlen shouted, though Roftome was already well on his way, swooping below a molten volley to see hundreds of ferotaurs advancing against Valeine's cornered force, which gave him a most creative idea.

"How would you feel about letting it have a better look at us?" he asked boldly, and Roftome sent him a suspicious look that slowly sharpened.

"I feel it would be most unwise," Roftome answered. "If you don't keep your head low." Then, without hesitation, they ascended closer to the approaching dragon, whose head cut from side to side in search of any telltale movement or scent, until they darted directly in front of its face. Roftome left no uncertainty to tales of his unmatched speed when they shot in a dive, dwarfed by the predator on their trail, its wretched call threatening to make their ears bleed. Still it failed to stall them as they led it over the enemy masses, which pressed forward thirty yards from Valeine and her men.

"Ready... be ready..." Morlen's voice rose while they bolted vertically down toward the tide of horns, feeling cold as the nearing creature sucked in all wind around them.

"Kill them!" bellowed Felkoth from above. "Kill them at once!"

Hearing the storm at their heels, Morlen gripped hard to Roftome's sides. "Now!" he yelled, and Roftome's wings spread wide to level them out in a parallel run just over the charging line of ferotaurs, while the jet of flame struck exactly upon their abandoned path of descent, pulverizing hundreds of foes on impact. Skimming above as many as possible while the conflagration followed closely at their backs, they created a fiery blockade between the city's defenders and all invading ground forces.

Feeling the dragon's wayward assault subside in their wake, Morlen and Roftome deftly rose out of view as it turned with a clumsy jolt to follow, slowly curling away from the battered legions below.

"We have to keep them on us," Morlen declared, looking over his shoulder while Roftome slowed enough to draw their enemy upward, and it rattled them again with another scream as the sealed gate remained beyond its attention.

Watching the tumultuous chase from below, Valeine was warmed by more than the flaming wall that rose ahead, barring those that would have destroyed her force. On all sides of her, men cheered for the eagle and rider who manipulated the city's would-be captor so easily.

Soon, many ferotaurs plunged desperately through the burning divide, stomping toward them drenched in fire with blades melting over their hands. Most collapsed in smoke while others sprinted wildly into the defenders' awaiting spears, swinging limbs of hot sludge against every parrying blow.

Her battalion could no longer serve any purpose within the gates, when all their enemies that continued to charge would suffer the same fate as those that smoldered here. Surely Felkoth would give them a path to circumvent this lethal obstruction, letting them spill out into the wide fields through which her people still retreated.

"Open the gates," she ordered, and a soldier returned to the central winch, retracting its bars. She grabbed her share of the long chains linked with the left gate's hefty iron rings, and pulled it narrowly open with dozens of her men while the rest squeezed through, two at a time.

Hearing the renewed efforts of other beasts that stumbled closer, she hastily turned and hammered the nearest between its scorched horns, letting her troops find safe passage as more steamed forward on blistered legs. After all her men had escaped, she stayed back, casting contempt on the swamp of stained metal and inhuman flesh, and looked up at the one who held their destruction at bay under great hazard to himself. Then, the last standing within her beloved city, she turned and left, striding outside to guard the fields with her remaining contingent.

She watched with apprehension, hoping her people had gotten far enough north to find protection as Felkoth circled back to release his impeded troops. Bloodsong's tail shattered the city's side wall, peppering nearby fields with rubble and dust, and the enemy flood poured out, rushing around the bend directly toward them with no obstacles in between.

Felkoth was on course to disintegrate her line before the

trampling rabble even arrived, his dragon enveloping them in a wave of silence while it drew in another breath. But just as the white-hot stream belted forth, Morlen and Roftome crashed talons-first into the left side of its face, making it veer hard off course with spouts of flame spiraling into air and snow.

Digging with all his might to stay latched upon Bloodsong's head, barely keeping Morlen astride, Roftome etched shallow scars into its jagged, rocky brow. "You will remember this eagle!" he declared. The dragon bucked relentlessly, finally hurling them off, but not before Roftome released a thick puddle of excrement into its red eyes, which clamped shut amid indignant, earsplitting wails. A burning rain erupted all around as Bloodsong lashed out in temporary blindness, swerving away erratically with them in its wake.

Tempted to give chase, though the creature was doubly lethal in its semi-impaired state, Morlen looked to Valeine and her men, who held their position against the charge that would overrun them in seconds.

"Ready spears!" Valeine repeated with pride, unafraid of the dense wave bent on consuming them. They had cheated death many times this night, and might yet again before the end. The ferotaurs pounded closer, shaking the snowy earth as impact was imminent. Then suddenly, a volley of arrows stormed down over her battalion's steady shoulders, dropping entire ranks of their attackers as she looked back in thrilled disbelief. Her brother Verald hovered at the head of at least two hundred Eaglemasters, swooping down to extract them from danger.

"Come on!" Verald called, beckoning her to his lowered eagle while those beside him did the same for others, his eyes only widening when she shook her head.

"Not before them!" she answered, gesturing for all of her men to find rescue first, with many still remaining on the ground. Huddles of foes began to penetrate their suppressing fire while more Eaglemasters busied themselves with gathering as many troops as possible. But Valeine allowed herself no relief, cracking one horned skull after another with diligent strokes of the Crystal Spear.

Then, in a splintering strike, Morlen and Roftome dove from high overhead to smash two nearby ferotaurs flat into the snow, joining her with sword and talons lashing out at the herd as Verald and his followers looked on in perplexity.

Almost all soldiers were now accounted for, Valeine saw, but the remaining few beside her would occupy every last ounce of space that the prince himself could transport. She refused to withdraw, until finally Morlen reached down to her.

"Quickly," he said, voice calm though he sat as a single rock in rising swells, and, after all others were lifted away, she clasped his extended arm and let it pull her up to sit behind him on Roftome's back. Spinning to deliver a deadly farewell, Roftome scattered many with a final swipe while Morlen and Valeine beat down any within grasp. All below stared fearfully at the blade and spear of crystal that moved together against them, both sparkling brightly when the eagle and riders pulled up, departing the fallen city with those above.

Morlen turned to catch up with the others, who slowed to see him more clearly. "They won't hold your city for long," he assured Valeine.

Had it not been for her brother's proximity, she might have kept her tight hold at Morlen's side. "My people?" she asked Verald, whose expression stifled her worry.

"Safe," he answered, though his attention seemed mainly on Morlen. "We flew with two hundred others who stayed behind to escort them upriver, along with your eagle."

She breathed a joyful sigh that felt cool on Morlen's neck, leading him to hope she heard equally good tidings before the flight's end, and he returned the prince's studying gaze, seeing gratitude over unease.

"Morlen," he said in reply to the inquisitive silence that Verald appeared more than content to prolong.

Trying to relieve Verald's obvious tension, Valeine's eyes asked him to show trust. "The fight would have been finished long before you arrived, brother, if it hadn't been for these two." She gave Roftome an affectionate pat as well, keeping her other hand tucked under Morlen's arm, which did not go unnoticed.

Morlen knew he had proven himself a useful ally, but more would have to be convinced, and immediately, if they were to divert Felkoth's advance before he struck again. "I have an idea," he began. "One that I believe may be our best chance of preventing what happened here from spreading farther. I'd like to discuss this before your king."

Verald continued to hold him with scrutiny, and gave no ready acknowledgment. "Never has there been an Eaglemaster from beyond our realm, nor any king, I trust, who would give one such an open welcome."

Glancing down at Roftome, who flew more gallantly, fiercely, than any eagle present, Morlen met the prince's suspicion, unthreatened. "I'm not master," he answered, "but friend."

The prince let his rigid, battle-ready posture slacken a bit at this, though not disarmed in the slightest. "Well, Morlen Eaglefriend," he replied, "I doubt my father has much desire to hear any man, let alone talk of action. But, I will ensure that you have an audience with him nonetheless, along with me, and any other who wishes to listen. You have earned that much, at least, from the Eaglemasters."

The capital rose before them now, its grayish-white walls projecting from the mountains. They glistened sleekly even in the dead of night, and hundreds of metallic glints illuminated the host that stood watch above, some aiming arrows until the identities of those approaching could be better discerned.

"You'd do well to hold your fire, gentlemen," Valeine called out to them. "Here arrive those who stood against the first waves of this plague within our realm, when you would not come to our defense. Hand them your provisions, and they'll go this very night into the mountains to claim carriers for themselves, though they are already more Eaglemasters than you."

Verald and his allegiant band settled to the walls, letting the now-seasoned youths disembark. They walked with scarred heads held humbly toward the open peaks ahead, to find eagles of their own.

Standing aside, the guards then turned all skepticism upon Morlen, who sat atop the eagle that had harshly cast most of them away, while their beloved Lady seemed so uncharacteristically content in his presence.

"Rouse the king," she bade them. "Though I doubt he enjoyed much sleep under the sounds of our distress."

Verald slowly turned a stiff face to her. "He sits below, unmoving since you left."

Her expression soured, as anticipated, and Morlen enjoyed the way she clenched his ribs. She soon became aware of it herself, and carefully eased her hand.

"Come," said Verald with little enthusiasm, his attention shifting mainly to Morlen. "This idea of yours had better be worth hearing, or I suspect he'll hold his silence till the very end."

Morlen nodded in return, and followed the group's descent toward the castle. He dismounted in the moonlit courtyard, seeing Valeine become caught in its silver glow as she stepped lightly down beside him, and proceeded with her through the open entrance, which was lined on either side by grim-faced guards.

Striding between the men who averted eyes in shame from the battle-stained Lady and her brother, they gathered in the great hall around a lone pale figure seated in its rear center. "He is not the king you seek," whispered Valeine. "Not anymore."

All present parted to allow Morlen a clear path, at the end of which slumped a sorry figure on the stout throne. King Valdis seemed to look past them toward the open archway, acknowledging no one, even as Morlen came to stand directly before him.

He was not old or feeble by any means, Morlen observed. In fact, if this man had a mind to harshly reject his entreaty and toss him out personally as nothing more than an intruder, such an action might prove no easy feat to repel.

"I come to you, as a ready and willing ally," Morlen began. "The only one you have tonight. And tomorrow will decide whether we succeed or fail to stop what is coming, if you join me, and face him."

Valdis's weary, colorless hands wrung tensely against one another, grinding dust to the marble floor at his feet while his gaze remained dedicated along a course just beside Morlen. "He is coming," he whispered, as though in a trance that no plea could lift.

"He has already come, Father!" Valeine hotly interjected. "He perches on the very seat you entrusted to me, looking to our remaining strongholds like each would give him only an hour's sport. There is no time, no tomorrow, but what we use to act, and act quickly, to show that slime what we truly think of him!"

Morlen watched her long after she spoke her piece, and lacked any compulsion to withdraw his attention. The king gave no stir, though, only holding an unblinking gaze in place as Morlen focused on him again.

"We have a chance to save this kingdom, *your* kingdom," he said. "Before it is swallowed whole by what has already taken your southernmost city, despite the men sacrificed there, despite those of your own flesh and blood who stood, when you wouldn't. There is still time to stand with them, and you can show them that there is a fight worth making. Because, sometimes we need our fathers to remind us what can be done."

Valdis's eyes shifted their focus, and found Morlen. They were awake, alert, and light still burned far within, even through anguish and indecision. "What can... be done..." his gravelly voice repeated.

Morlen, heart hammering at this opportunity, stood tall and drew in a calm breath with which to deliver his plan.

"I will attack Korindelf," he answered, glad to receive ringing silence instead of outward dissent. "I have strong allies in the East. The shriekers still hold many thousands there, numbers that dwindle each day under their guard. They keep the city ready for Felkoth's return, because they feel his presence strongly, as he feels their hunger, their obedience, their distress.

"He will feel their distress tomorrow at first light, and its severe sting will be enough to draw him and his fire-breather away from your lands, leaving you free to drive out the invaders he brought tonight and meet him at Korindelf, with me."

All eyes in the hall held to Morlen firmly, knowing any flinch could topple the fragile promise of hope in his proposal, so fragile that none could immediately take it to heart.

"You speak as if this were the Battle of Korindelf," said Prince Verald. "Only now the scales are tipped much more considerably in the enemy's favor. And how are we to gain the upper hand over the Tyrant Prince and his dragon when we arrive to spring this trap, since they had no trouble shattering hundreds of Eaglemasters in a matter of minutes?"

The king grumbled achingly, dragging stiff arms up the throne's broad sides to support himself, and stared at Morlen with far greater intensity while the rest observed them closely.

"Would you have me watch again?" Valdis asked, his voice smoother now, though just as grave. "Would you have us fly headlong to our destruction while you stand below?"

Morlen shook his head, speaking to deliver comfort and courage. "Fly to me," he said. "Have him think you mean to charge. Then, just when he prepares to meet you, drop low enough to disembark, and the eagles will pull them upward as you join me on the field."

Again, the palpable quiet held many stifled objections all around, though the king, it appeared, still had an ear to lend. "You mean to separate us from our carriers, as a diversion?" he asked. "Merely buy ourselves time on the ground while our flock perishes above, until he returns to finish us?"

"I mean to separate him from *his*," Morlen answered. "He controls the sky; thus, he thinks he controls you. So remove yourselves from his arena, and force him into yours. His seat within the creature's grasp is still vulnerable, and, with enough eagles swarming him, he's sure to seek refuge below, where he'll find us instead."

Glancing at all who listened, Morlen could finally see more daring in their faces now, even in the prince, whose initial resistance seemed diminished. There was almost a yearning now, to believe, trust, that this course was worth pursuing, that he was worth joining.

"An Eaglemaster is deadlier on the ground than in the sky," said Morlen, glimpsing Valeine, whose eyes were very much on him and no one else. "Leave him no choice but to discover this for himself."

Valdis kept very still for a long while, as though the slightest shuffle might answer the call of the one before him, whom he continued to study.

"Eaglefriend," the prince and those beside him whispered around the king, a murmur that traveled throughout the entire crowd until finally reaching Morlen himself, who nodded to make official introduction.

"Morlen," he said plainly to Valdis, keeping an unbroken watch on him, though it was only briefly returned before the king drifted low again.

"I… am sorry," he replied, casting a dejected wave over all.

"Father…" Valeine urgently stepped forward, hoping to stop what she knew was coming.

Making no effort now to elevate his slouched form, Valdis looked past them once more. "I"—he began, sounding choked— "free all forces here to join this campaign, if they so choose. But…" He broke off, almost hesitantly. "I will not. I must remain here. This is my final word to all Eaglemasters, and to you, young Morlen. Go tomorrow, to Korindelf. And may you strike a true blow, before the end."

Then, sinking again beneath a tremendous weight that had seemed momentarily to lift, the king signified for them to take their leave.

Her cheeks having lost their flush, Valeine stood beside Morlen with droplets glistening in the corners of her eyes, which bored deep into the king's face while the crowd slowly filed out of the hall. Finally, she too left, and her brother with her.

With the sense there was nothing more to be said, believing that perhaps his call to act still resonated within the king's mind, Morlen turned to follow those who had listened and made his way out into the courtyard, where Verald and Valeine were ready to meet him.

"The Eaglemasters are with you," said the prince, with a nod of newfound respect. "Whether my father heard your words or not, *we* have. Tomorrow, when the Tyrant Prince departs our lost city, we'll know that you have given your signal. And you will see us following behind him at Korindelf, to stand, and fight, at your side." With that, he extended his arm, and, wasting no time, Morlen gladly took it.

"Captains," Verald said in the voice none dared question, "assemble your companies, and order your men promptly rejoined with their carriers, or risk never being called Eaglemasters again!"

A satisfied clamor rang out through the capital while many took flight to spread the message, and the crowd quickly dispersed with great purpose as dawn was near. Soon, only Morlen and Valeine remained in place, and neither appeared intent on being moved, until Verald swept proudly overhead. "Come on," he urged his sister. "The keeper of the Crystal Spear ought to be ready to lead this army, if we're to fly to battle!"

Sending up a curt glance of acknowledgment and dismissal, she still found her feet quite fixed to the ground, her hand suddenly on a deliberate course toward Morlen's arm when Roftome landed with a powerful flap of his great wings.

"The city men agree to fight?" he eagerly asked Morlen, who distractedly looked from Valeine through the open castle entrance, pulling himself up to Roftome's back.

"All but one," he replied, and sensed his regret at this to be tenfold in her, along with a mutual wish to delay their parting. Facing her again, he felt strangely relaxed in having no words, and in her willingness to prolong their silence.

Then, he finally ushered Roftome upward, skimming along the airborne ranks of many Eaglemasters, all of whom recognized him now. Rising farther above, he began to catch lyrics being sung among them, with each verse boldly passed from one man to another while the army busily prepared, and he listened.

"To their mountains long ago he came

He was Veldeam the Wise

The eagles knew him by his name

His voice, and his keen eyes

But Veldeam's noble heart was sore

For he'd lost his dearest friend

In parted paths so long before

And he searched until the end

In the East, he answered the shriekers' call

And his friend he never found

For the Dark Blade struck to bring his fall

And the eagles' cries did sound

But in their mountains he still walks

He is Veldeam the Wise

The eagles know him by his name

His voice, and his keen eyes. "

Giving in to a gentle wave of hope that came with a bolstering wind, Morlen left the Eaglemasters' capital as Roftome aimed toward Korindelf, which was now caressed by a slowly rising sun.

And, still quiet within the bustling great hall, King Valdis felt the sting of each face that hardened sorrowfully at the sight of him, limp and unmoved as they made ready to fly out.

Where was the hero with the Crystal Blade? He had played the glorious arrival so many times in his mind that it was almost solid. But why would he not come now, when it seemed the most opportune time, while his own forces rallied so eagerly? And what incentive did he have to join with this Eaglefriend—this Morlen?

After seeing what his forces would be up against, how could he go without being assured of victory, by the savior he'd so long awaited? Even if Morlen was as strong as they seemed to think—what then, if he did answer his call to fly with them? Would he give them a reason to believe that they could turn the tide? He could not even turn his own face from the archway through which no one entered, but many departed. If the one for whom he watched would only step forward now, and relieve him of his burden, he would gladly rise up with him.

But, it finally began to set in: No one was coming. No one but Felkoth, who would cover every inch of the realm in death and ash. His remaining options were clear. He could sit and let his enemy deliver him such a fate, or strike out and help the Eaglemasters determine their own.

They would be leaving shortly, with or without him, as soon as Eaglefriend made his move. If he led, they would still follow, but if he remained here, they would not look back. Time for deliberation was over; he had to decide now.

Would he stay? Or, would he go?

CHAPTER FIFTEEN

THE SECOND BATTLE OF KORINDELF

"ARE YOU SURE this scheme of yours will work?" Roftome
muttered when they passed over the outskirts of Korindelf.
"Meeting them on the ground seems most unwise."

Morlen's brows rose fondly while he looked toward the far-off
Isle, its center a sprawling, blackened mass surrounded by lush forest. He still sensed his old companions safe within, even with such
distance remaining in between. "I'm sure only that I'll be there,
ready," he answered.

Now he was able to make out enemy droves massing in the
fields outside the city walls. He clutched the Goldshard's jagged outline against his chest, and they held course for the hostile response that awaited them, nearing the city as dawn began to
creep up the blurred horizon.

"Bring down the intruder!" A powerful scream broke out
within the underlying host, which recklessly fired hundreds of
arrows that failed to cause even a stir of Roftome's wings.

"Summon your master here, now," Morlen bellowed down to

them. "Then flee back into the South! And today, his hold over you will be broken." Surrounding winds shook as they barked in collective opposition, and more opportunistic shots stretched higher. But Morlen would not be deterred. "This city, these people, are yours no longer, whether you choose to stay, or leave," he called. "But leave, now, and call your master to face what he has brought upon himself, and you will not have to face it with him."

Spiteful arrows whipped past his shoulders to deliver an unequivocal answer from the endless packs, and Morlen's features hardened as he leaned forward while Roftome gracefully wove through the snare. "Then, if blood is what you want," he said, unthreatened, "come and take mine."

Swooping downward to whet their enemies' already brimming appetite, Morlen and Roftome passed over rows of thrashing gray heads, soaring toward the Isle. The pouncing brood tirelessly hunted behind them.

"Well," said Roftome, keeping low in plain sight, "if on the ground is where you insist on meeting them, let us hope you don't do it alone."

Vividly remembering his frantic escape from Korindelf a year before, Morlen looked ahead to the mystic realm that had sheltered him then and was comfortable knowing he would take no refuge there, this time. "Let's just make sure they pursue us all the way," he replied, and Roftome maintained his moderate speed as the scent in their wake swam to the drooling creatures.

"Pursue *you*, you mean," retorted Roftome. "I'll be safely watching from above, long before they close this gap."

Laying an encouraging hand on his companion's smooth-feathered back once more, Morlen said, "They won't be the ones to close it."

Miles away from the city, Morlen glanced over his shoulder,

emboldened to see that they still gave chase in full force, even as the Isle's murky borders towered a short distance ahead.

"Drop me just at the edge," he said, as the time for their parting came near at hand.

And Roftome, still wary to deliver him to his chosen destination, inquired finally, "This is truly what you—"

"Yes," Morlen answered, leaving no room for doubt as Roftome hovered close to the ground. Dismounting lightly on grass that protruded through thin snow, Morlen looked up at him reassuringly. "Be ready when Bloodsong arrives. Surround it with the other eagles, and force it to release its master to us."

Roftome's lethal gaze held him gently from above. "My watch will be on you, first and foremost," he said stubbornly. "So give me no cause to break from the others." Then, Roftome rose high over the glistening fields that were flooded by a sea of teeth and claws. And Morlen stood alone, unshaken as it came.

With the Isle's familiar warmth at his back, he released all thoughts of danger and slowly came to feel its inhabitants again, one by one lighting up within his mind, which reached back toward them in greeting. Widespread embers far behind soon burned more brightly at the edge of his vision, joining beside others until tens became dozens, and dozens quickly brought numbers even greater as he drew them now like a beacon.

The ground trembled as the shriekers drew nearer, only minutes from closing in, but he kept his focus on the radiant clusters at his heels. They were coming. He could feel them more strongly now. Hundreds upon hundreds, speeding gladly to meet him, to run together, as they'd once done.

He watched the writhing gray throngs narrow the divide with claws extended and dripping fangs bared. The innumerable lights were racing closer behind him, and the gray tide ahead came screaming ever louder while he held his ground.

Brilliant rays filled his periphery, burning against the nearing shadow as the shriekers only a hundred yards off prepared to devour him, letting not even the foreboding Isle slow them from their prey. He knew they were with him now, ready to go forward into those that stamped so hungrily toward him.

He drew the Crystal Blade with a twinkling slice, and suddenly a thousand unfettered roars shattered every menacing howl as the great lions leapt hundreds at a time from the Isle's mists to join him. They charged with tremendous force through the storming wave, whose front ranks crumbled beneath stout manes and crushing paws. And Morlen plunged ahead with them into the savage masses that splintered back across the fields they'd so furiously traversed.

He repelled all before him with each fierce swing of the Crystal Blade, batting off one after another that dared spring with knifing claws upon the lions' broad backs. Driving them back toward the city, he knew there would soon be no doubt in Felkoth's mind that his kingdom was in dire jeopardy. Now he would have no choice but to relinquish his foothold in the Eaglemasters' realm and come here, to Korindelf, where all would finally meet him.

Submerged in spiked horns and blackened, gnawing teeth, the city of Veleseor sat broken in Felkoth's shadow while he stood, uncontested, within Bloodsong's grasp. With his minor wounds from the previous night's affairs bandaged and concealed, he spat at thoughts of the boy who'd acted so tirelessly to stall him, aiding the Eaglemasters' people in their northward escape. He'd bought them nothing more than a few hours before their inevitable undoing.

All four remaining cities whitened beneath this, their final dawn, and he stirred at the sound of Bloodsong's rumbling throat, which ached to liquefy their foundations and give his new herds a long-desired feast. But... there was something sharp, digging into him like an insect's prod, drawing his attention to the Dark Blade, which, he now realized with a start, rang with the shrill cries of ambush from Korindelf. It was being taken, right from his own clutches! And, there were many assailants, breaking through the lines he'd commanded to defend, at all costs! The city would soon fall, and his servants along with it, unless he intervened.

Looking down upon the tide ready to spread destruction throughout the Eaglemasters' realm, he judged from Valdis's inaction that they would be quite undisturbed if he left for a short while. And if he should come upon any Eaglemasters at Korindelf, perhaps launching this assault to lure him away from their lands, it would only speed him faster to drown every last one of Valdis's people in fire.

"Hold the city!" he fumed harshly to the ferotaurs. "And do not stray before my return!" Then, giving them no second glance, he urged his carrier out with livid determination to reach Korindelf, anxious to crush all that he would find.

The blood-spattered creatures kept watch over their newly claimed territory in his stead, scraping every bone left to tell of their enemies' defeat in anticipation of spoils the day would yet bring. But shortly after their leader's abrupt departure, a strange storm cloud began to gather in the northern sky, drifting quickly in low winds, and growing significantly in size. He was long gone before they could tell that its course was deliberate, their dim minds discerning thousands of forms within, all coming for them at a speed that sought to devastate without answer.

"Take cover!" many shouted in alarm, all lifting large scraps of armor or rubble, even the corpses of their slain brothers, in preparation for what rapidly descended. Soon finding themselves under the Eaglemasters' far-reaching shroud, they realized every defense was futile against the deluge that befell their ranks, pummeling to the ground one wave after another.

Hundreds toppled in haphazard pushes for retreat while thousands scrambled out of the city's broken wall, overfilling scattered boats in desperate haste to cross the river, and many fell to watery graves. The riddled fleets rowed back toward their own sequestered territory, toward the vast remainder of ferotaurs that had waited to be ferried over but now only cowered at their airborne enemies.

Then, the Eaglemasters suddenly abated all efforts to pursue, as though satisfied that they would not trespass again while their forces drowned on every side. Rising above in a darting eastward flock to address more pressing matters, they flew behind the distant trail of Felkoth and his dragon, following him, unsuspected, to Korindelf.

Morlen's sword and body became one staggering mallet against all shriekers that jumped forward, and he thinned their ranks for several arduous hours with the lions stampeding around him. Their wretched yelps did not go unnoticed by their king either, he realized, finally glimpsing an unmistakable dark shape close on the horizon.

Having anticipated the inevitable moment with great pain, he could not escape it now as it blew down like a corrosive breeze. Bloodsong announced destruction to all adversaries, seizing the sure-footed lions while his ready arms slackened as well, exposing them to more vigorous attacks that did not hesitate.

Gray swells lurched over him, slashing, pulling down against any attempt to shake free as the dreadful sound fell louder, heavier. Seeing the thick hindquarters of many beside him suddenly give way beneath the hostile surge, Morlen drew on what energy he still had to leap upward while he thrust the Crystal Blade through those sinking him. And Roftome flew down to his aid, heaving away many that wriggled and spat in his grip.

"The city men are on their way," Roftome alerted, and Morlen soon found a great deal of hope restored, scanning out to glimpse the airborne fleet that stealthily gained. But, they would not arrive before Felkoth had a chance to land a critical blow here, where all could be lost in one breath.

Glaring with disdain at the approaching monstrosity, Roftome spread his own wings to their full span in open challenge. "It will not have satisfaction, not while I fly," he declared, and bolted far above, undaunted, to engage Felkoth's most threatening servant for a second time.

Morlen could only watch him go for a few short moments before returning to the wailing forces at hand, and rallied the lions from defense into a gallant attack as ripping claws and fangs clashed viciously upon one another. The Crystal Blade led them forward in his quickening hands despite the scream of death that drew so close.

Dipping beneath the foul creature's narrow line of sight, Roftome made for its well-cradled master, sure that an assault on him would disrupt its collision with those below. It began a steep descent that abruptly halted as he shot against its clasped talons, scratching and rattling until Felkoth commanded a sharp turn upward, where he met them again. This time he latched between its eyes as he'd done before, pecking determinedly until its flailing head whipped him off and launched a spout of flame, which he easily evaded.

Its vision dulled by a veil of smoke, Bloodsong swiped hard in all directions while Roftome stabbed his talons into the center of its granite back. The colossal tail soared in a quick reflex to squash him on the spot, smashing with a terrible clatter between its own wings after its target lightly sprang off in a dodge. The dragon sank through billowing dust before it recovered from the blow, holding tightly to its irate master.

Then, as the sky finally cleared, no eye or ear could miss what came. The Eaglemasters had arrived, belting a fearsome note of defiance while aimed directly at Felkoth. At the front of their ranks, King Valdis flew with the Crystal Spear thrust out to lead a heavy charge, his son and daughter following on either side.

Bloodsong went forth to immerse them in their own flaming ruin, and the Eaglemasters held formation behind their king to meet it head-on, even as the creature's agonizing scream enveloped them. Then, with distance closing between them and their foe, Valdis suddenly sped into a sharp dive with all Eaglemasters far beneath the dragon, which struggled to turn while it pursued them lower toward the battle.

They looked down in wonder at the valiant lions, whose ancient majesty was summoned and gathered now by one, and one alone, deep in lethal territory.

"Our ally fights bravely on the ground," Valdis called out to all, who heard him clearly as they neared the shriekers. "Let us do the same!" With that, he lunged from the back of his eagle, rolling through their enemies to spring gracefully to his feet with the Crystal Spear battering a circle around him. Every Eaglemaster followed suit, disembarking from their bearers in a wave of red and silver that crashed through the whining gray tide. Unencumbered by their riders, the flock swarmed as one against the closing dragon, drawing it above the fray while Felkoth bellowed angrily in its grasp, backing away from the incessant prods of their attacks.

Valdis unleashed a flurry of crippling strikes against every brute within reach, bringing down two with one swing while taking another that tackled him from the side and hoisting it across his shoulders, hurling it into one more that rushed him.

Prince Verald, surrounded by six that stood taller than he,

buried his spear into the first that pounced, and then silenced two more with a swift draw of his sword, which delivered a quick end to the remaining three that darted in without sinking a single claw or fang.

Morlen watched the Eaglemasters cleave through the ranks on his left, with Valdis far out in front, unscathed by the rocking swells while other men fought hard to keep up in his wake. And, he sensed *her* close also, perhaps searching for him as he now searched for her.

Valeine leapt forward, smashing every snout that bore down on her, and harbored no fear as she saw her father alone, moving weightlessly. Taking in the vast number of radiant lions on their right flank, whose prowess had until this moment been the stuff of dream and lore for generations of her people, she knew there was only one who could unite such distant worlds. She could not see him yet, blocked from sight as he was by so many that fought around the path he forged, but, she knew he was there, in the very thick of danger.

Flooding all ears with a deathly scream, Bloodsong slithered and flipped high overhead beneath the eagles' relentless net, which glided around each blast to leave Felkoth no safety within its hold. And, through each violent somersault that did nothing but disorient him under the raptors' attack, Felkoth knew it would be only a matter of moments before he stumbled too far, yielding his neck to their beaks.

Well-alerted to its master's peril, Bloodsong spiraled vertically upward, its tail a chopping windmill that pulverized scores to feathery mulch while their brothers whistled in retribution. Those who were able struck Felkoth's seat more aggressively than before, until his rising groans left the dragon no option but to lower him away from their assault.

Pursuing closely as Bloodsong changed course, the eagles

recognized that they'd accomplished their task when it began an urgent plunge toward the battle. But once Felkoth was unloaded from its grasp, it would become much more volatile, free to exert any destructive maneuver, and they would not be able to keep it in check for long. They wove all around as it neared their allies on the field, allowing it no other movement but to protect its master, until finally, it released him into the ample fold of his shriekers.

Roftome pounced stubbornly onto Bloodsong's jagged brow once more, covering its red eyes with his wings so that it would be afraid to crash through the fray, knowing its master was somewhere within. But this proved to be a tenuous ploy at best when the enraged creature spun out again, rocking back and forth while the other eagles swarmed to drag it higher, ducking every unpredictable blow.

Meanwhile, keenly aware that Felkoth had finally joined them on the ground, Morlen and the Eaglemasters tore forward with new determination, bent on bringing their coordinated campaign to fruition.

Only now, up close, did Felkoth begin to take in the magnitude of forces rallying together against him, from Valdis and his brash troops to the stomping lions and the boy, the boy with *his* prize, who had led them here. They would have no pleasure, no victory. And all would burn upon these very fields they'd come so desperately to take. Marching beside his loyal beasts, he pointed the Dark Blade firmly out toward all enemies, and prepared to drench it in their death.

Having bridged the gap between himself and many of the Eaglemasters, Morlen looked more closely among them for Valeine, but she was still too difficult to spot inside the skirmish. King Valdis, though, was in sight of everyone, crumpling an entire pack with three devastating swipes of the Crystal Spear as they tried to bar his passage farther, until he became an unsinkable island within their tumultuous center.

Morlen delved harder ahead, hoping to reach him, and Felkoth's jeering face in the distant crowd drove his blade even faster. There was no telling who would engage the Tyrant Prince first, since he stood surrounded by the shriekers, aligned between both forces that hammered against him. Every Eaglemaster slanted in his direction, and all foes they encountered were nothing more than mere hurdles before their primary target.

Breaking through to the rightmost edge of her countrymen, Valeine knew that if she could just cross a few more yards, she would find Morlen. Together they could repel the rest while her father fought Felkoth, although she knew Valdis was not the closest of the Eaglemasters to his position. They would buy him time.

Watching as the other Eaglemasters held nothing back to fragment the defensive wave, she felled every enemy holding her off while trying to catch up. One by one, Felkoth cut each challenger down with the poisonous Dark Blade and reveled in their dying gasps, his face contorting with greater enjoyment as more filled their place, all of them falling by his wrathful hands.

Bolting forward, she was abruptly pulled left by an outstretched claw that ripped across her shoulder, dragging her around to face a growling wretch that beat across her cheek as she ran it through. She fell back from the blow without her spear, into two more that excitedly caught her with fingers that sliced into her sides, until she hastily drew her sword, taking their heads in one stroke. Another grabbed both of her arms and forced them over her head, and she could feel its wet breath on the side of her neck as it opened stained jaws that she cracked with the back of her head, slamming her elbow into its temple to drive it many paces sideways.

Still on both feet, the seething foe careened straight at her while she prepared a threatening defense, one she never got a chance to land as Morlen sprinted in to deal a finishing strike, sending it in silence to the ground. They were pushed against one another by the tightening struggle around them, and Morlen felt quite safe with her hands suddenly on his, breathing in what she breathed out an inch away.

Yanked off balance by the writhing clusters on every side, they kept close, carving a path forward through the shriekers' formation. Felkoth stood not far ahead, overpowering any who poured in. Shoulder to shoulder, the pair became a moving wall that no enemy could withstand, and soon they entered the front lines beside Verald, whose heart rose to see his sister in fair condition, as well as the company she kept.

"A fine day it's been, Eaglefriend," he greeted, marshaling those with him to spread around Felkoth and his barking guards, tentatively closing in. But, they were denied their chance to strike at the Tyrant Prince when, drilling through his fortified circle, King Valdis emerged with the Crystal Spear held at the ready. Looking at Felkoth, who turned just a few strides off to meet his gaze with none in between, Valdis offered no rebuke or demand, only a certainty that every step and breath that followed would be greater than what his enemy could return.

Morlen and the Eaglemasters meshed together, weapons poised against the ring of beasts that now cast attention inward upon their master and the one who had entered, and everyone watched for the scene to unfold.

Without one second's rest, Valdis released a deep shout and threw a deadly slash that Felkoth held inches from his own throat with a ringing parry, pushing hard to wedge a gap between them. But Valdis shoved him back and moved forward with a whistling slice of the spear's base that flew just over Felkoth's head when he ducked, stabbing out with the Dark Blade, a strike Valdis narrowly parried.

Valdis's ensuing thrust missed by a hair's breadth when Felkoth spun to the side and leapt to swing the Dark Blade toward the king's head, but the Crystal Spear batted the sword wide off guard, and Valdis smashed his clenched fist into Felkoth's pursed mouth, knocking him flat on his back.

Felkoth sat up, spitting blood, and Valdis meant to finish him before he reached his feet, swinging the spear's sharp-horned end like an axe for his skull, but he dodged the weapon, which became entangled in black knots of his hair.

Dragging him in like a netted fish, Valdis pulled Felkoth's head upward and drew a dagger from his hip sheath, aiming its point for his captive's exposed throat. In an instant Felkoth drew a knife of his own, cutting his hair free while he whipped his leg around to bash Valdis's feet off the ground, dropping him with a loud clatter.

Before Felkoth could drive his knife through the plated chest lying before him, Valdis kicked it out of his raised hand and rattled him sideways with the butt of his spear, and both of them rolled to get up before the other. Felkoth lunged, but Valdis would not be moved, halting every route the Dark Blade took to end him with tireless spins of the Crystal Spear. Each swing only spurred Felkoth further, until Valdis went again on the offensive, driving their path as Felkoth fought to find any weakness he could exploit, unable to even graze Valdis's deftly weaving hands.

Worry began to stiffen Felkoth's face, and everyone gathering around could see it as plain as the blood that still trickled from his gashed lip. Valdis saw it as well, feeling the slight fatigue in each of Felkoth's breathy, futile attempts. But soon, all on the field suddenly remembered the unstable threat above when Bloodsong pierced them with another freezing call, descending through a thick mat of eagles to belt a stream of fire that narrowly missed the crowd. It scalded and smoked over those who quickly scattered in an uproar, and the shriekers dove against Morlen and his allies one more time.

Breaking through their onslaught, Morlen labored to reach Valdis, bringing down any that tried to bleed him along the way, until they had to go to the ground again as the dragon's fire scorched many in another pass. The combatants rose cautiously to their feet in a thick haze, searching dizzily for friend and foe while the smoke slowly cleared.

Suddenly Morlen saw Valdis, staring right at him across a short distance, and also at the Crystal Blade in his possession, a sight that filled the king's face with an odd look of confusion and then understanding. At that moment, slinking from the shadows, Felkoth drove the Dark Blade through Valdis's middle, and Morlen, yelling out in vain, rushed through the embattled rows toward them.

Felkoth savored each second, slowly withdrawing his sword while Valdis still stood, spear in hand, and Bloodsong swooped down with open talons to snatch up its master, lifting him to safety as the eagles chased them from Korindelf.

Finally reaching Valdis, Morlen gripped his arm and shoulder tightly as he sagged off balance, gently bringing him down to lie on his back. The veins of his face began darkening to a greenish-black, and yet he looked up at Morlen, lacking any pain.

"You... carry the Crystal Blade," Valdis said breathily, with a tone that held no surprise. "I didn't know... but still I came." His chest rose and fell less noticeably, and soon Verald and Valeine rushed to them, kneeling at their father's side. Around them, the Eaglemasters and lions drove all remaining enemies from the fields in broken clusters that whimpered at their king's departure, retreating far toward the Dead Plains.

Korindelf stood soaked in rays that tore through the surrounding white curtain as Valdis's voice grew quieter. "We met him well today, young Eaglefriend... Morlen," he said. Then, his limp arm gathered enough strength to lift the Crystal Spear out before him. "Take this… for me," he bade. "And meet him once more."

Glancing at Verald and Valeine, whose countenances bolstered their father's request, Morlen accepted the Crystal Spear from his unshaking hand, which folded lightly upon his body beneath the hands of his children. They held him warmly, until even the cold creeping through his fingers could not diminish the glow he gave off when he became still.

Bowing their heads, all three said nothing, letting his words be the last that resonated with them, and Morlen kept the entrusted spear ready, hoping to bear it with honor in his stead.

Roftome suddenly broke the settling silence, dipping toward him from the sky as the other eagles struggled to hinder the dragon's escape. "He goes to burn their people," he called to Morlen, who stood when he landed with no injury but a few singed feathers. And, by Bloodsong's speeding path, it seemed clear that Felkoth drove for the Eaglemasters' unguarded cities, resolving to destroy them in exchange for his defeat here.

He climbed atop Roftome's back, sitting poised to fly out with the Crystal Spear. Turning to Valeine as she rose with her brother, he said, "Your father's people will have less to fear when this is through."

Valeine's face brightened in a way that Morlen held as tightly as memory allowed, and he remained in place for a long moment, until Roftome understood the delay yet gave no stir to break it. Then Morlen finally spurred their flight to catch up with Felkoth in Bloodsong's unyielding grasp.

The Eaglemasters below raised many cheers as he and Roftome passed, and their proud shouts of "Eaglefriend! Eaglefriend!" struck his ear pleasantly more than a few times before he left them and the regained city of Korindelf miles behind.

CHAPTER SIXTEEN

A ROAR FOR BLOODSONG

THE SWARM OF eagles threw every talon and beak at Bloodsong, like a fluid web expanding and self-mending straight ahead while Morlen and Roftome quickly gained on them. Clasping the Crystal Spear tightly against his side, Morlen had no intention of joining their intricate weave, making instead to crest over them and their maddened quarry, which would not be stalled for long.

Watching them flow around each strike that sought to obliterate all in its path, Morlen felt his heart drop amid the creature's bursting screams while dozens were engulfed in one molten breath. Bloodsong ripped through their net, driven more fiercely by Felkoth in now open skies toward the Eaglemasters' realm.

But, despite the ruin of so many, the flock was not deterred, regrouping to maintain pursuit until Morlen and Roftome hailed them from above. At this, every eagle gradually halted, recognizing that the two companions meant to go on alone.

On seeing the air graciously yielded, Morlen looked ahead to Bloodsong's narrow lead, and glimpsed the lone peak that towered just outside the Isle's southwestern edge. Thinking of the tactical advantage it could pose if Felkoth were unseated upon it, he directed Roftome into a slight descent alongside the unsuspecting dragon.

Felkoth peered vigilantly out in all directions and saw them swoop on his left, sharply turning Bloodsong toward them only to be drenched in a scornful gust when Roftome darted forward. Leading him over the Isle, Morlen and Roftome made for the distant mountain at a purposefully enticing pace, one they came to regret when Bloodsong immersed them in another vengeful call that slowed their every fiber. Pain and death became Morlen's only thoughts, creeping within a heavy bile that ate away at him until the shrill onslaught subsided, leaving them mere seconds to careen sideways and avoid the torrent of flame.

Batting his seared cloak, Morlen did the same to Roftome's smoking tail feathers, though the speed they picked up snuffed out every darkened clump. Bloodsong followed in their wake, pushed vehemently by Felkoth to ensure nothing remained of them but vapor. To avoid presenting another clear shot, Roftome swerved in and out of the dragon's vision, luring it and its master farther toward the single peak that rose a few miles away.

Another foul cry smothered them, and Morlen ground his teeth in despair while Roftome's wings barely remained open. As the clamor dimmed beneath one more telltale gulp of air, it was all they could do to stay aloft, let alone dodge the jet of liquid fire that shot close behind. Morlen folded hard against Roftome's rigid spine, compelling the magnificent bird to tap every remaining ounce of agility and spin them downward just beneath the burning stream.

Leveling out below a sheet of smoke, Morlen caught what little breath he could through the heat. Roftome made no utterance at all, expending every available pocket of energy on their sunken propulsion forward, until they found themselves in line with the peak's rocky summit.

As if kicking through deadly rapids for the only protruding

refuge, they flew onward with their enemies still in tow, and finally perched atop a jagged ridge of the wide mountaintop, facing out as Bloodsong descended for the kill. Bathed in swallowing silence that forewent what would be the worst they'd yet heard, Morlen and Roftome knew only that they would not be found sitting when it came—that they would meet it, together.

"We'll leave no cloud untouched," said Morlen, fondly remembering their plans to scour every inch of sky when this was finished, and readied himself while Bloodsong approached with gathering force.

"And no peak unexplored," replied Roftome, equally at ease.

"Go now," Morlen urged, bracing for the sonic impact as Roftome soared up from their high platform to match the dragon's altitude, charging head-on with distance shrinking fast.

Bloodsong seized every muscle in their bodies with a palpable outcry that tenderized and embalmed, slowly undoing them from the inside out while they plunged deeper in a dedicated arc that no blast could disrupt. Morlen dug where all was submerged and choking, grabbing hold of any recollection of light and air, and bellowed so loud that the forcible tendrils of sorrow and fear unraveled at his own echoing voice. It drove back that of the wicked creature, which cried forth more harshly, trying to drown him out. But Morlen was louder, his shout reverberating through the outstretched wail's center as the divide shortened between them and collision, until Bloodsong could bear the sound no longer, lifting up its stony head. And Morlen hurled the Crystal Spear into its newly exposed chest, puncturing rock and gushing flame to pierce its brittle heart.

Throat writhing around a gurgled rasp that soon fell silent, Bloodsong sank into a limp dive, still holding Felkoth in its clutches as Morlen and Roftome coasted above, and crashed with a splintering skid through plumes of thick brown dust across the great mountain peak.

Banking to face the billowing site, Roftome cut through smoke and hovered in triumphant observation, until Morlen bade him to fly lower and jumped down with the Crystal Blade in hand. He landed lightly upon the spacious summit, which was gashed and strewn with a trail of popping hot sludge that led through the fumes to Bloodsong's crumbled, broken remains. But Felkoth was not among them, he realized as he pivoted calmly to survey the wreckage's murky perimeter. Roftome searched as well, past scattered bits of floating debris. He must have leapt free just before running aground, and was likely crouching now in some trench, waiting to leap out and strike.

"It truly has transformed you from what you were when you first took it." The chill voice caused Morlen to turn toward the shadowy outline of a tall figure that stepped toward him through the steam. "Stripped from my reach, in the hold of a boy more delicate and incapable than any I've seen, and returned to me by the very same, now almost unrecognizable."

Felkoth emerged unharmed, with the Dark Blade held casually ready, and Morlen's hand immediately twitched toward the Goldshard, pocketed so carefully against his pounding chest. Resisting the urge to hold it now was more taxing than any battle he'd yet faced. He'd been able to let it fade to the back of his mind at each challenge, trusting that he would prevail while the confrontation for which he needed it most still lay ahead. But now that he faced that fight, all he could see was its bright gleaming outline to which he owed every victory. And he would be naked without it.

With a satisfied snarl, Felkoth lunged and swung the Dark Blade for Morlen's neck, and Morlen met the blow with his own gleaming sword. The clattering force staggered him backward through the uncertain terrain, while Roftome circled attentively above.

Morlen slashed downward as though to split a log in two, aiming to quell Felkoth's momentum, but too late, as Felkoth's parry overbalanced the weight of his attack and left his guard open for a heavy thrust. Avoiding it in a daring sidestep that sent him stumbling, Morlen rotated sharply to defend against Felkoth's next strike, and his shaky stance only wobbled farther under the assault. But Morlen stabilized his footing, though hard-pressed to maintain it under Felkoth's relentless advance, well aware he could afford to lose no more ground.

Deflecting a wide chop aimed at his gut, Morlen countered with a high swish that only threw his arms off center as Felkoth elbowed his cheekbone, rocking his overextended form. Hearing Felkoth pounce after his clumsy recoil, Morlen twisted around with a ringing horizontal slice that Felkoth halted before bombarding him with more tireless bursts.

Every heated clang drove Morlen to focus on the inescapable Dark Blade, knowing even a minor graze would bring death, while he repelled it over and over. In the face of such perilous vulnerability, his mind soon began to crumple under the same blinding flash that had once brought solace. Why was it failing him now, of all times? Perhaps he wasn't fully trusting in it.

With each near miss of the cursed sword bringing him closer to his end, Morlen tried to rely more deeply on the Goldshard. But, his mind gradually constricted, as though suppressing so much in exchange for protection.

Ever on the offensive, each stroke weakening Morlen's tenuous position, Felkoth pushed him farther back from the peak's center, moving him steadily toward its edge. Morlen returned Felkoth's fire with fading vigor as his efforts proved to be in vain.

He refused to be herded so easily and set both feet firmly to balance a forward stab, struggling to keep his hold when Felkoth batted away the attack and followed with a diagonal slash he barely had time to block. Thighs quivering, Morlen sprang up and lashed out broadly for Felkoth's head, which ducked below the opportunistic cut. Then Felkoth kicked just below his ribs with a steel-toed boot, knocking his breath away and nearly taking him to his knees in pain. He quickly moved backward to avoid the Dark Blade, stumbling again, and caught himself as he staggered near the rim that curved yards behind.

"It hasn't served you as well as you'd hoped?" mocked Felkoth, quite relaxed while Morlen breathed through the nauseating pain, the Crystal Blade loose in his grasp. "A worm that sprouts wings may still be squashed."

Felkoth pressed in to finish him, but Morlen held firm, ducking the high swing to throw a straight hit that was harshly cast down while Felkoth's knuckles drove hard into his temple, spinning him sideways with his sword defensively raised through blurred vision. Coils squeezed tighter around his faltering mind, where all was buried beneath the terribly bright gold, the only thing that could help him prevail. It had made him strong enough, fast enough... He knew it had. It would not fail him. It would help him win this struggle. It had to.

He reared back and executed a desperate strike that barely moved the Dark Blade on impact, and Felkoth shoved him closer to the dizzying edge. "Give it to me, or I'll cut you just like your father, and that bird-straddling fool."

Morlen surged forward, paying little heed to the deadly instrument's proximity to his own thrashing limbs, and felt so much in himself that could taste the surface yet sank deeper each moment it was put aside for something else. Felkoth was openly unthreatened by his renewed assault, neutralizing each weak attempt before knocking him away with the back of his fist. Morlen went at him again, blades colliding at shoulder height, then higher when Morlen withdrew and struck for his pale throat. But Felkoth only enjoyed watching him bleed his last reserves dry, and finally pried his arms apart and wrenched the Crystal Blade from his limp hand with a powerful blow that sent it flying off the mountain, over the edge.

Looking with dread as his sword arced a mournful goodbye through the open air and plummeted toward some distant resting place, Morlen glimpsed a dash of white that sped down in the same direction just as Felkoth beat him to the ground. His hair matted by dirt and blood, he rolled frantically to dodge while the Dark Blade smashed a rock to powder where his head had lain a second earlier, twisting both legs away from the attacks that followed. Then, sliding a hand into the pocket over his rattling heart, he clung tightly to the one thing that would save him, withdrawing it in an urgent bolt to stand upright again as Felkoth abruptly ceased pursuit.

Morlen pressed the Goldshard against his body like a tiny shield, sharp and smooth, knowing the power it had given him would re-emerge at any second. But, that certainty only muddled his mind further, drowning him the longer he held out for what would not come.

He was going to die, he realized as he backed slowly toward the sheer cliff while Felkoth inched in to flay him. But then, suddenly appearing on his right, Roftome ascended with the Crystal Blade firmly clasped in his talons, and quickly tossed it to him from above. "Show him a true fight, Morlen!" he called.

Urgently reaching up to catch it, fingers locking securely around its marble grip, Morlen now held his sword in one hand, and the Goldshard in the other. And Felkoth charged with the Dark Blade raised high to deliver a crippling slash, one that would require both of his arms immediately to defend. But, if he relinquished the Goldshard, all of its effects would be undone, leaving him the way he'd been before turning to it for strength—weak, and afraid.

He had no time, merely a fraction of a second to decide, and still his head swam dizzily with all that begged to be freed from beneath the repressive veil.

Felkoth brought the Dark Blade whistling down, and Morlen released his hold on the Goldshard's jagged shape, dropping it to clamp both hands around the base of his sword, ready to meet the worst. As the relic struck the ground at their feet, it burst in a tumultuous cloud of golden dust that knocked both of them flat to either side. Felkoth growled bitterly, slinking up onto all fours with his face twisted in horror at the wispy remains of his long-sought prize, which dissipated in the wind.

"No!" He shuddered, scooping up what little his fingers could before it vanished, and cast all focus upon Morlen, waiting to watch him shrivel and cower. Morlen, too, expected a reverse transformation to take him as he stood, bracing for the ripping pain that would contract his muscles and dim his spirit to what it had previously been. But, no change occurred, even after Felkoth rose in front of him.

"Why are you no different?" Felkoth seethed, scrutinizing Morlen's form. "Everything it gave you is now destroyed."

Morlen knew this to be true as well, yet felt altogether the same—except lighter, as though some long-worn restraint had been thrown off, and the waters of his mind now flowed freely without the dam he had imposed.

"Because," said Morlen with new understanding, "it gave me nothing."

Felkoth scowled, his confusion overshadowed only by disdain. He at least would not be denied this singular pleasure, the pleasure of tearing through the one who'd foiled him at every turn and watching his innards spill. Resuming his advance, he intended to open Morlen from chest to waist. Morlen wove around the slice easily, needing not even to raise his sword when Felkoth brought on an angry flurry meant to kill a slower foe.

"What is this?" Felkoth spat, but Morlen did not share his

surprise, deflecting every persistent thrust and cut with speed that was, and always had been, his.

Irked at how precarious it became to fight with one hand, which had more than sufficed up to this point, Felkoth clenched both together to launch an attack that Morlen nullified, until soon he could hold no ground that Morlen had a mind to take. And Morlen continued to halt the Dark Blade wherever it flew, driving Felkoth into a frenzy that further compromised his position as he threw his entire weight behind killing blows.

Letting him miss by a feather's thickness, Morlen spun Felkoth with each step. "Do you think your blade is a threat to me?" he asked, recalling Matufinn's taunt while darting past another vicious lunge. "I'm already gone before it's thrown."

Felkoth tried to take off Morlen's head, but Morlen flowed beneath his swipe and kicked him over the unforgiving rocks. Springing up to stand, scuffed and disheveled, Felkoth thought Morlen would surely charge. But the dividing space remained intact with Morlen relaxed on the other side, even as he sprinted holding the Dark Blade out like a beast's horn.

Morlen swept the weighty stab aside, and Felkoth's shoulder barreled into his chest as though it was a brick wall. Stunned by the bash, Felkoth collected himself to return fiercer hits in response. But Morlen moved too fluidly, battering him farther with each clash of their blades all the way to where they'd started, at the peak's center.

Tripping through stone fragments and smoldering slime that littered Bloodsong's tomb, Felkoth struggled against Morlen's unfaltering stride and cursed every effortless path of the Crystal Blade that thwarted his attempts at an offensive. Only one tiny cut was needed to end this, one slash of flesh, but his careless blows either missed or were parried. He could not endure such disgrace another heartbeat, and harnessed what little was left in him to unleash a final vertical blow that Morlen could not possibly withstand.

As the Dark Blade came thundering down to crack his head open, Morlen swung his sword with all the strength he possessed and shattered its vile metal into shards that blew back to pierce Felkoth's neck and face.

Felkoth drew an icy breath, teetering away half a pace with nothing but its hilt in his hand, and gazed on in shock, more beaten by the impervious look his enemy now gave than by his fatal wounds.

"Who are you?" asked Felkoth fearfully, veins rupturing under sallow skin.

Morlen stepped closer, peering deep into the malice of Felkoth's eyes, malice that rushed to sink him. Then suddenly a swell of laughter shook from his core as he felt no urge whatsoever to avert his own, and it raucously carried through each second the outreaching shadow brushed but could not take hold of him. And in such rare fullness, he knew.

"Morlen of the Blessed Ones," he answered, turning with the Crystal Blade lowered at his side to walk out toward the summit rim.

This was the last thing Felkoth heard as his buckling legs gave way, collapsing flat into a blanket of ash where all would waste and scatter.

Standing at the high edge of the world, over the Isle's distantly remembered shelter and cold stretching fields stained by death, Morlen gazed out, feeling great promise and hope in all that remained to be discovered, though he could not expect what lay ahead.

He would greet it when it came, whether danger or good fortune, and knew only that—in this very moment—he was nothing less than whole.

CHAPTER SEVENTEEN

FAREWELLS

A SWIFT GUST passed over Morlen's shoulder, drawing him around as Nottleforf materialized a few paces ahead, beaming at him with pride. Feeling as though it had been ages since they'd last parted, Morlen approached him comfortably, knowing it would not just be a wizard or a mentor who listened. "The Goldshard never had any power to offer, did it?"

Nottleforf's ancient brow relaxed above his luminous eyes, and he softly shook his grayish head. "No," he replied. "None but what you gave it, in your mind, so that you could finally see what Matufinn helped you uncover.

"The admonition to Korindelf's kings regarding its power drove them to be industrious and resourceful, reserving it for future generations who might need it more desperately than they. Had any of them turned to it before you, he would have had to face the same harsh lesson you did: the greatest power we have is the immeasurability of ourselves."

"Yet you told me never to use it, when you first gave it to me," said Morlen.

"Because I knew that Matufinn first needed to help draw away the curtain you'd raised against your capabilities. And after you'd gotten a clear glimpse of that potential, your trust in the Goldshard kept you a step ahead of your fear. But when we hold too long to that which shields us from our fear entirely, we forget what it is to be brave in the first place. We cling so hard to the rock beneath us that our only hope is to hear the kind soul who calls out for us to jump, and see the view that we've been missing."

Morlen became quiet at this open admission, and Nottleforf met his gaze more humbly, withdrawing nothing.

"I spent so long hoping you would see yourself, as I knew one day you could," said Nottleforf. "I think, deep down, I hoped you would see me too, see what I lacked the courage and clarity to face on my own." His throat emitted a subtle rumble. "For a very long time, I have been Nottleforf. But, I have always been Morthadus; I know that, now. And you, Morlen, are one whom I have yet to match in heart."

Morlen looked down at the Crystal Blade in his hand, glad to finally have cause to sheathe it indefinitely, and basked in a cool wind made by Roftome's landing at his side, patting his folded wings in a glad reunion.

"Where shall we go now?" asked Roftome, not yet ready for rest.

And Morlen glanced up at him with equal zeal. "Anywhere," he answered, seeing endless possibilities for their further adventures. "Everywhere."

Climbing atop his welcoming seat, Morlen ushered Roftome to the peak's center, and wrenched the Crystal Spear from Bloodsong's cracked chest in preparation to leave.

"Korindelf is without a king," said Nottleforf as they came back toward him. "It is yours, by right."

"No," Morlen replied fondly. "I think Korindelf would do just fine without one for a long while. But," he mused, "perhaps a high guardian might suit her well. Would you be willing?"

Nottleforf raised an obliging chin. "I was, long ago," he answered steadfastly. "I shall be again. Besides, with you keeping watch over all lands from the skies, what troublesome duties could possibly encumber my many other pressing affairs?"

Morlen nodded warmly at him, knowing this was not good-bye, and then lifted away, making once again for Korindelf, where the Eaglemasters looked to the smoking summit for his return.

Day faded to cool, still evening when Morlen and Roftome descended to meet the Eaglemasters outside Korindelf. Its soiled people trembled out from captivity to open air, and broken families were reunited, piece by piece. Children throughout the city were emancipated from Felkoth's supporters, who were shackled and gagged to be taken to work in Veldere's silver mines.

"They have much to rebuild," said Verald while Morlen dismounted, surveying the downtrodden, malnourished masses. "Much that has been lost, that may never be renewed. But we will always be behind them, with every step, Eaglefriend. I swear it." He extended a king's hand of loyalty and friendship, which Morlen took firmly with his own, though his attention was held by none but Valeine, who looked at him now as she had many times before.

Valdis's body lay on the unmoving back of his perched eagle, Clodion, who maintained regal poise in grief, and Morlen strode reverently to his side. Gently, he lifted one of the fallen king's folded arms and placed the Crystal Spear beneath it, against his still chest.

Nodding in respect, Verald climbed atop his own carrier, directing the other Eaglemasters to follow suit, and Morlen felt the brilliant approach of many energies, turning to face the great lions with affection. He gazed toward the Isle in which he'd dwelt as one of their own, and conveyed a surge of gratitude for the happiness they'd shared in that place, where he did not intend to return.

The ancient host grew heavy with the understanding that he would not run with them again, but would not harbor such sadness in their hearts for long. Holding instead to the lingering radiance of the one who had drawn them out, they traversed the fields with splendor that all beheld, and passed again through the mists that would forever house them.

Mounted to lead the Eaglemasters' assembled ranks, Verald looked down to address Morlen before departing. "We will bear our dead to rest," he said, readying to leave. "Then return at first light with provisions for all people here, so the rebirth of Korindelf may finally begin. And she will forever have a powerful ally in the Eaglemasters, as will you, Morlen Eaglefriend, wherever you may be."

They rose together and soared as one red flame burning in the wake of Clodion, who bore Valdis far ahead into broad open skies that for once revealed no enemy on any side.

Morlen and Roftome spent the next days surveying Korindelf's continued reconstruction. The city's people slowly transitioned back into the lives stolen from them, reclaiming homes abandoned and in disrepair, with scars of forced entry that evoked memories too cold for even the most comforting fire to erase.

But fallow pastures would thrive again, in time, as would craftsmen re-hone their chosen trades, commerce and lively activity surging once more through the city's streets and village squares. Perhaps even a fresh crop of defenders would soon grow, under the Eaglemasters' strict tutelage, though from which direction the next threat might emerge remained unknown.

Parting clouds yielded countless roads before the two companions while they let every crossing breeze and tailwind steer them farther, higher, until vast reaches of sky and earth were theirs to discover.

"I would often call any high-nestled perch near food and stream my home," said Roftome, as the Eagle Mountains extended wide below. "But, my home must not be a place where I encounter no new shape or texture, no new challenge, or hope."

"Nor mine," replied Morlen, warming one hand within his densely feathered side as they aimed for no particular destination.

They coasted weightlessly over ranges that glistened, inviting them to explore the deep, dangerous paths and concealed wonders, and Roftome said, "Together, we may find those things."

Morlen held his hand tighter against his companion, needing no further shelter from the cold. "Together, we will," he said.

They passed above cliffs that overlooked the Eaglemasters' realm, when a reflected glare from the nearest mountainside shone in a way reminiscent of their last foray through these heights. It drew them closer until both could make out the tall, transparent form that grew more solid as they approached, coalescing into the same armor-clad man they'd met once before.

They landed a short distance away, and Morlen stepped down, suddenly recalling the Eaglemasters' song at sight of the regal figure, whose elegant silver plating and helm shone in the sunlight.

"My kin hold you in great favor." The specter's smooth voice carried far across the icy slope. "You and your friend have illuminated much, and may again, where more shadows creep. I know the richness forged in such a bond, and the joy, also, while it remains unbroken." His young, faded eyes echoed long-remembered victories laced with regret and guilt, for which Morlen could not help but suspect the cause.

Remembering their last exchange, Morlen said, "Your friend,

whom you lost." He paused at the sullen aura this seemed to evoke. "You *did* find him again, didn't you?"

No initial response came, and the man all but blended into their frozen surroundings until he finally said, "Only what he had become."

Morlen felt the bite of grief this confession carried, knowing more would soon follow as he asked, "And, what remained between you?"

The ancient warrior became quieter than the high solitude in which they stood, until he replied, "Only pain. Before he struck me down, and I him."

Morlen's gaze immediately centered on the severe slice carved through the thick pauldron before him, a mortal wound from a weapon he remembered well.

The man nodded at his unspoken understanding. "You have broken the Dark Blade, which slew me in an age long past; but still I feel its sting, for it was delivered by one I held dear. We were like family, driven apart by forces beyond our control, till our efforts to not be conquered by them brought us face to face as kings—I of the Eaglemasters, and he, of the shriekers. What pains me the most is not the cut he inflicted on mere flesh, nor the thrust of my spear through his heart, but rather the look in his eyes as he swung to end me, as though there was no going back."

Morlen swayed in a heavy wind that passed through the one before him, and took comfort leaning with an arm outstretched against Roftome's folded wing. The stranger's presence began to withdraw, vanishing, though Morlen held every long stride in sight as long as he could.

"Farewell, Morlen and Roftome." His words resounded through the peaks. And, blurred by a vaporous expanse ahead, he concluded, "She looks for you, from her city."

Then, after a gust that left them both quite on their own,

Morlen and Roftome felt no scathing chill or numbness, but only peace in one another's company. The ghostly king's final words drove Morlen's mind toward Veleseor, and to the one he'd first met there, who made chaos and certain peril seem less daunting. She was there now, beginning to rebuild a place for her people, a place he would very much like to preserve, and be welcome in, as long as it was hers.

"Are you up for paying the city men another visit?" Morlen asked, reclaiming his place on Roftome's back.

"I sense the city men, and women, would look favorably upon our presence," Roftome replied, obliging without reservation.

Surging upward, they plotted a course for well-known terrain, spurred by the refreshing lack of a plan or a goal. Morlen was unsure whether he went merely to reinforce what it felt like to be near her, or to tell her he would not return again for some time. But, regardless, he hoped to find her there, and hoped even more that she would be glad upon his arrival, whatever it might bring.

Valeine stood proudly within her retaken seat of command at the fragile southern divide, where a billowing pyre swelled with those that had come to conquer and failed. Her newly anointed contingent of Eaglemasters stoked the warning flare to their enemies with heaping scoops of all that remained throughout the city, letting it smolder at the river to a pile of cracked horns that would give pause to any wishing to cross. But, her watch stayed fixed primarily on friendly skies, willing them to open and reveal the one who could come as he had before, and realize he needn't wander to find his place.

Morlen looked fondly down at the battered stronghold, and knew that its broken walls being mended brick by brick were safe as long as she stood within. Descending, he knew even the most enthusiastic hail from below would mean little next to the look of greeting he sought from her. She gave it long before he landed, and its reward was instantaneous.

After dismounting with no trace of trepidation or uncertainty, he walked forward to meet her as she strode toward him until they came face to face, neither of them feeling clumsy in their mutual loss for words. The scent of her hair alone made the divine apples into a distant memory, and her skin flushed in a warm, unabashed sheen.

"When you roam around up there," she said, "what do you see?"

Morlen tried to envision the boundless heights that mere moments before had been laid out at his fingertips. "Places I might go," he replied. "Where I discover something greater than I would anywhere else."

Her fair cheeks gained a bit more color now. "And you came here."

"I did," he said tentatively, "because, there is much more that we are still going to have to confront. And I wanted you to know that whenever it comes here, so will I."

Her expression sank, though it wasn't cold. "But until then, what?"

Glancing toward Roftome, who waited patiently behind, he then returned her unbroken stare that quietly knifed him.

"Will death be all that draws you?" she pressed. "Will all the life that you've helped restore go un-enjoyed while you leave to unearth some far-off mystery? What about the one here, now?"

Morlen prepared to turn, though finding himself partially anchored. "It will always be my greatest reason to remember where I've been, and to come back."

Then, knowing any further words would only spoil their parting, he returned to Roftome and silently took to the air once more, though no distance gained could diminish the pull he felt from her watch. They climbed welcoming gusts and slopes of fog, and yet the exhilaration brought on by such an open domain was somewhat lesser now. Roftome seemed to detect this in him also, exerting less forceful bursts to keep them from straying too far.

"Morlen," said Roftome, when his slowing drew no protest. "A great adventure is calling you, one that it may not be wise to forsake. As long as I fly and breathe, I am your friend, and I am with you. There will always be new places for us to go, new allies and enemies to meet. And we will go. We will meet them, together. But she looks to you now, and it may not always be so."

They eventually came to tread air in place, and Morlen craned his head toward the underlying city, hoping that she still held him in sight. He could not wait until later, not another month, or day.

She had watched until they shrank from view, and continued to stare at the area where they vanished. Just as she made to look away, a tiny point reappeared, drawing nearer and nearer as they descended toward her again. Her heart grew dangerously light while she could almost make out both of their distinctive outlines.

Speeding downward again through every ruffling breeze, Morlen and Roftome enjoyed a wealth of riches in this flight alone, and in the certainty it was but one of many to come.

They rushed faster, closer, still high above. Morlen already knew she hadn't moved, that she saw him, the way he saw her.

"She is smiling," said Roftome, smugly.

And Morlen smiled too.

THE END

About the Author

Charles Laurence Murray was born in 1989 and grew up in San Diego, California. He spent many days lost in the humming, spark-scattering clashes between Luke Skywalker and Darth Vader, caught up in a charge with the Riders of Rohan, and enthralled by the cadence and poise of Doc Holliday emerging from the shadows to face Johnny Ringo. When he was thirteen, he became obsessed with the idea of an eagle-riding, sword-wielding hero and developed it over the years into an epic, four-part series.

Morlen and Roftome will return for more adventures as *The Tale of Eaglefriend* continues. For news about forthcoming books and deals, visit authorclmurray.com and subscribe.

Made in the USA
Lexington, KY
29 April 2018